Groupie

OMNIBUS PRESS
LONDON · NEW YORK · SYDNEY

Exclusive Distributors
Book Sales Limited,
8/9 Frith Street,
London W1V 5TZ, UK.

Music Sales Corporation,
257 Park Avenue South,
New York, NY 10010, USA.

Music Sales Pty Limited,
120 Rothschild Avenue, Rosebery,
NSW 2018, Australia.

To the Music Trade only:
Music Sales Limited,
8/9, Frith Street,
London W1V 5TZ, UK.

Printed and bound in Gt. Britain by Hartnolls Ltd, Bodmin, Cornwall

A catalogue record for this book is available from the British Library.

Visit Omnibus Press at http://www.musicsales.co.uk

Preface to the 1997 Edition

For all its reputation as a hotbed of cultural advance, the Sixties was no great sponsor of fiction. As for the "underground", "counter-culture" or "alternative society", less still. There were manifestos galore, but little creative prose. It might still read, but generally it did not write. The hippie bookshelf drew on other times and places and the first "acid generation" lacked its Irving Welsh. The underground press would in time prove to have been the formative seedbed for a variety of writers, but not just yet. What there was was minimal. There was the ill-fated *Agro* ("When Skinheads and Hell's Angels meet, there's only one outcome . . .") by the pseudonymous Nick Fury; a pulp level roman-a-clef that fell foul of one of its models, who promptly had it injuncted out of the bookshops. There was Thom Keyes' *All Night Stand*, another docudrama, based not that loosely on The Beatles as they moved from poverty to Beatlemania. But best of all was *Groupie*, published in 1969 and written by Jenny Fabian and Johnny Byrne. A fictionalized first-person anecdotage of life and times in the world of late-Sixties London "underground" rock'n'roll.

The groupie, defined sniffily by *The Times* as a girl who "deliberately provokes sexual relations with pop stars", was hardly a Sixties phenomenon. She had been around for years: jazzmen had called her a band rat, Australians a band moll. In the end, as The Rolling Stones would sum it up in a song title, she was a star-fucker, the prerequisite of successful entertainers across the ages, bartering her sex for a proxy taste of their glories.

But if she was no novelty to those inside the music business, she was still pretty strong meat for the mass public. Even the hip were relatively uninformed until San Francisco publisher Jann Wenner, anxious to launch his new rock-orientated magazine in the UK with more than the usual grab-bag of hacks and canapes, hit the British newsstands with his rag. *Rolling Stone* issue 27 was largely devoted to the world of the groupie, lookers mostly, and mainly West Coast sirens, although the pair that really had the fans back on their collective heels were a homely duo self-titled The Plaster Casters, whose speciality was taking back to their Chicago home plaster clones of superstar cock.

But *Rolling Stone* was American and all this remained pretty esoteric for Mr Average, who'd just about got his mind around such assaults on his consciousness as MBEs for The Beatles, and The Rolling Stones refusing to mount the revolve on television's small-screen music-hall, *Sunday Night at the London Palladium*. The fact that some girls, girls who indeed might be his own daughter, were willing, let alone desperate, to offer themselves up as virgin (-ish) sacrifices to these self same gods of rocky horror, was not something upon which he wished to dwell. Miniskirts, beloved of the media, were all very well in their place, but they were not, repeat not, to be dropped unceremoniously at the foot of some squalid hippie waterbed, or tossed cheerfully amid the empty bottles and dead joints bestrewing some hotel floor.

Later, much later, there would be other books, usually blow-and-tell confessionals, emanating from various major-league star-fuckers but Fabian and Byrne's *Groupie* was a ground-breaker. As the promo copy put it, "Read the sensational story, in her own words, of Katie, a nineteen-year-old Groupie, as she 'pulls' from pop group to pop group." It was, as was soon made clear, largely autobiographical. Fabian, a junior journo on *The Daily Telegraph*, had gravitated almost by accident into the rock world. Starting with Syd Barrett of Pink Floyd, she moved through a number of relationships, every one if not quite a star, then certainly central to contemporary rock. As she put it for the paperback blurb, "If you're a groupie you wear freaky clothes, take a fair amount of drugs and go with the boys in the the good groups . . . the really inventive musical ones." As the Liverpool poet Adrian Henri had it, hymning Merseyside's homegrown versions in *Daughters of Albion*: "Beautiful boys with bright red guitars / In the spaces between the stars."

Turning experience into art was not, however, a conscious move. Fabian had met Byrne through a mutual friend, Spike Hawkins, poet, former beat and bridge to the emergent counter-culture. "I didn't suggest writing *Groupie*. What happened was I was sleeping with Andy Summers at the time. I'd told Johnny about Syd and then there was Andy, and I told him where I was going and what I was doing, and he said 'You really should write about this' and I said, 'Well, I can't write about it' and Johnny said 'You write it just as you want and I'll help you with it. We'll just do it as a team.' I had nothing to lose and it quite amused me."

It amused many others too. The book proved an enormous sensation. Perhaps unsurprisingly: for most of its length *Groupie* worshipped the holy teen trinity – sex, drugs and rock'n'roll – and a few years later might have vanished amidst the brief, if lucrative vogue for *Confessions of a . . .* pulp. But *Groupie* was more than that. The fact that Fabian, far from being an inarticulate scrubber down on her knees outside some provincial stage-door, was authentically middle class, and clever with it, only helped the bandwagon. She gained a certain celebrity, the media loved her: she pontificated on late-night television; *The Sunday Times*, then the apogee of middle class chic, ran a deliciously voyeuristic feature asking, "What would you do if your daughter . . .", then kept the story going for another week or so with the answers. (Tribute to the changing times, they were by no means universally negative.) For many, unused to slang's by-ways, she even broadened the language. Aside from "pull" and the slang terms for a variety of drugs, "plating", Katie's synonym for her favourite activity fellatio gained a hitherto unknown publicity. (It came from the rhyming slang "plate of meat" equalling "eat", itself another slang term for oral sex). Indeed, the lexicographers must have loved her: *Groupie* gets 22 citations in the Oxford English Dictionary, from "downer" to "trippy" and "spliff" to "uptight", a mini-lexicon of Sixties-speak.

Perhaps more surprisingly she gained very good reviews from the unlikeliest of pundits. Arthur Koestler, the echt Mitteleuropa intellectual, ostensibly the least predictable of worshippers, loved it; Desmond Morris, he of *The Naked Ape*, followed suit. Giving allowance for the excess enthusiasms of any era (look no further than the brief intellectual infatuation with The Spice Girls) they were not wrong. Morris told readers to see it as a sociological document, and whatever the initial intention of Fabian's reminiscing, or Byrne's editorial expertise, that's what it became. It may have excited the less sophisticated readers who took the hype at face value (the paperback proudly terms itself "Unexpurgated" but no-one ever aimed a blue pencil – even in that era of censorship battles, the most benighted moraliser realised this would have been a case much too far) but its real charm, especially as viewed three decades on, is the degree to which it accurately reflects what was going on.

For a start there's the milieu, a world in which the counterculture bordered on the rock business, with the odd foray into glossy journalism. The duo produced a laid-back style that echoed the counterculture's accepting attitude to supposedly sensational activities that (then and sadly now) could still send shivers down suburban spines. Radicals might have shouted in suitably apocalyptic tones but the hippie end of the "underground" didn't make that much fuss. For all the sex – and nearly thirty years on one can be surprised by quite how much *Groupie* offers – it's not especially "sexy"; the attitude to drugs is nothing if not matter-of-fact. If Katie plated some rock-biz executive or dropped her crushed velvets for some star, then so she did (her main worry was "Is sperm fattening?"); if she smoked a joint, dropped a tab, did a Mandy or an upper, then so what. Needs must. As for the rock'n'roll, as Fabian was at pains to make clear, this was not bubblegum, but the cutting edge. Like morals reputations change, but Katie's pseudonymous roll call (with band names conveniently in italics in the original version) masks such Sixties stalwarts as the Floyd, Spooky Tooth, The Animals, The Soft Machine, Family, The Nice, Aynsley Dunbar and Jimi Hendrix.

The backdrops, for those who lived it and for anyone with a yen for the period, are wonderfully evocative. Reading behind their thinly disguised *noms-de-plume,* one finds The Speakeasy, the rock industry's favourite hangout; Middle Earth, the hippie equivalent, and the Roundhouse, one of its successors; Thea Porter, a couturiere who offered the ultimate in silks, satins and other gorgeous fabrics. And for real Sixties trivia fans, spot the upper class hack with a monster penis and a propensity for waving it in the back of taxis.

But in the end the over-riding sense is one of a woman if not wholly triumphant, then utterly in control. One never for a moment sees Katie as subservient, as exploited, as a victim. Instead, in the language of a later era, she seems empowered. Acquiescent, complaisant, foolish, but never dumb. The males, conversely, seem almost universally thick. Vain, egocentric, demanding, like petulant children. But this is the Sixties, an era when the "sexual revolution" was a strictly male indulgence. Katie plays a conscious role, but her intelligence never slips.

As the century vanishes the Sixties – mythologised into unreco-
gnisability by propagandists of every type – remain its pivotal decade,
a yardstick for a myriad of comparisons and complaints. And as the
cliché – has it, the past is indeed another country and, yes, we did
do things differently then. For those who want to know just how,
Groupie remains an admirable guide.

Jonathon Green, January 1997.

CHAPTER ONE

I realised soon after pulling Nigel Bishop that I'd done something very clever. It was a much better scene to turn up at clubs with the group than being one of many in the audience. It wasn't that I had minded being part of an audience, I just hadn't known any better. Now I had the privilege of the dressing rooms I also seemed to have a new identity. I *knew* the Satin Odyssey, and that was a pretty cool thing to be able to say. The Satin Odyssey are the first underground group to get anywhere. They started down at UFO, which is an underground club for people on that scene, like me. In fact, it was the only club where you could hear the really original groups like the Satin play. They were the first group to open people up to sound and colour, and I took my first trip down there when the Satin were playing, and the experience took my mind right out and I don't think it came back the same.

Nigel was their manager, and I hadn't really felt like being pulled by him until I found out who he was. I had been impressed, and thought what a groove to get back-stage and meet the Satin. Ben in particular, everybody was talking about him and saying how weird he was. He wrote for the group, and his mind, through his words and music, came over in fragments, like signals from a freaked-out fairy-land, where nothing made sense and everything held meaning. And I used to watch his shadowy figure on stage, and wonder about him. It had been difficult to see his face with all those colours flashing and swirling over him, but what I saw I liked. And when I saw it in the bare light of the dressing room I liked it even more. He had this thin nose which separated the sunken circles under his very dark eyes, and a pale skin that was stretched almost unbearably tight over the bones of his face. He was tall and thin, and his eyes had the polished look I'd seen in other people who had taken too many trips in too short a time. I found him completely removed from the other three in the group; he was very withdrawn and

1

smiled a lot to himself. As I got to know them all better I realised that the others and Nigel were worried about him. They muttered that he might freak right out soon if he didn't watch it. They complained that it was impossible to get new group things together with him when he was in this state. They weren't the only ones failing to get through to Ben. I was trying to let him know I fancied him, but it seemed hopeless, so I didn't push it.

Anyway, I was enjoying this new scene. The Satin had started making real bread now, and their shows were always packed. Underground groups were suddenly commercial, and straight industry people were moving into our scene and exploiting it. Imitators changed their equipment, got light shows, and followed where the Satin led. And the Satin were important, and there I was, being seen around with them. With Nigel, that is. I didn't know many of the faces yet, so I kept myself in the background, or stuck with Nigel and listened to him talking business. Everyone seemed to talk business, and I wished I knew more about it all. But I gradually started sussing things out, fitting names to faces and picking up little bits of knowledge here and there. And it made me feel one-up that I knew about these things.

Some of the group's image and importance rubbed off onto me, and my friends and people like that were always asking me questions about the Satin. I had a sort of status, because now they could say they knew someone who knew the Satin. And when Nigel took me on gigs I could feel the stage-door groupies' envy, and I found I liked to be envied. I was different to them, because I was with the group and they weren't and they wanted to be. Though I was well aware that without Nigel I would be back in the audience again, for, on my own, what was I – a 19-year-old groover who had just happened to pull a face. I'd sussed out the competition from the senior groupies, the type of chicks I saw at places like The Joint. The Joint is a nightclub for the pop-elite where nearly everybody is somebody. Ben didn't seem to notice all the pretty chicks that managed to find some excuse to talk to the group, but I watched the others getting it together, and I noticed that the girls had got classier now the group was bigger. One or two of these chicks lasted, but more came and went, and I wondered what happened to them. Maybe they ended up like Roxanna, a very obviously senior groupie I met at The Joint one night when the Satin were playing down there.

She came over to our table and said Hello, great to see you all.
She obviously knew them, though I didn't know her. She sat down,
and I watched. She had long dark hair and a fantastic figure, though
her face wasn't all that special. She spoke fast in a decisive way, as
though she really knew what she was talking about, in a rather
obvious educated accent. I was a bit knocked out by her, by her
confidence, and by the way she seemed to know everyone down
there.

"Hello, Tony," she would call out to some shadowy figure sitting
at another table, "I want to talk to you in a minute." Then she would
dash off and sit at this table and that, engrossed in conversation with
these different faces. I could never have done that. It made me
realise there was a long way to go before I could be like her, and
when I realised that, I also realised that I envied her just like the
stage-door groupies envied me. I wanted to leap about saying hi to
everyone too, I wanted to call these famous people by their first
names and speak to them in their own language. She seemed pretty
flash, and I wondered if she was for real. I asked Nigel what her
scene was and he said she pulled pop musicians, the best and the
grooviest around. Did she have a job, I asked. No, chicks like
Roxanna didn't have jobs. Unless it was something in the pop
business, their's was a full-time occupation, he told me.

I wondered if she got hung up on the guys she pulled, and if so,
what happened then. I mean, I get hung up on guys, and if I had
to dash about pulling groovy musicians I'd probably get hung up
on someone somewhere along the way, because I'm gullible, I
believe things people say to me. I mean I even believe telly ads and
things like that. Anyway, I was impressed and I envied her scene,
and wondered how I would do if I tried.

During all the gigs Nigel took me to I made as much contact as
I could with Ben. Nigel often left me alone in the dressing rooms
while he hustled with promoters and stage managers, and Ben would
sometimes talk to me. He showed me how to roll spliffs – as he
called them – so that I could roll for him. Though I was still Nigel's
chick I tried very hard to let Ben know how I felt about him. But
he was so stoned all the time that without being completely uncool,
I doubt if my message got across. He may well have interpreted my
longing eyes as transitory hallucinations or something. And I really
did want him, to me he was the actual *thing* that Nigel only repre-

sented. Although I dug the status I got from being Nigel's chick there was even more prestige in being Ben's. But only an incident of some kind could make this happen, and I just had to wait for my opportunity.

At the Oxford Summer Ball it happened. All in all it was a pretty busy day. Our flat got busted in the afternoon. I live in a large pad with two guys and another chick. One of the guys does light shows at UFO and the other is a recently dropped-out encyclopaedia salesman who now manages a bad, nowhere group. The chick is called Wendy, and she does nothing in particular except loon about. But she's very intelligent, and I get on well with her.

I suppose we looked pretty suspect, the guys with their long hair and acid clothes, me with my Jimi Hendrix head and all the people going in and out late at night. It was a nuisance getting busted, it meant wasting time and bread on solicitors and appearing in court, and the nagging thought at the back of my mind that I might be treated as an example and put away. Although it was quite fashionable to be busted, everyone groovy seemed to be having the same trouble. And ours was a dramatic bust – nine fuzz, two women fuzz, and two hash hounds. It took them ages to search the place and I was the only one who had anything, the others were just lucky not to have had anything around that day. After I'd been through all the bad scenes at the police station and I had been bailed, I found that I'd missed my lift to the gig. But Nigel rang up from Oxford and told me to come up by train, and he would send Bat, the second roadie, to meet me at the station.

It was quite late when Bat took me to the college where it was all happening. There were all these students and deb chicks in long dresses looning about with guys in DJs, all getting stoned on strawberries and cream and champers. Nigel was grooving around with some people he had been to college with, so I got Bat to take me to where the group was. They said the whole thing was too much for them, and as they had plenty of time before they were due to play, we decided to split down to the river and turn on. I managed to sit with Ben on a punt somewhere apart from the others and rolled some spliffs for him. There was this warm mist creeping along the river, and the sounds of the water lapping against the sides of the boat made us both feel relaxed and peaceful. I told Ben how groovy it was to be here with him, and quite suddenly he put his arm round me and started talking about Japanese temples. I sat leaning against him, and wondered if I was getting anywhere. I was afraid to speak, I didn't want to interrupt his voice or spoil the almost transcendental mood I was in. Though maybe I felt more on the edge of victory than transcendental. I didn't really understand what Ben was talking about, but it didn't matter. We stayed there until it was time for them to go back and play.

Nigel was a bit uptight when I got back, and wanted to know what was going on between me and Ben. I handed him a flower that someone had given me, and that seemed to do instead of an explanation. Then I escaped to watch the show from the light tower. The Satin were pretty good, and had quite an effect on the students, who probably hadn't seen anything like them before. Being a bit stoned, the strobes seemed especially effective tonight; from where I watched it was like the entire concert platform lifted into the air and jerked sideways in movements of sudden frenzy. The contrast of the quiet electronic pluckings of Ben's guitar and the sheer volume they worked up to as they all gradually joined in to form a tune, left me breathless. But I managed to get it together to go over and stand by the stage just before they finished. I had to fight my way through a mob of longdressed chicks who had gathered there, saying how super, and trying to attract the group's attention. I was sure there was very little holding them back from grabbing at the group like out-of-town groupies.

When it was time to go, the distribution of the passengers between car and van had to be decided. Normally I travelled in the car with Nigel, but I knew Ben would be in the van, so I hid behind a hot dog stand outside and watched Nigel drive furiously away without me. Then I emerged and said,

"Oh, has the car gone?"

"You're in the van with us," Ben said.

The back of the van was full, so I sat in the front with Ben, and Boris, the roadie. I could feel the curious eyes of the others on us from the back. This was my first ride in a group van, but I was so hung up on wanting Ben that I forgot to savour it. Side by side we sat, with a silent Boris driving very fast. The night was finishing now and we were into the early morning, with a huge red sun climbing its way up in front of us.

"Lean on my shoulder if you're tired," Ben said, and incredibly wide awake I leant, and closed my eyes. It stayed like that for a long time. Then, as we neared London, I realised that I would have to get something more positive together, for nothing was settled yet, except that I was blowing my scene with Nigel. I sat up and felt a little panicky. I alternated between looking grimly ahead and then questioningly at Ben. He didn't seem to notice me and I just didn't know what to do. Then, blowing my cool completely, I leaned over and asked him straight out if he was going to stay at my place, but he just gave a superior smile and stayed dumb.

Boris knew where I lived and made for my place first. The van drew up, and I slid the door open and climbed reluctantly out. Ben moved over into my place and then casually swung his legs out on to the ground. "Too much," my mind flashed. "He's coming with me." With the others staring at us out of the van's windows we waved our goodbyes and went into the house. We went upstairs and into the flat, then down the passage and into my room. And now, having wanted him for such a long time, here he was, alone with me in my room.

We wasted time exchanging vague remarks and smoking a couple of joints. Finally Ben reached down and untied his gymshoes. He always wore gymshoes, as a sort of protest about all the money they were making.

"Let's go to bed," he said.

We undressed silently and got in beside each other. At first we just lay there, he on his back, me on my side looking at him. I pulled back the covers and ran my hand over his body. In the half light of the room his long thin body looked longer and thinner, and his paleness was emphasised by the absence of hair. I kissed his nipples and after that I ran my tongue gently round his navel. He liked it. I felt his body stiffen and his erection came rising up hard. He shoved his hands into my hair and held my head steady. I wondered whether I should plate him. I hadn't done much of that, but I knew guys on the scene liked it because Nigel had told me so. So I covered him with my mouth, and started doing things with my lips and tongue. His hands still in my hair seemed to lose their strength. He never spoke or made a sound and hardly moved; he just lay flat on his back with his eyes wide open, and kind of blank. It took a long time and I enjoyed every minute of it. Not like with Nigel, who used to go berserk every time he got into bed and fuck me so hard I'd sometimes end up on the floor. This was cooler and somehow much sexier, and I really worked at controlling it for him. I'd take him to the edge and, feeling the tension rising in his body, I'd bring him right back and circle him around and then up again and back again and so on for a long, long time. Then it happened and I thought his body would crack under the strain, the way it buckled. He tasted sweet, and when it finished I found there were tears in my eyes. He lay in exactly the same position he had started in and still he hadn't spoken. It didn't matter. I didn't know where Ben's mind was at; it was enough to be lying there beside him. When I woke up early in the afternoon he had gone.

It was just as well it happened when it did with Ben, because soon after our night together, he freaked out completely. He turned up at my place without any warning to take me on a gig, and looked really ill. He wasn't speaking to anyone and his face was deathly white and beaded with sweat. He went on to play and I noticed halfway through the first set he wasn't singing and hardly playing a note. The bass player was covering up for him well, so not many people noticed. I just had to ask someone about him, so I cornered Nigel. Nigel had accepted the new situation with me rather sourly, but he didn't mind telling me.

"Nobody's talking about it," Nigel said. "We've been expecting something like this to happen. His mind is blown to pieces by all the acid he's dropped this summer. You won't be able to help him," he added, "though I wish somebody could."

After the first set Ben said he wanted to get away from the club and sit somewhere quiet. So we took a taxi back to my flat, promising to return in time for the second set. He sat down and suddenly started talking about all the people who were now putting down the group because they had made it. I told him there would always be people like that. But he believed the group had sold out, and he couldn't reconcile what he wanted to do with what he was actually doing. Commercialism had nothing to do with being a religious artist, he said. I wanted to help, but didn't really understand what was wrong. They were the best and grooviest musicians around. They could play where they liked and what they liked, and still make more bread than they needed. They were in a position to experiment with new musical ideas, and there was nothing Ben couldn't do if he had just half a mind to get it together. I just didn't

7

understand. It was like his mind was burning up right in front of my eyes. I'd tripped and turned on, perhaps not enough to realise what he was going through, but certainly enough to know what acid did to minds. But this beautiful pop musician, shivering and pouring out his torture and miseries, was something else. He seemed to have lost touch with reality, and there's no convincing someone like that. So I kept silent and just listened. When it was time to go he rose without argument and we went back for the second set.

This time he made no bones about his problem, nor the effect it was having on him. He went on stage, silent, pale and sweaty again, and just sat on the floor with his guitar in his lap. He stayed like that for the whole set. It was the last time he played for the Satin, and the last time I saw him. He left for some Spanish monastery to find himself. The Satin got themselves a new lead guitarist. They were established and could do without Ben. For me, the Satin's magic went with him.

CHAPTER TWO

My drug case came and went. I got off with a small fine by playing it very straight and saying that I had just been trying to find out what it was all about, and that I didn't like it, and I was sorry and never again. I had crammed a hat over my hair, which resembled an exploded brillo pad, and worn a sensible dress. But it was a pretty scary experience that I wouldn't like to go through again in a hurry. A few days later I got the sack from my job. I held a junior post on a newspaper, and, although I was good at my job, I used to take the occasional day off to groove, which made them a bit uptight with me. When the news of my trial came through, the editor flipped, because it gave the name of the paper I worked for, which he didn't dig at all. He said that by keeping me on it looked as though he was condoning pot-smoking, which he couldn't afford to do in these controversial times.

"OK," I said, "You'd better fire me." It wasn't that I sympathised with his problem or anything. It was just that I would be quite glad to get away from working with all these straight people, who were now looking at me as though I had committed a *real* crime. I had been working there for nearly a year, and although sorry to leave the few people I liked, I didn't really mind because I felt I had to move on; I wanted a job on the pop scene that might bring me the sort of Roxanna power I wanted. I had enough money to keep me going until something turned up.

On my last day I bumped into Reginald Chatterton outside the darkroom. He's a well-known freelance writer on the glossies, and did the occasional piece for our paper. I'd met him around the office a few times, and although he looks very straight he was nice to talk to. He's rather a witty writer, and I dug him because he had everything going for him. When I told him what had happened he said he was sorry, and asked me out to dinner that night. I thought that would be a groove, he'd be bound to take me somewhere trendy, and maybe I could hustle some connections and work through him. He'd be quite a good pull, even though he wasn't on the music scene.

So I split from the office immediately. I reckoned it was time to do something with my hair, so I went and talked it over with Gavin. He said my frizz had just about had it, and anyway, too many people had Hendrix-heads now. He suggested a Brian Jones. Gavin's always one step in front, he has to be, working at one of the best salons in London. So a Brian Jones it was, and for the first time in months I was aware of my hair hanging round my face, and when I swung it, it fell across my eyes. I had this long fringe that I could look out of but which people couldn't look in through, and the hours spent going through the straightening out process had been well worth it. I also blew a lot of bread at Thea Porter's, my favourite shop as yet undiscovered by too many people, and bought some crushed velvet trousers and a thin silk shirt with enormous sleeves.

Reginald took me to Cosimos on the Kings Road, where all the clientele were faces on his particular scene. Every time a face entered the waiters exploded into a sort of servile minuet of bowing and scraping which didn't stop until the face was seated. Reginald and I had got the same treatment, and I really dug it. Although it had been great going out to eat with the Satin, there were always so many of us that I felt I might have escaped attention. This time they *had* to notice me. Conversation roared from table to table and waiters glided about with notes from faces trying to pull other faces' chicks, and this is where it all happened for these types.

Reginald had put on a pair of sunglasses to look cool, so I retaliated by wearing these evil shades with reflecting lenses which looked like an American cop's sunglasses. Nobody could see where I was looking, and it really freaked them out. I didn't say much at dinner, because guys kept coming up to Reginald and saying "Hel-*lo* there" and talking shop. He was getting pissed and shouting jolly remarks to different tables. When we got back to his pad – a groovy split level place on the Embankment – he started going through this terribly dated seduction scene, feeling around on the top of my clothes and trying to force his hand down my new trousers, which can't take all that much strain. So I told him to hang about, and took my top layer off, leaving on my bra and knickers, because it was obvious that Reginald was one of those guys who had a fixed laying routine and I might just be spoiling things for him with too many premature actions. Well, he could fumble away for all he liked at my bra and knickers, but my Thea Porter trousers were something else. Reginald got to work again as soon as I lay down, and sure enough I was right about him. It took him hours to get it all together. He went through these really wild routines with his trousers on and almost came several times before actually getting out of them. Not having me to undress, I suppose the compulsion was still there, for he started to undress himself by degrees. After a bout of rubbing, groaning and fumbling, he sat upright quite suddenly and took off his watch. Then back to me, and some more of the same before he shot up again and removed his shirt. It took him ages to get down to his underpants, and they took the longest to come off. In the process my knickers were a write-off and my bra was without hooks, but there he was kneeling beside me in his underpants, which were sagging under the weight of his erection. It seemed huge. I reached out and felt it. It was the largest one I'd ever seen. I tried to pull his pants down to get a good look, but Reginald jibbed a bit and said something about it being unendurable. Unendurable! What was *he* talking about? I was the one who was going to have to endure *that* inside me. But when we finally made it to the bed, and it was right there between my legs and inside me, it wasn't so bad, it only hurt when it was going in and when he occasionally thrust it hard inside me.

It was all terribly conventional and well-behaved in bed with Reginald. He murmured fond words and called me darling as he worked at it. His was a well-bred passion which rose to a text-book climax and stifled cries of "I'm coming, my darling, I'm coming", and then hoarse gasps, after which he held me suffocatingly close and fondled my back, telling me, "How super and right it had all seemed". I had never known anything like it in my life. I mean, the guys I slept with were just not like Reginald. Few of them ever spoke while making it, and none of them were romantic in the phoney but nice way he was, but it was a new scene and a weird groove that rather appealed to me. I had my doubts about being able to plate him without choking, but tried to have a go all the same. Before I could get anything together he stopped me, saying, "Sorry, darling, kinky sex isn't for me; come up now". I dutifully moved up beside him.

"Don't you like that sort of thing, Reginald?" I asked him.

11

"It's perversion, darling, I *can't stand* it." I was amazed. Surely plating wasn't perverted?

"Do you think I'm perverted, then?" I asked him.

"Not really, just a trifle misled," he said.

"But why do you think plating is perverted? Everyone I know does it," I said.

"Well, I don't know the type of people that you go around with, but I'm obviously not like them. I think it's a beastly thing."

"Why?" I wanted to know, and he told me why perversion was a beastly thing. Apparently he had the horrors when some chick had freaked out and insisted on licking him all over. I mean all over, in an unstoppable way. He was too much, this Reginald, and I decided I would see him again.

So we start going out a bit together, and although I dig him for what he is, he's not my romantic scene at all. Meanwhile, a lot of changes were happening on the scene. UFO was dead, closed down by the fuzz and various other pressures, but there is a new underground music scene happening, a sort of breadhead's version of UFO called The Other Kingdom. It's rather grim and sordid down there at the beginning and people aren't too happy with the stone floor, but it's the only place of its kind around, and some really incredible new groups are appearing down there, including The Transfer Project and Relation. I spend quite a lot of time down there grooving and getting to know the management because they're the sort of people that might be able to help me get the sort of job I wanted. I don't feel like trying to make The Joint scene on my own yet, and I don't like going round with other chicks. Besides, I don't know any chicks who go down to The Joint.

* * *

And then I came across Roxanna again. It must have been a couple of months since I'd last seen her. She had been so together and sure of herself at The Joint that it was a shock to see her now, pale and hollow-eyed, and wearing nondescript clothes. Ted, the guy who lived in my flat, the one who managed the group, had met her at some function or other, and she was in trouble. She said she had nowhere to stay, and Ted had brought her back to our pad; I mean, she was a good pull from any guy's point of view. He left her in my

12

room while he went to buy some food to feed her. She remembered me all right, and I was curious to know what had brought her down so much in such a short time. She was tense and shivered a lot, but her voice still had a artificial edge to it. She didn't look at all well. I made her some coffee, and that broke the ice between us a little.

"I feel terrible," she said.

I agreed she didn't look too hot, and then asked what had happened.

"I took this OD," she explained.

"Is that an overdose?" I asked.

"What else?" And she looked at me sharply as though I should have known better.

"What did you do that for?"

"I was down, really down . . ." she laughed a little hysterically. "I'm always trying to kill myself." But making sure she didn't succeed, I thought. Anyhow, I couldn't imagine why she wanted to kill herself when she seemed to have so many things together.

"It's that bastard Roger," she went on. "He's thrown me out and is refusing to speak to me."

Roger led one of the best groups on the scene. He was a groupie's El Dorado, and she had been living with him for over a year.

"That's bad," I said, and the silence and a sympathetic ear prodded her on.

"Oh, I'm used to it, you know, but he's never gone so far before. He's really putting me through it this time, changing the lock and putting my cases outside." Roxanna paused, and then laughed confidently. "I'll give him three weeks."

"Three weeks?" I asked.

"Yeah, three weeks before he wants me back. He'll soon get tired of that Swedish bird . . . do you know, he flew her over just because she's got big boobs . . ."

She seemed very matter-of-fact about it all, and I wondered what was the point of an overdose. She started telling me about her scene with Roger, but it didn't quite ring true, and I started seeing through all her cool talk. She had been living with him for about a year and a half, but the relationship had broken down about six months ago. It seemed that she refused to admit this, claiming that it had changed into something different, like she didn't mind him having other chicks around, but she always made sure he came back to her.

You have to be pretty cool to take that sort of scene, I thought. Then she went into her groupie thing. In the groupie stakes, she told me, you usually started small and ended up with the biggest; that is, if you made it. And by that time the ones you had when they were small had often made it big, so you'd have quite a few good names to your credit. She had made it because she had the looks and was groovy, and had the confidence to get it together.

She seemed to have pulled all the best musicians around, and I noticed it was always the leader of the group. I liked the way she called all these guys by their christian names, assuming, of course, that I just had to know who she was talking about. It made me wonder whether I'd ever be in a position to do that, though now I was beginning to wonder whether her particular position was as cool as I had first thought, because here she was, she had pulled them all and ended up living with one of the best known. But it seemed that underneath it all she was a terrified chick, because she couldn't hold her scenes together any more, and, having had the best, she couldn't start downgrading her pulls now. From the way she told it, it struck me that something else was needed apart from looks and being groovy, to successfully get things together. Grooving around with lots of famous guys who lived constantly in the public eye and who spent enormous amounts of bread didn't mean that you were equal to them, like she thought. She was twenty-three, and I am nineteen, so I had plenty of time to try her scene. Not that I wanted to be like *her.*

However, it was interesting to listen to Roxanna talking about these guys, even if she did seem to have missed out somewhere along the way. And she did know them, and she had slept with them, which was more than I had. Apart from Nigel, I'd only had Ben, and nobody knew about that, it hadn't lasted long enough. Then she told me how this one wouldn't make it with the light on, and that one had it eight times a night, and another only wanted it once a week, and so on. And she even knew about the ones she hadn't had, because groupies like to tell other groupies who they've scored and what they are like.

"I'm really messed up now, though," she continued. "It's like I've got a frozen mind. As for sex, forget it. I stopped sleeping with Roger ages ago."

I didn't have much to say. I'm no good at offering sympathy, because I rarely feel it. I personally try to work out all my problems for myself, without talking about them too much. I know what most of these problems are, but it takes more than knowing to overcome them. I'm apt to be uncool with guys I like, giving myself away so that they can take advantage of me. And even when they know, and make me suffer all kinds of paranoid hell, I still go on taking it from them because that's the way I am and it's a problem. Though there's nothing like a bit of paranoia to keep one in one's place; at least, that's what I've been told by guys I liked enough to make me feel like this. Still, I hoped I'd never delude myself the way she seemed to. I reckoned it was no good putting on a together image if you were all screwed up inside, because people would soon suss you out and drop you. Be yourself until you could afford the luxury of being the person you wanted to be. And you couldn't be the person you wanted to be until you had a certain amount of power and bread and the right kind of confidence, and you wouldn't get these until you learned through experience. That's how it is on most scenes, and mine was no different. Roxanna was still explaining things. "Everyone thinks of me as Roger's chick, you know, which annoys him," she said. "He won't take me round with him any more because he doesn't want people to think we are having a scene. But I still use his surname when I sign myself in anywhere, just to let them know. He'll have me back soon, wait and see. He always takes care of me when I'm down. He took care of me when I had the baby . . ."

"Was it his?" I asked.

Roxanna shook her head. "I can't tell you that. Anyway, it's with foster parents now. I've given up a lot for that guy. He'll remember that as soon as he's fed up with the Swedish chick's boobs."

She seemed over confident to me. Putting her cases outside the door and changing the lock struck me as a pretty strong hint. Then Ted came back with some frozen food, and started chatting her up. But she kept putting him down. She had a very sharp tongue, and I suppose he was far too small a face for her to bother with.

"I can't bear being touched," she confided in me when he was out of the room, "would you mind if I stayed in here tonight?"

"Of course not," I said, looking forward to more revelations. Better than the music papers any time.

15

CHAPTER THREE

Ted made another attempt to pull Roxanna. They had the flat to themselves all day because I'd gone to do some typing for some bohemian poet I knew. When I got home in the evening, he was still at it, following her from room to room, making her tea and generally chatting her up. I don't know how Roxanna had behaved towards him before I came home, but as soon as I was in and we were lying on my double mattress watching telly she started putting him down. Maybe she was doing it because I was around, or again, like she said, sex didn't turn her on. Whatever the reason, it was fascinating to watch her at it. And the nastier she became the less Ted seemed to notice. He laughed at her and thought she was really witty. She put him down because of his age, his looks, and when he started name-dropping and coming on about how good his group was, she really let fly.

"Look," she said, "I don't want to know about you because you're a loser and I haven't got time for people like that. Now leave me alone, there's a darling, you're hanging me up."

It was rude and patronising all at once, and it rather shook him, and threw him into an offended silence. Then I joined forces with her, because his big talk really did seem pathetic in comparison to the scene she'd been on, and I don't like people to talk big unless they are big; it sounds foolish. Ted got uptight and left us.

"He's OK really," Roxanna said, after he'd gone, "but he's a drag . . . I mean *where* is he?"

"I'm not interested," I said. "He was uncool, I think, because he fancied you."

Roxanna tossed the hair out of her face disdainfully.

"Yeah . . . well let him go and pull some scrubber, that's more his thing. I couldn't possibly sleep with him." She paused. "Have you had him?"

"No, he's not my scene," I told her, which was true. I regarded

Ted as a mildly irritating friend. Roxanna turned and looked me straight in the face.

"What is your scene?"

Group members are my scene, I thought, but I couldn't tell her that because she'd ask me who I'd had and I'd only had Ben. I didn't want her to think me a failed groupie or something.

"Not guys like Ted. I used to go out with one of the Satin," I said. I felt I had to let her know about the Satin at least, because they were big.

"Yes, that's right," she said. "It was the Satin I saw you with that time down at The Joint."

"Yes, that was me. I wasn't sure if you'd remembered me."

"Oh, I remembered seeing you, but I wasn't sure who you were with at the time. The Satin are groovy . . . which one was yours?"

"Ben," I said, "lead guitarist."

"That guy was too much . . . Roger knew him. I never quite got it together, I was going through some bad scenes at that time. He freaked out, didn't he?"

"Yes," I said.

"And what now?" she asked.

"Oh, there are guys around," I said casually. "People mostly on the scene. Do you know Reginald Chatterton?"

"Is he a group?" she asked.

"No, he's a writer," I said defensively.

"Oh, well then, I haven't heard of him."

I'd have to learn not to drop Reginald's name, I thought. Maybe it would be better to drop Reginald.

"So you only sleep with guys," she said.

"Well . . . yes," I said, thoughtfully. I wasn't quite sure what she meant.

"What about chicks?" she asked.

"What about them?" I said.

"Do you go with chicks?"

"Sometimes," I lied. Although I've never gone with a chick, I'd thought about it often enough, and the way she spoke made it sound as if I should know about chicks.

"Yes, I thought so," she said. "Most chicks on the group scene go with other chicks . . . and you're on the group scene, aren't you?"

"Not really," I said, feeling now a little out of my depth.

17

She was surprised. "Oh, I thought you were. You look the type."

Did I? Were people able to point at me and say, "There's a groupie"? I didn't think that would be a good thing.

"Why do I look the type?" I asked.

"Nearly everything about you. Your friends, your hair, your clothes . . . though I must admit that you don't talk like one."

"Just as well," I said. No names to drop, I thought.

"Yeah, I know what you mean." She yawned and stretched. "God, I'm tired. Let's watch telly in bed."

So we rather coyly undressed with our backs to each other. This might be interesting, I thought. Last night she'd slept on a mattress we'd brought in from another room, tonight it seemed things would be different. In a weird kind of way I began to look forward to what was going to happen, or not happen for that matter, if she didn't try to make me or if I wouldn't let her when it came to the crunch. Also, I was curious to see what her body looked like naked – I had to admit she had an incredible figure dressed. I've often wondered about other chick's bodies because I have hangups about mine. I think most chicks have this feeling. Although I've never had any complaints, and like examining myself in full length mirrors, I still have doubts.

I put my nightgown on and turned round to see Roxanna still naked and caught a glimpse of her breasts. They were wider and flatter than mine, with more at each side, and her nipples stood out more than mine did. My eyes moved down over her body, and she seemed to have more actual curves and was definitely more voluptuous than me. I could understand how she managed to pull a lot of groovy guys with a body like that. Then she slipped on the nightgown I had lent her and smiled at me.

"What are you staring at?"

"You," I said. I had never seen a chick naked before, but she wasn't to know that.

Roxanna peered at herself down her nightgown, then up at me again.

"You've seen it before, haven't you?"

"Each body is different," I said, and didn't like how that sounded.

"Let's have a look at you," she said.

Terrified to be uncool about it, I lifted up my nightgown and held it above my head. My face hidden by the material, I felt her

18

eyes probe my body with a sense of almost physical contact. After a moment I let my nightgown drop.

"It's cold," I said, and made for the bed. I wasn't sure what Roxanna was up to. She made it sound as though she went for chicks though she hadn't actually said so. She now assumed that I did the same, and I wondered what was going to happen. I mean, she'd told me that she didn't dig sex any more. Perhaps she meant with guys. Anyway, I was far too shy to make the first move and I rather hoped she would do it for me. What a groove, I thought, to sleep with a chick who had had all those faces. I might even get to meet some of them through her. Third hand glory. But it was a start.

In bed I noticed that our legs were touching, and from time to time I noticed that she moved hers up and down against mine. When something on telly made her laugh she would lean right against me, and hang her head in front of me giggling. And she'd never quite move back to where she'd come from.

"Where do you have your hair done?" she suddenly asked me.

"At Leonard's . . . why?"

"I've never seen hair cut quite like that before," she said, and ran her fingers along my cheek where my hair ended.

"You've got freckles too," she went on, peering at my nose.

"Yes, I know," I said.

"I've got a terrible nose," she confessed.

"You can hang your clothes on it," I said, trying a nervous joke, because her nose did turn up in a very pronounced way.

"Very funny," she said, and pushed me. She was still treating me in a very superior manner, and didn't like it at all when I got at her.

"Do you get excited when you have a chick next to you? I mean in bed?" Roxanna let her hand slide down my belly, and I could feel my muscles tighten reflexively.

"Sure," I said, "but I feel like that when I'm with a guy too."

She put her hand between my legs. "Are you excited now?"

"I am a bit, I suppose."

"It doesn't feel like you are," she said, rubbing her hand against me.

"Well, I am," I said. And when I thought about it I was. Because a hand is a hand and a clitoris is a clitoris and when you can feel

19

the pleasure beginning to rise up inside you, it doesn't really matter about the sex of the hand.

"I'm only saying it because you're not very wet," she went on.

"Well, it takes a bit of time," I explained.

"I don't," she said, and moved my hand towards her. "Feel it?"

I put my hand between her legs and applied the tiniest pressure.

"Have you ever made it with a Les . . . a real Les?" I asked her.

She pulled back a little way from me and laughed.

"You mean a short back and sides, a pepper and mustard tweed dike . . . is that what you mean?"

"Yes," I said, "that's what I mean."

"Not on your life . . ." She paused and gave me one of her sharp looks. "Hey, you don't think I'm a dike, do you?"

"No, of course not," I said. Well, she couldn't be a *real* dike, not after all the scenes she'd had with guys.

"And I don't dig dikes," she said, "I think they're sick, I can't be doing with the rubber things they strap on. No, making it with a chick for me is like making it with a guy without the hangups."

"So how do you do it, then?" I asked.

Without warning she kissed me. I was glad her breath didn't smell, I hate smelly breath. After a bit I kissed her back, and it was weird. I had to keep telling myself that it was a chick I held in my arms, that this was a chick's mouth against mine. The pleasure I could feel was the same I felt when I was with a guy and it rather amazed me. The pressure of our hands and mouth were different, however, more gentle, less urgent.

"Come on," she said, and took her nightgown off.

This is it, I told myself, I hope she doesn't suss me. I stripped as well, and before I knew what was happening she was down between my legs and her tongue was inside me. It took me some time to get into it because I'm rather inhibited about being plated, and usually only enjoy it when I've been going with someone for a long time and we know each other's habits. I had to close my eyes and concentrate on the feeling. I could vaguely feel Roxanna moving about and she was making small liquid sounds which seemed to carry around the room. My body began to move too, gradually at first then more as the feeling began to overpower me. Roxanna's hands shot up and tightened painfully on my breasts. She was almost as frenzied as me now, and feeling the tension gathering in me, she began to rake my body with her fingers. I couldn't take much more of it. It was driving me mad, and she never let up for a moment. Finally it happened, and I gave myself up to it and my mind went blank for a moment. Then, when I'd recovered a little, she pushed me down and I followed her example. I used my tongue tentatively at first, but even this was enough to make her writhe and groan. It tasted different to a man, it was more salty. And I thought this is what a man must taste. She pulled me away from her, and brought her mouth down to mine, kissing me frantically. Her hips were still grinding away spasmodically and I put my hand down there and found the right place for my finger, but she was moving around so much it was difficult to keep in position. When she came it was very dramatic. She squealed and gasped and flung herself into the air. She's very noisy, I thought, as she lay heaving beside me, saying "Oh, oh, oh," over and over again. It's almost like doing it to yourself, I thought, there's nothing to it. And I felt quite pleased that I'd managed so well.

After a while Roxanna resumed her poise, and, back in our night-gowns again, we lay down to sleep. But she felt very talkative, and started repeating stories she had already told me. Although it was interesting at first, it soon became very boring. It was another of her Roger stories, and the way she told it made it sound so false, like she was exaggerating the whole thing. I fell asleep at the point where he'd decided to take her shopping in the Edgware Road.

Roxanna stayed three weeks, though we never made it again. It wasn't that I hadn't liked her. I had – it was just that I was starting not to dig her. She continued to put Ted down, and she was rude to Wendy and John, the light show guy, as well. And I was bored with hearing how Jimmy insisted on turning out the light before he got undressed. I was bored with shopping expeditions in the Kings Road. I was fed up with Eddie's moodiness, and I was thoroughly pissed off with Roger. I noticed that she never once mentioned their music, which was surely one of the most interesting things about these guys. Sure, she went on gigs, but only to groove around back-stage, it seemed. If I was going to be a groupie I wasn't going to be like her. I had to be turned on to a guy's music before I could be turned on to him, because the sound he was making was part of his whole thing. And if I couldn't groove to his music I didn't think I could groove to him. That was one of the main reasons why I had dug Ben so much, his incredible sounds. Though maybe if I met a musician, and got turned on to him as a person, his music would automatically turn me on. I didn't really know, but I wanted to find out about it all. I also wanted to get rid of Roxanna, who was now hanging me up and hadn't even introduced me to anybody. So I started putting out offhand vibrations, criticising her, and telling her she should get herself together and find a pad.

"I'll have some money from Roger tomorrow," she would promise, and "Roger will have me back soon, don't worry". I told her bullshit. If she wanted Roger back, she'd get him quicker if she showed that she didn't really need him – though I didn't think he wanted her back at all and I didn't blame him. Finally, after three weeks, instead of moving back with Roger as she had originally predicted, she met a promoter somewhere, and he had offered her a job and a room in his pad. That sounded pretty suspect to me, but she was full of herself now. Telling me over and over again how pleased she was to be able to graft again.

"So many times I've almost got it together and somehow just not making it," she said. "Like when I was producing for the Rainbow People."

Never heard of them, I thought. And until she moved out I got the complete history of her failed business career, and this she managed to tell as if it were a success story or something. More name dropping. People "in the business" this time, but it made little impact on me, because by now I thought of her as a failure. To me she was a chick who had little except her body, and those who had used it didn't seem to want it any more.

She could only go one way from now on, I felt, and that was down. There was a lesson here somewhere, I thought. Maybe I was underestimating the toughness of the scene when I believed I could do better than her. Maybe I wouldn't pull so many faces, but I'd cover up my mistakes better than she did, and I'd make sure I'd got a work scene together so I had a sort of security. I wouldn't be too ambitious, I'd let it happen gradually, and if it didn't happen at all then I could back out without losing face. Anyway, I had no further use for Roxanna, she was finished and I wanted her out of the way so that I could start.

CHAPTER FOUR

So one night there I am down at The Other Kingdom to see the
Transfer Project, this incredible group Zach Franks formed from
his Big Sound Bank since he took acid. They have really got the
light show scene together, too. They are the first in England to use
overhead projectors, and the great swirls of primary colours racing
round behind them plus their enormous sound hits you so hard
you almost fall over.

I'm talking to the Other Kingdom DJ, who is small and pretty
and has brown hair cut exactly like mine, when I become aware of
one of the Transfer staring at me. He is standing in the opening to
the stage eating a huge ham roll very ferociously. He seems to have
rather a long nose and is small and skinny. This staring goes on for
quite a while, and I'm rather intrigued. When they go on to play I
give him an all-over scrutiny; I'm sitting on the side of the stage so
I can watch him without him noticing. I like what I see; he's girlish
and his fair hair curls onto his shoulders. He plays lead and his
skinny arms coming out of his tee-shirt really turn me on.

When they finish their set he comes over to where I am and starts
staring again. Suddenly he says hello.

"Hello," I say.

"I'm Davey," he says, and I notice quiet Cockney overtones to his
voice.

"I'm Katie," I say, and don't take my eyes off him.

"You look sad," he says, looking pretty glum himself.

"Do I?"

"Yeah," he says, "you don't look happy."

"Well, I'm not sad."

His eyes widen while he thinks of something to say. And they're
beautiful eyes and I want to have eyes like that.

"Maybe it's the natural repose of my features," I add.

"I like that," he says, dead serious.

23

"Like what?"

"The natural repose of your features," he says, savouring the feel of the words in his mouth.

"It's true," I say.

He smiles at me thoughtfully. "I know what you mean. I have the same problem." And I think that I want to see him again. So I casually tell him that I've been invited to this new boutique opening and would he like to come along. He says yes and we arrange to meet.

Before he came to take me to the opening I wondered whether I would still like him in broad daylight. Although I had dug him, he had struck me as being slightly faded and weedy. However, when he turned up, I still found him attractive, though I couldn't quite work out why. It wasn't just that he was in a group, either. His clothes were great because although they were obviously carefully thought out, they didn't look contrived in the fashionable sense. He had this great Afghan jacket and faded rust trousers and skinny black tee-shirt. And his boots were a good shape and didn't look too new. I noticed that his hair was so soft it looked almost unreal.

I rolled a couple of joints for us before going, and we tentatively chatted. He was polite and straightforward and didn't seem to have any particular image. None of Ben's romantic despair; in fact he put down the talented freaks on the scene because they were destroying themselves and their music in the process. He reckoned that living was the most important thing that had to be done, and he admired people with systematic life plans, people who were complete and very much together. He was very pragmatic and treated pop music as a job rather than artistic creation, but he was good at his job and he dug his work, and that was a good way to be. So here was a member of one of the underground's currently most popular groups talking in such a together way that it rather unnerved me. And fascinated me.

It was good when people at the boutique recognised him with me, though both of us stayed quietly with our backs to a wall, slightly stoned, while it happened all around us. Then I felt his arm round my waist and I thought no mental blocks about this one. We split. After a somewhat self-conscious meal we went back to my place and slowly felt our way into each other's minds. He was very self-assured and worked out, with no hangups that I could find. His blue-green eyes concentrated on me while he spoke and I wondered what he saw. By the time we got into bed I was nervous. His confidence and coolness were making me feel gauche and useless. So I was dry and tight and reluctant to respond, never mind about initiatives. I was knocked out by the perfection of his genitals. They were compact and beautifully symmetrical, and I reflected that this was the first time I had ever found genitals worth looking at with appreciation.

The second time it was more relaxed and our movements coincided well. His strength was strange coming from such a frail body, and he really knew what it was all about. Afterwards I sat up and examined him while he lay slightly curled up and lost in the proportions of the bed. I flattened my face on his shoulder and breathed in his smell. It was a lovely smell, and it was mingled with Fenjal. That was a coincidence, because I use Fenjal in *my* bath as well. Then I stared at his face. Lying in repose I found his features faultless, and his mouth, slightly parted, was soft and girlish. That was it. Instant infatuation.

From then on he came round constantly, even dropping in on the way back from gigs if they passed by before about half-past three in the mornings. We didn't go out much, except sometimes to eat or to a movie. We spent a lot of time in bed. Davey destroyed whatever hangups I might have had about sex and my body. He made me very aware of my body and really turned me on to pleasure in a way that no one had before. He liked being plated, so I really got down to it. He said I was the best plater he had ever met and maybe he was right. There was nothing I couldn't do with him. I swallowed so much of him that even when he was away on gigs the taste of him would stay in my mouth for days. We had discussed the taste of sperm and I told him everyone's was different. He wondered whether if he ate bananas for a week, his sperm would taste of bananas. He never bothered to plate me, but that didn't worry me. I reckon now it can't be as groovy to plate a chick. I adored him. I would spend hours looking at his face and wondering what was so beautiful about it. His nose was too long and his eyes too weak (he wore contact lenses to straighten them and also to darken them) but the whole combination with that incredible mouth and soft hair was faultless. There was not one thing I could fault him on physically, and naked he was as sure of himself as when clothed. I loved just gazing at him and touching him. It was unbelievable.

He liked sexual diversions. He hit me with his leather belt one night to see if I liked it. I did, because it was him hitting me, but he found he didn't like hitting me, so that was abandoned. He said I generated a crudeness in him he hadn't noticed before and it was one of the things which he really dug about me. We played a lot of games in bed. We worked out some strange new positions and had competitions to see which one of us could come up with the most interesting and practical one. We sometimes sat for hours with his erection inside me just staring into each other's faces without moving. He said it was a Yoga form of love-making. We pretended it was the first night again, and the last. I had to seduce him, then he would seduce me, each of us seeing how long we could resist the other. I'd touch him up while he watched the television to see if I could make him come during the commercials. He got me to masturbate while he watched, then he'd do the same. Sometimes we masturbated together to see who would come first. This masturbation scene was something I had been into before. I mean, I was taught to masturbate by a far-out guy who studied William Reich, attended Reichian courses, and had built himself an Orgone Accumulator, whatever that was. To Reich, and his followers the orgasm was all important, and when this guy discovered that I wasn't having orgasms with him he became very concerned in a crusading sort of way to rescue me from my plight. For weeks he tried to make it happen for me. We tried control, positions, suggestion, but everything failed – perhaps I was trying too hard. Then, one night, with the desperation of defeat beginning to haunt him, he grabbed hold of my clitoris and started working on it with his fingers and thumb. At first it was uncomfortable and irritating, but I suffered it silently for the sake of the experiment, and because the prospect of a future without orgasms, as sketched out by this guy, was pretty grim. Then something different began to happen. He must have been touching me in a slightly different place because sensation began spreading through my body and flooding my mind, until I became all sensation and blank-minded. It nearly finished me when I came. I was holding my breath, concentrating on this incredible feeling, until I nearly burst, so when it became too much there was not only what I felt like a vaginal explosion but an oral one as well,

26

as I let go of my breath with a high-pitched gasp. I lay there panting, and then he did it again, just to make sure that it wasn't an accident. He now had to persuade me to do it for myself and I was shocked and put up a stubborn resistance, because I had never played with myself and really believed it wasn't a nice thing to do. But the temptation to recapture the sensation, a sensation that shredded my mind and senses, was too great, and I started doing it alone. I soon got it all worked out, and it was such a groove, almost therapeutic like the guy had said. I was rushing to my room at all hours of the day, locking the door and masturbating. I shunned everyone, including the guy who had taught me, and just worked on myself in privacy. And when it was all over, when the need began to wane, I was more than a little relieved that my skin hadn't turned blotchy and pitted, and that my nose hadn't fallen off; dark forebodings which had troubled me just below the surface of things. Well, I was only just fifteen at the time.

I still haven't had orgasms in the normal way – I mean lots of chicks claim they come first time round. Sometimes it happens when a guy masturbates me, but they have to learn the right way to do it. If they can, they're away, but not many do, and I won't show them how. This doesn't mean that I don't get pleasure from sex. I love the physical contact, and love giving pleasure, and I'm good at it. It gives me almost a feeling of artistic achievement when I know I have really satisfied someone. But it does take a long time for me to get a compatible sex scene together. I know I'm not frigid but I also know I haven't got a great capacity, because if the person I'm having a scene with insists on it every night it becomes a mechanical process, inevitably turning me right off. But I never have the courage to tell them, and when they suspect and insist on trying to make it happen for me I get uptight, because it's usually an ego thing with them, as most guys are obsessed with making chicks have orgasms, and it's a big let-down for them when them when they can't get it together. It takes someone I really dig and who really wants to understand to make it good for me. Davey was like that. He took frankness to the point of crudity to find out, and to understand he had to worm the information out of me. It's very rare for a guy to take the trouble to do that, and this was the first time a guy got that deeply into me.

Anyway, I felt very self-conscious with Davey at first, but when I saw how much it excited him I started to dig it, and we reached a peak one week when we did nothing but masturbate when we were in bed together.

We talked a lot as well. We talked about his spiritual scene and how he dug Gurdjieff and re-incarnation, transmigration of souls and Nirvana. I didn't know too much about all this; there were a lot of plausible theories around these days, but the way Davey laid his down they just had to be the right ones. He sometimes got uptight when talking about souls, saying I was laughing at him, but I wasn't; I just found it so strange that he should be so intense about it all. He told me that the only proper way to trip was to follow Timothy Leary's book, *The Psychedelic Experience*, and move from phase to phase. If you do this properly you will reach the point where this White Light is supposed to hit you in a blinding flash of self-realisation. Everything is wiped out by this White Light and your body and soul are atomized and flow into the life energy force. Now I've felt my soul leave my body on quite a few trips, but hadn't noticed this accompanying White Light that he was talking about. He accused me of never having tripped properly.

So we took a trip together, and a very solemn affair it was too, with Davey reading the changes from *The Psychedelic Experience*. He was trance-like and intent on reaching his mind-climax, but I couldn't concentrate. Too many walls were bending and colours changing, and I couldn't get the words or ideas together in my mind, I had all these important things to say, and Davey's enraptured voice sounded all wrong. What was he going on about? He advised me about the horrors and what to do if I got them. But I don't get the horrors, they just don't seem to be my scene. The really screwed-up ones inside, these are your horror candidates. Acid melts their defences and everything bad inside begins to feed on itself. That's when the mind is jolted into an attack of the unmentionables. We spoke about this for what seemed to be a long time, but you can never be sure about things when you trip out, and then we quarrelled about it, and began in rapid alternations to hate and love each other with great intensity. Davey got annoyed with me because I was distracting him from concentrating on reaching the White Light. He said tripping was a ritual, not a groove, and people who looned about on trips didn't know where it was at. He set such high standards of performance for himself in everything that even his tripping had to be as perfect as possible. Anyway, he finally got there, and stood up with his arms outstretched to greet his White Light. It didn't matter than his trousers suddenly descended around his ankles because he wasn't there, he was distributed into everything everywhere and I knew how he felt. All in all it was a groovy trip and I came out of it feeling closer to him than ever.

In order to impress Davey I made an intense effort to get a work scene together. "Getting it together" was his favourite expression, and he couldn't stand chicks who "weren't together". He made no allowances for chicks who failed in this respect. So get it together I did. Using the contacts I had kept from the newspaper, I managed to get commissioned by a glossy magazine to do a feature on the "hippy boutiques", as they called them, that were springing up everywhere. I didn't have much to do as it was mainly photos, but it impressed Davey. He went and got his sitar and played to give me inspiration while I brooded over my typewriter. He was also pleased when I hustled a job working for the Rome Festival, a week-long festival of pop music to be held in Rome. I was given the job of writing and editing the weekly newsletter, and doing publicity, which meant I would be grooving around meeting important people on the scene.

But the Festival soon ran into financial trouble. The groups were cut from fifty to twenty, the week to four days, and I ended up as the equipment manager, trying to get PAs and amplifiers together to satisfy all the groups. I didn't know the difference between a Farfisa and a duck's arse before I started, but what I didn't know I pretended and caught on fast. I learned to lie tolerably well, and the Festival people found me indispensable for soothing the ragged nerves of conned businessmen. Sometimes Davey came with me as I went round agencies on Festival business, and he'd watch silently while I went through my hustles, and when I'd got what I'd come for he would nod gravely at me, pleased at my ability to handle these tough experienced guys.

CHAPTER FIVE

The more I got into Davey the more I felt I loved him and depended on him. And as this gradually happened my hang-ups began to assert themselves. I couldn't believe that he felt the same way about me, and I was terrified that he might find another chick. I got quite desperate about this, and suffered paranoid fantasies about him pulling lots of teeny-boppers and groupies when he was away on gigs, because he never made any bones about being attracted to other chicks. And the thought of this when he was away made me jealous and evil. He knew it too, and didn't dig it – coolness was his motto – but that only made me worse because I couldn't help it. Finally it began to bring him down, and a lot of the initial happiness went out of our scene. He began to criticise my attitude and often complained that he felt guilty if he didn't spend every spare evening with me, and he didn't see why he should feel guilty, especially as he loved me, and would be getting a flat together for us. I knew if I was making him feel like that I must cool it, and I tried, but wasn't very successful. I couldn't stop myself from telling him how I felt, and he couldn't believe I loved him as much as I claimed to.

Going on gigs with Davey didn't help much either. It was a different scene from the Satin. The Transfer didn't dress up or groove, they were just doing a job, and Davey could never understand why I wanted to come along with him. But he took me to most of the local gigs, and standing in the audience while they played, I'd hear the suburban groupies discussing which one they dug the most, and it was nearly always Davey, and this mixed me up even more. I was proud, of course, that they fancied him, but a bit jealously uptight to hear them discussing him like he was a prize stallion. He's mine, I'd think grimly. And when he wasn't on stage I'd stick as close to him as possible to let them know. Davey dug his fans, and told me not to make it so obvious that we were together, and in the dressing rooms I'd have to sit in a corner and watch him chatting them

30

up while he signed autographs, which really annoyed me. Then something happened which really put us through some changes.

Davey's group, Transfer Project, although favoured by the underground and doing very well around London, just weren't making enough bread or getting the required number of bookings out of town. Zach, the leader of the group, had been asked by Den Casey to join The Savage on one of their big American tours, and had refused. However, when pressured again on Den's latest visit, he accepted, and that meant the end of the Transfer. Although Zach really dug the music he was making with the Transfer, the money and travel abroad were too tempting, and besides they didn't seem to be getting anywhere. Without Zach the group would be lost. Everyone dug the way he played the organ and his freaky performance on stage really knocked the audience out. It would be impossible to replace him, so the group would have to disband, which made everyone on the scene sad and angry at the unawareness of the provincial people who couldn't groove to his music.

That meant that in a few weeks Davey would be out of work. He started talking in a worried way about his future. He got offers from middling groups but turned them all down. His idea was to either make a lot of money and travel, or play with people who were making a sound he really dug. The Dream Battery filled both these requirements, they were going over really big in the States, and as they were friends of his and due back in England soon, he intended to approach them. But he was worried and moody and even hinted darkly that he would flee to this remote island called the Bird of Paradise Isle which he'd hankered after since he'd seen *Swiss Family Robinson*. And all these possibilities of him going away made me moody too, and we weren't much help to each other and had quite a few cold scenes.

It didn't help, either, that the Rome Festival had turned into a complete fiasco. The Americans who had come over to set it up, waving impressive contracts and spouting millions, turned out to be nothing more than freaks. Everybody in sight was being sued and the whole situation was getting out of hand. A lot of money went down the drain and underground prestige suffered a setback. It was sad because the original conception was brilliant and it could have worked with real organisation and more front money. A huge sports stadium seating eighteen thousand people listening to non-stop sounds for a week by groups from practically every country in the world. Fleets of aeroplanes would shuttle people to and fro, and it was intended to airlift the entire West Coast music scene en bloc to Europe. A wild shout which fizzled out with a whimper. Everyone associated with it felt very brought down, which was a drag because it could have been such a good thing, and great to be able to say one had worked for a successful festival. I didn't even make it to Rome. The ticket I was given I sold to Wendy because I didn't want to leave Davey. I wanted to go just to see what it was like, and it's groovy to go to things, but I just couldn't go without Davey, especially with his mutterings about going away soon.

When The Dream Battery arrived in England, Davey got it all together in his efficient way and came bouncing in one evening all pleased with himself.

"I'm joining The Dream Battery."

My heart clumped to the bottom of my expensive boots.

"That's great, Davey," I said.

"Yeah, we're going to the States."

He must have seen something in my face because he came over and put his arms round me.

"Come on," he said, "don't bring me down. Be happy for me."

"I am happy."

"Be honest. You're not."

"When are you going?" I asked desperately.

He let go of me and threw himself down on the bed.

"In about a month."

"A month?" I repeated stupidly.

"You're not happy at all, and that's a drag. You know it's the best thing that could happen for me."

He was right. I had known it was coming and I'd tried to prepare myself, but he was right, I felt very brought down. How could we groove together if I knew he was going away? Faithfulness, and "I'll write", and "everything will be the same when I get back", didn't come into it. We could both have said these things, but they would have been false, and Davey and I had always been straight with each other.

It took me two doomy weeks to get myself together. Davey complained that I was bringing him down, and started sleeping nights at his pad, saying he had a lot to get together. I started asserting myself in various ways. I dressed the way I really wanted to – Davey hated me wearing long dresses and freaky clothes; he had me shorten my skirts and dresses to ridiculous heights; he really dug legs and as I have good ones he said I should show as much of them as possible. When he began rehearsing with The Battery I stayed away, despite the fact that he actually invited me along once or twice and I wanted to go. Even my way of talking to him changed. It seemed important to me that he shouldn't go away thinking that I'd fallen to pieces just because he was leaving. I had to show him that I could take his absence as much as I dug his presence. Big things were going to happen to him in the States which meant that he would be moving on in status as well as experience. He would not be the same Davey when he came back, and he wouldn't be back for six months. I dimly realised that I would have to move in the same direction if there was to be any scene between us in the future. I found contacts I had make working for the Rome Festival useful for getting a new job, and I started pursuing some of them. Davey obviously noticed the change in me but said nothing; he sussed out what was going through my mind and understood why I wanted to get new things together for myself. What he dug most of all, he told me, was that he wouldn't have to leave with the memory of bad scenes fresh in his mind. We would write to each other, that much we were sure of, the rest would have to wait and see. Underneath it all, however, I was desolate at the knowledge that he was leaving me. Once he'd gone I'd work it all out on some new guy, but meanwhile he was here, and with him I was OK, but a few times I went out on my own and got very confused about guys chatting me up. Though unresponsive, I don't think I could have resisted a serious sex pull from somebody really determined.

And that's how things were until I contacted this guy at the Fund Agency. His name was Pat Blessing, a straight hustler of about 30 who spoke very fast Cockney. He had offered me a job while I was doing the rounds of the Festival, and here I was coming back to see if the offer was still open. One of the reasons why I hadn't been round to see him earlier was because I knew he fancied me, which was cool, but he knew some of Davey's friends and that sort of thing made me wary. I knew there was the possibility of a serious pull, but thought so what, the money and the position he was offering as his assistant would be worth whatever he threw at me.

The Fund Offices are in the West End. There are about six offices in all, and lots of groups, personal managers, roadies, producers, pluggers and bookers grooving around. They drink coffee, play sounds and make interminable phone calls in an atmosphere of paranoid competition. I found Pat in his office, which had a gold carpet on the floor, a sofa, two enormous stereo speakers and this specially built desk which is right-angled in shape and has sound equipment set down into the surface. And there's a framed series of gold and silver discs hanging against William Morris wallpaper. Pat was swivelling gently from side to side in his director-type chair and he was wearing some groovy shades. I sat on the sofa and he rang through on the intercom for some coffee. By the time the coffee arrived, we'd talked and I'd managed to suss out a few things. He seemed keen for me to start work, but said it all depended on the guy who owned the Agency. This guy was in the States, but would be back soon. I was not to worry, everything was cool. Then he turned to sex and started talking very frankly about his birds. Between sips of coffee and drags at my gold-tipped menthol I made my little contribution and that encouraged him. He leant back in his swivel chair and stared contemplatively at the ceiling.

"Me – I don't charver birds."

That must have been a lie. "I wouldn't have thought that," I said.

"No, straight." He gave me a very serious look. "I *like* to charver birds, but I never do."

"Why not?"

He shrugged. "Well, you can't tell these days, can you?"

"I don't know," I said, "tell me why not."

"Well, I'm telling you you can't because all these flower children are poxed up. You just can't tell where they've been, can you?" And he was still staring hard at me.

"That's the chance you take," I said. "Besides, who gives it to them? And stop staring at *me*."

"*I* don't take that chance," he said.

"Well, *I'm* not poxed up. In fact, I've never had it."

"I didn't mean *that*," he said swiftly.

"Neither did I," I said.

"Yes, I don't charver girls," he paused and looked at me intently. "But I'm not against the occasional plate."

I said nothing.

"Do you plate, Katie?"

"Of course," I said. I cannot see any reason for lying about my sex habits, even to a virtual stranger. To be able to talk about sex in a completely frank way is a help, but it doesn't mean *that* much in the long run.

"Plating without sex is just the thing for me," he said.

I said I knew what he meant.

"Yes," he went on, "it keeps it all on a fairly impersonal basis."

"That's often a good thing," I said.

"I wouldn't mind if you plated me," he said significantly.

I said nothing and his eyes went back to the ceiling, which he frowned at this time. After a pause I got through by sipping cold coffee, he suddenly swivelled down on me again.

"Would you like a massage then?"

I didn't want to be unfriendly, and I really like being massaged, so I calmly said yes. He sprang from his chair and came round to me, making me lie face down on the sofa. He began to knead my neck and shoulders. Then he got me to open my blouse so that he could get at my bare skin. He was brilliant with his hands and it made me tingle all over. I felt the least I could do in return was to plate him, which I did swiftly and efficiently. He complemented me and asked me to come round again in a few days. He hoped he could get me the job as he thought I would be a cool and discreet chick to have around the office. Not that he cared about anything people said of him – he knew where *he* was at, but all the same we needn't be indiscreet, need we? Nodding his head wisely, he showed me out of his office. I stopped to chat to one of the Ghost Engine in the reception, and while he was raving on about his latest record scene I became aware of a sharp-featured face watching me from behind a partially closed door. I asked the telephone chick who it was, but before she could answer, the intercom went and I heard her say, "Yes, OK, Ray, I'll send her in". She turned to me. "That's Ray, he wants you to go in."

"Who's Ray?" I asked. I guessed it was the one in the door. Sure enough, the telephone chick pointed out the door from which the face had appeared.

"Who is he?" I asked again. "I don't remember seeing him around here before."

"That's Ray Laurel," she said. "He's our publicist. He's new."

I was suspicious. "What does he want?"

The telephone chick smiled quite mindlessly and said "I don't know really. He says to go in for coffee and penguins".

"Oh, does he? Well, that's all right then, I like coffee and penguins. See you," I said to the Ghost Engine guy and went in.

Ray was thin and had a sharp nose that looked as if it would strike oil if he fell over. He darted about in short stabbing bouts of movement, sitting me down, introducing himself and handing me the promised coffee and penguins. His office was identical to Pat's except that it had framed glossy photos of himself with groups of famous and groovy people taken at important show biz functions. He flopped down onto his swivel chair and began to rock to and fro in a fretful way.

"Tell me, Katie," he said, "what did Pat want with you?"

"Just business," I said warily.

He gave me a frustrated look. "Don't give me that love, he was talking about me, wasn't he?"

"No."

"It's all right, I *know*. He was putting me down, wasn't he?"

"Look," I said firmly. "I don't even know you. Why should he talk about you?"

"Don't you see," he said, all fast and desperate, "that's what I don't know. I mean, I'm new here, aren't I . . . competition . . . see?"

"He said nothing about you."

"Did he try to pull you?" he asked worriedly.

"You mind your own business," I said without malice.

"Did he tell you to watch out for me?"

"Why should he have done that?"

"He always does, you know, he always warns the chicks against me."

"Well, he didn't."

Ray stopped rocking and went into a broody silence. This guy was too much. I couldn't keep up with him.

"Don't get uptight," I said encouragingly. "He never mentioned you."

He sprang up and paced around. "I tell you I won't stand for all this plotting. This aggravation has to stop or I'll split and take my contacts with me. *Then* where will they be." He paused and fixed me with a burning look. "What fantastic bristols you have."

I looked down at them in surprise, for they were hardly noticeable under my loose waistcoat.

"Do you really think so?"

"Yes, I do," he said, all tense.

"Why do you call them bristols?" I asked.

"It's just the way I talk," he said. "Tell me, did he plate you?"

"It's none of your business," I said primly.

"Did you plate *him*?"

"I told you . . ." I said.

"Do you plate?" he asked.

"Yes."

"Shall I plate you?" he asked, nose pointed in the air as sharp as a guillotine.

"No," I said.

"Will you plate me?"

"Why should I?" I said.

"Did you plate *him*?"

"Oh, forget it," I said impatiently, and made a move to go.

"All right," he said, and unzipped his fly.

"There you are," he said with satisfaction. "Let's see what you can do with *that*."

"You'd better put it back," I said, uneasily. "Someone might come in." I mean the door was open. Ray didn't seem to hear. He looked down at himself in dismay. "What . . .? Put *that* back?"

"Yes, you'd better," I said.

Ray gave me an aggrieved look. "You didn't tell *him* to put it back."

"I didn't ask him to take it out either."

"You mean you took it out for him?" Ray said swiftly. I remained silent. The room seemed full of his erection, and it was a magnet for my eyes.

"Look at the state you've got me into," Ray said dolefully. "Why won't you anyway?"

"Why should I?"

"You did it for *him*."

"He's the boss," I said, and walked out.

I continued to call round at the office, although under no illusions about the job. It was good for me to move around on that scene and get my face and my name known. Ray never tried it on me

37

again, and we got on all right from then on. Pat, however, demanded his due from time to time, and though it didn't hang me up, it was all rather uninteresting for me, rather a means to an end. I dug being around the offices, and I was driven home in the management car, given meals, records and posters. When I was with Davey, I didn't feel any shame, because, like one of them said, plating can be one of those scenes that works on an impersonal level. I mean there are some guys I would plate, but never hold hands with, like these guys for example. My only worry was that sperm might be fattening.

CHAPTER SIX

So Davey is going to the States any day now, though there seem to be various hangups over visas. Also, he has moved out to Dulwich with one of the group so that he can practise. He's got so much to do that I really feel left behind at Queens Gardens. I feel restless and lost and can't stand being alone in my room anymore. The other people in the flat are not much help either. John is setting up this light and sound plastic dome scene for some grooving deb friend, so he's busy at that. Ted is hustling twenty-four hours to promote his group, and Wendy is having an intense scene with some drummer and isn't at home much. I'm very down, all tensed up with Davey's imminent departure, hating him for going but wanting him gone and sort of not knowing what to do with myself.

I go and suss out the scene at Theo's pad. Theo is a writer I used to go out with. He has this big incredible pad in Kensington where elite and semi-elite film people, writers, and scene people generally, pour in and out. Theo has two of his friends from way back living there with him. These three have been writing and grooving together for about eight years. Theo made a lot of bread with his first book last year and immediately moved himself and his friends into this mansion pad, all balconies, big rooms, fitted carpets, cool sounds and groovy distracting objects. One of these guys is a writer called Johnny and we're good friends though we've never had a scene together. The other guy, Mark, is also an old boy friend but that's been finished a long time now. He's a poet and lives with this tall blonde American chick whom he usually calls B.G. or Blonde Giant. Though I like Theo and have known him a long time, it's difficult to be real friends with him because he's on such an ego trip that, if I didn't known him as well as I do, I would consider him an unpleasant power head despite all his groovy superficialities. All three are such different types. Each is talented and imaginative in his own particular way and they have this close affection for each other which comes across and slightly sets them apart from other scenes. If they didn't have this going for themselves it's doubtful whether they could survive the paranoia and savage uptightness which comes from three such guys living on top of each other and attempting to lead very together type lives while being stoned most of the time.

However, there is no doubt about who is king of the castle. Theo has all the bread, and is making more by writing film scripts. He has assumed the mantle of responsibility for what he calls his "family", which is cool, so he makes the bread, pays the rent, seeks the credit and works hard at allowing the others to bask but not shine. While I'm not absolutely convinced that I want to get myself into all that, I reckon I'll suss it out anyway.

Anyway, Theo and Johnny think it would be nice if I moved in because I'm cool and I can help Blonde Giant make tea and tidy up after smoking scenes and generally be a groovy accessory. Johnny intends to go away for a while very soon and when he does I can have his big room. Until then I can stay in the small room which has the colour telly, because the people in there are going. These people are two of Theo's freaky protégés. One is a guy who can do incredible things with wires and telephones. At the moment he is making a computer in the kitchen. Theo has persuaded a young millionaire to put bread into this wire genius. The computer will be able to forecast horse results, stock market trends and useful things like that. However, he is sharing the kitchen space with Theo's second protégé who is a speed freak and looks like one of Tolkien's Hobbits. This guy invents light machines and his mind can't seem to get it together with his mouth, because nobody can understand what he says. And these two are unbelievably jealous of each other and have the wildest territorial wars in the kitchen area, not to mention the sabotage which goes on whenever one or the other is not around. They are moving out and getting separate work scenes because people are afraid of what they might do to each other if things get worse. So I've come at a good time.

I tell Davey what I intend to do, and he's quite impressed but disapproves at the same time. Meanwhile I rent my room at Queens Gardens to some struggling musician on a temporary basis, because I feel I may well want to retreat back to my own company, though I reckon to stay at Theo's long enough for something to happen.

Things always happen at Theo's. There's only one hang-up: Theo hates pop musicians. Except people like the Beatles and Stones. That's because *they're* on a different scene – they've got real power, not just the sex power of some group on the make. So I'm not reckoning on meeting any group members there, but maybe that's just as well. After Davey a change of profession might be cool for a time.

The first week I'm there I have to sleep in Theo's room; he's away visiting some titled groovers in Scotland. He has this enormous bed made out of antique worm-eaten wood. It has black sheets and a white fur cover, and takes up a lot of the floor space, which is covered by a white fluffy carpet. The walls are white, too; at least those parts of the walls that aren't covered by tinted mirrors. Johnny hasn't gone away yet; he's having a fragmented scene with this young chick called Mara who wants to be a dancer and who walks around the flat showing her middle and a lot of her black-knickered bottom. She speaks in this terribly loud upper-class voice, which is really weird, because she only came to this country five years ago when her diplomat father defected from somewhere in Eastern Europe. Big T can't stand her because she rejected him, and I think she's driving Johnny mad.

Before Davey leaves we got out for the last time. We're going to see the movie *2001*, and so, to really blow our minds, we take some tincture. We can hardly speak when we come out of the cinema, and just sit overcome while we eat some food. Back at Theo's we get stoned some more, I think we both feel like wiping the last few hours we have together clean out of our minds. Davey seems a bit out of place there and is rather reserved. He reckons the atmosphere in Theo's pad was a bit too hedonistic, and could see me getting carried away. Why should he care, I say, he's going away. Yes, he says, he supposes he is. But he warns me to think about things and to get myself together. I tell him that moving out of Bayswater and onto a new scene is the first step in getting myself together. I was being cool about it all and speaking to him in my new detached way. I had to let him know I wasn't going to vegetate in England and cry over him. I'd got over the initial shock and almost didn't care what effect my words had on him.

We watched ourselves making it in the mirrors. I was so stoned and weird that it was like I was watching vaguely familiar people

going through their paces in a blue movie. I noticed how Davey
dilated his nostrils like he does when he plays the guitar. And I
noticed for the millionth time how beautiful I found his skinny
body, and for the first time how interesting it was to see his erection
going in and out of me. I arranged myself so that I looked good in
the mirror, and watched the expression on my face. I tried making
it look kind of ecstatic and sexy and then I'd look at him and he'd
be looking at me, and our eyes would meet in the mirror. Often
during the long time it took us to do all our different things together,
my mind switched off and my body took over completely. Sensations
built up and splashed around inside me as I lay with my eyes closed,
my body moving involuntarily and my mind a warm quiet presence
inside my head. Davey asked me once why I was crying, but I wasn't
crying, and I told him so, whereupon he suddenly became incredibly
tender and began kissing my face and my eyes. The images in the
mirrors became confused and there seemed to be a time lapse
between what was happening here and what I was seeing over there,
and I couldn't work out which came first, but then it wouldn't
matter any more because I'd be back in my body again with my
open eyes just seeing the mirror images as freaky hallucinations. I
tried to watch myself plating him, because I've always wondered
what I looked like, and when I caught a glimpse it looked strange
and unnatural.

We talked afterwards and I think Davey was a trifle disappointed
I was taking his departure so well, having made so many bad scenes
before. I'm sure he had expected tears and drama, but I'd used
them all up. I often find I can't cry at the right moment, though
when the moment and the person are gone the tears come. When
Davey left the following morning, after fond clutchings and fare-
wells, they still hadn't come. I knew I'd miss him but already I was
getting over round one. The weeks of waiting had been agony, now
it was almost a relief. We would have to go right back to the beginning and start again when he came back, and I would be ready for
him.

CHAPTER SEVEN

A couple of nights later Mara wants me to go The Joint with her. She often goes grooving off without Johnny, claiming she's meeting producers and people who want her to dance for them. I hadn't been to The Joint for a long time and the thought of all those groovy group members I would see down there was too tempting.

It's good to go out, I told myself, and I know I'm still hung-up on the group scene. So I dress up and wear a Japanese robe with long hanging sleeves, very short and held together with a brooch, and calico shorts underneath. It's all rather sexy because it's always falling open.

Anyway, we get into The Joint and it's Sunday, which is a drag night; there's nobody I recognise from the groups or anything. Mara's like a bait. She is wearing thin silk trousers which are rolled down over her hips so low you can almost see her crotch; then there is a large flesh gap all the way up to her breasts, which are just about contained by a tiny sleeveless halter thing, all sequins and coloured threads. She sits there, moving to the music, her breasts coming at you from all directions, with a life of their own, almost, and you just *have* to watch.

The group on that night are Jubal Early Blowback, who I've heard of because they were booked to play at the Rome Festival but never got there on account of all the cancellation hangups on the last day. I see them setting their gear up on stage, and I notice this guy with a moustache and an interesting face, a typical blues player's face. Blues players are a different breed to your pop musicians. They all have this untidy hair, Zapata moustaches and wear indifferent clothes, and Jubal are a Blues group. I really didn't know anything. I'd never seen any of these guys before and I wondered if the guy I was looking at was Jubal Early, but it turned out that Jubal Early is the drummer, and this guy is the bass. They come on and play and they're not bad, and I fancy this guy with the moustache, though they've all got moustaches except Jubal Early who's somewhat ugly but a good drummer. They have this funny little singer called Hector who stands at the organ and sings in a croaky soulful voice. He's got grey in his hair but he's sweet. Their lead guitarist is attractive and is wearing a snakeskin jacket, but I dig the bass player most; he's called Max and I decide to stare at him.

We were sitting at a table quite close to the stage so I stared at him, just stared. I did nothing else but stare and every time he looked up from his guitar he noticed me, because he noticed Mara. Like you notice Mara, then you look on and you notice me. It was good. He starts getting uptight on stage, trying not to look, then looking furtively, and there I'd be, still staring. They finish their first set, and he's at the bar having a drink. So I go up and talk to Jill, the chick behind the bar, and sort of brush against him, so he notices me again, but now I'm pretending I don't notice him and that confuses him and he thinks maybe he's imagining things. He should have been assertive and asked if I wanted a drink or something, but he doesn't and that's the way it stays until he goes back to play their second set and I start staring all over again.

About half-way through, a group of rather noisy guys come in and sit at the table opposite. I look over and there's some of Relation. I recognise them because I've seen them play down at the Kingdom, and, though somewhat new to London, they got off to a good start and everyone on the scene digs them and reckons they will make it. Relation are really weird to look at. Their clothes aren't wild or anything, but there is a bizarre touch about them that's interesting. None of them attract me at all. They've got the kind of faces I don't suppose I'd look twice at if they didn't belong to Relation; all battered and sharp – it's difficult to explain. They are making a lot of noise and drinking. People are saying hi to them, and they wave to Jubal Early, who waves back, and then Spike, the vocalist with Relation, who looks tall, spasmodic and stroby on stage, gets up and sings with them. He has this groovy strained voice, and it's so great to hear, that I forgot to stare for a while.

When the set finished, everyone is going, and we're just sitting there with some guys talking to us when suddenly all Relation are around us and they sit down too. Then the Jubal Early appear and they gather round Relation and suddenly it's all happening, and it's freaking Mara out. She's saying to everyone, "Hi, I'm Mara, I'm a virgin, and I dance, and I'm going to America to dance in a new star-studded production", and of course she's not going to do any such thing. They look and listen and can't believe that there's a chick like this. Their eyes go kind of blank when she speaks and they can't decide whether she's a joke or a groovy freak. They turn to me, wondering if I'm a joke too, and I say "Hello, I used to work for the Rome Festival and I had a terrible hustle getting all your equipment together". This got them all excited and they told me how they had met the Byrds in Rome and what a groovy time they had, even if the Festival was a flop.

Soon I am talking away to their bass, Joe. He's got blue twinkly eyes, a slightly beaky nose, and lots of soft dark curls. Natural ones. I reckon I prefer him to Max, who close up is a bit heavy featured, and anyway Relation are a better group than Jubal Early Blowback.

By now Max has got into staring at *me*, and I'm staring at Joe, and The Joint is closing around us. Mara is telling everyone what a groovy pad she has, and invites them back for a smoke. But nobody can make up their minds except Joe and Max, and we finally end up with them, and set off walking. Joe keeps talking away to me, and Max is trying to join in without much success. He got my message all right, the only trouble is that it has ended, and he doesn't know yet. Neither of them are paying much attention to Mara who is gliding and swooping about, quite out of her skull with excitement, and being much too freaky for either of these guys to even *think* about getting her together.

We become very silent as we creep into Theo's. We both know that if Johnny is awake he's going to be very uptight with Mara because she said she'd be back by two and it's now half-past five, and this is a scene they have had many times before. However, everything is quiet inside, and we put some sounds on and set the light machine going. So far everything is cool, and Mara and I are looking for some smoke but there doesn't seem to be any about so we go into the kitchen where the anti-bust stash is kept, but there's none there either. But it's OK because Max remembers that he has some, and he starts rolling. That gives me a chance to sit back on the sofa and talk to Joe, while Max, ignored, gets the joint together. We smoke and watch Mara who is grooving alone to the sounds. She twists her body and spreads and flicks her hair with a sort of naïve abandon, while at the same time jiggling her breasts and sticking her behind out like she's asking for it.

Then suddenly Johnny comes rushing in wearing a chick's green-striped beach robe and a hat. He takes an amazed glance around the room and calls Mara outside in a very weird voice. Mara is immediately nervous and very uptight. She pales and flounces after him, saying, "Oh bother Johnny", to no one in particular. We settle back uneasily and I tell Joe what the scene is between them. We hear their voices raised in the passage and after a while they drift down to the other end of the flat. After half an hour they don't seem to be coming back and now Max is getting fidgety because I'm not taking any notice of him. He stands up and looks at me accusingly. "You shouldn't be like that when I'm like this," he announces, and disappears, and I can't imagine what he means, but it leaves me and Joe alone, which is cool, and in pretty quick time we end up in Theo's bed. And maybe the skin cover, fluffy carpets, and tinted mirrors put him off because he's not very good at it, but he's nice and warm and I go to sleep digging him just the same.

The next morning, I try to get him up and out before Theo comes back. But Joe has to go to some photographic session and it's taking him ages to get himself together. He moans because he's still wearing the clothes he had on last night. Then he starts fiddling around with his hair, back-combing and pushing it into shape until he is finally satisfied. We are still there when Theo wanders into the room and takes in the scene with a sweep of his tinted specs. He always wears tinted specs, and he has a full broody face. Theo puts down his small suitcase, and starts pacing round the room. Joe stares at him, not understanding this scene at all.

"Who's he?" Theo asks, not looking at Joe.

"That's Joe," I tell him, "I hope you don't mind." Joe looked even more bewildered. I get up and start making Theo's bed. I hadn't told him anything about Theo, and all sorts of things were going through his head. Theo paced on, grumbling.

"I wish you wouldn't bring people like that around here . . . especially not in my bed . . ."

"Oh, well, I'm sorry, Theodore," I said. I always call him Theodore when I'm annoyed with him, because he doesn't like it.

"I'm very cross," he said, "I've had a very bad journey, and I want some tea, immediately . . ." He went out abruptly.

46

Joe made some kind of stifled sound and said he'd split and ring me later. I gave him my number just before he got out of the door.

When I took Theo his tea, I had to tell him who Joe was and which group he played for. He listened superciliously and said "Really, Katie", and, spreading his legs, asked me to "suck him off" to make him less uptight. Maybe if he'd asked me to plate him, I might just have obliged, feeling guilty as I did about the bed, but the "suck me off" expression together with the cracks about Joe, didn't make me feel very co-operative. So I said, "No, I can't really manage it right now".

He gave me a disappointed look and asked me to roll him a joint instead, which I did, and then I wandered off for a bath, hoping Theo would forget about Joe.

* * *

I rang the bell and the door was opened by this guy wearing a straw hat with untidy black hair sticking out under it, and his eyes obscured by shabby steel-rimmed shades. I said hello, and asked if Joe was in. He considered me cautiously for a moment.

"No," he said.

"Look," I explained, "I arranged with Joe to come round at six, and it's six now . . . so surely he's in."

"Well, he's not."

I got uptight. "Why not?"

"How should I know?" he said, raising his eyebrows.

I felt at a loss. "Well, can I wait then?"

"There's nowhere to wait."

I looked behind him. The hall was full of equipment; surely I could wait there?

"I'll wait in the hall," I said. Who was this guy, and who did he think he was putting me through all this, like I was begging for Joe's company? He certainly wasn't in the group, so who was he?

"Oh, very well," he said, "you can wait in Wank's room. *He* doesn't matter because he's just been sacked."

He let me inside, and I'd barely closed the door behind me when he turned and said: "We've just been busted."

"That's terrible," I said, "did they find anything?"

"They said they found a piece of charge on Joe's mantelpiece. He's at the station now, being bailed out."

"What a drag," I said. "Why didn't you tell me all this to start with?"

He didn't answer, just stared at me.

"What's your name?" I asked.

"Grant." And he marched to the end of the hall and pushed into a small room which was in absolute chaos, as though the fuzz had just turned it over.

"That's Wank . . . and his room is always like this . . ." Grant turned to Wank who rose up off the mattress pit and stared at us.

"Go to the kitchen and clear it out," he said, and Wank slid out of the room without a word. This guy seemed to have authority, whoever he was. "We're spring-cleaning; that's why you can't wait in *my* room . . ." and Grant sniffed distastefully several times at Wank's room and disappeared.

Keeping the door open, I balanced myself precariously on the mattress which seemed to have something immovable like a large, heavy rock under it and waited. This was the house where the group and their roadies lived. It was a small terrace thing, in very bad nick, and from where I sat I could see the narrow hall, the walls of which were all swirling colour, exploding women, and acid flowers, plus the odd monster or two. After a while I heard someone coming softly down the stairs and looked out. It was a quiet, abstracted looking guy, with a bucket in one hand and a bobbled hat on his head. He said hello very politely, and I said I was Katie and I was waiting for Joe. He said he was Wyatt and he was painting his room. I recognised him as the one in the group who played the wind instruments. He went off and I went back to the mattress.

Shortly after that, Grant came stomping down the stairs and into the room. He stared at me for a moment, and then said, in a very grudging way, that I could now wait in his room as he was finished spring-cleaning. I got up and followed him upstairs, and he plunged into this sort of boxroom about the size of a large cupboard. I went in after him and found myself treading mattress. There was no floor space at all. A double mattress took up the entire floor, and covering the ceiling and curtaining the door were these large printed squares which come from the Antique Market in the King's Road. Bits of material cut off some of the walls here and there. Peering behind them I found rows of clothing hanging from hooks screwed into the wall. I also found a disconnected sink, a TV facing the wrong way, and a small record player, all of which just fitted into the tiny space between the mattress and the walls. On one corner of the mattress a small table was lodged securely, full of books and boxes of sixpences. There was a large gaily painted steam radio hanging in a corner blaring forth music, and a heavy electric fire screwed into another corner gave out heat. The rest of the wall space was covered with lots of posters and cartoons of Peanuts and things like that. I was told to take my boots off the mattress, so I sat with my feet sticking out onto the landing.

"Unless you want to take your boots off," Grant added generously.

He was floundering around on the mattress, straightening corners, and throwing bits of rubbish out the window. I couldn't believe this guy. He was so unfriendly that he intrigued me. But I didn't dig him at all. He hadn't even asked my name, and it was really like he didn't care about letting you know he didn't care. I noticed he had a broken front tooth.

I could see Wyatt balanced on a ladder in his room on the first floor, and I watched him painting his room slowly as this obnoxious guy kept fidgeting behind me. I heard the front door open and looking down I was in time to see Joe unlocking his door and go into his room. Grant came out and glared at me through his glasses.

"You'd better not let Joe catch you up here with me . . ."

"What's that?" I asked.

"He might think I was trying to pull you."

"Rubbish," I said, and tried to rise with dignity from the mattress. I went downstairs, and into Joe's room.

Joe seemed pleased to see me. He kissed me and said hello several times. He said that he'd been planted and that he was worried about his court case. But he was soon smiling again after he'd changed his jumper and put on a record. His room was much larger than Grant's and all dark tones in different colours. He has a small narrow bed, a little wooden table, some shelves with a lot of rather pointless objects littering them, and a few trashy books. Then he flashed out a bottle of wine, and before I have finished my first glass, he's trying to make it with me. I can't understand the hurry, I mean he had me last night, so why can't he wait until later when we get into bed? It's not like he's got to prove anything. But saying no is a hangup, so I let him, and it's not much better than the first time – too quick, too mechanical, and no variation at all.

But lying there beside him afterwards, I still found that I liked him. He got out some digestives, and we sat around eating them, and finishing the wine. He told me that the others would be coming back soon, so I got my knickers and boots on before they all came pouring into his room wanting to know what had happened at the station. Nobody paid any attention to me as I finished dressing, and I kept my mouth shut and listened as they went on to talk about music in their funny provincial accents. I was knocked out at being surrounded by them all, and getting quite hung up on Joe.

* * *

So we start having this scene, and I'm hardly at Theo's at all. And when I am, it's a drag because everybody is always quarrelling, and Johnny has finally broken with Mara, and he's uptight and so is everybody else, and there's an air of gathering crisis about the place that makes it very difficult to be there. So I see a lot of Joe, and although I dig him, it's not the same as Davey. We don't seem very together, and I'm having a very hard time trying to suss him out. There isn't any mind probing or discovering, only grooving and sex, and that still isn't very interesting with Joe. We never talk about it though, we just *do* it, silently, and without passion in his narrow little bed which has too many covers and only one pillow. He has to have it because of his asthmatic tendencies – or so he says. I can't understand why I'm so fond of him. I wash his socks, mend his trousers, make sure he takes his allergy pills and make love to him. All in all, he isn't very healthy, and he looks as if he takes too many drugs, though his mind is far from being freaked out.

Relation have now been in London for about six months and they have come a long way already. Joe, like most of the guys in his group, is beginning to play the pop star bit, and he digs it. He's very cool, a bit too cool perhaps, because it's not that he's mysterious with it or anything; he hasn't got that kind of depth. Being what he is, he accepts that he doesn't have to put himself out to get groovy chicks – they come to him.

Spike, the singer, seems to be the weirdest of the lot. He's always darting about making strange remarks, like he's on a permanent trip or something. All of them are from the same district in Nottingham, and there's a closeness between them that comes from knowing each other inside out.

I enjoyed being part of their scene. Everybody was talking about the sound they made. As a group their music was very distinctive and different, though before they could hit it really big, they had to get through to a wider audience. Spike's incredible voice played a big part in their sound effect – harmony teetering on the edge of hysteria, and Joe's electric violin, and Wyatt's various wind instruments added a strange sound that hadn't been heard before. No one else had a line-up like theirs.

I liked watching Joe play. On stage he was very cool. When he wasn't playing his violin, he would lean against his amps, while he plucked his bass, he body still, his fingers barely moving, and one foot tapping out the rhythm. Spike did a lot of arm-waving, side-stepping, and gyrating, all of which was pretty freaky to watch. He looked like he was under a strobe, but he wasn't. Paul, the drummer, was very energetic, and kept his head constantly turned to one side as if it had been stuck on wrong, but he was really watching Eric, the lead, for the changes. Eric and Wyatt only made occasional trance-like movements – all the action was left to Spike. Grant would sit behind them on the stage, wearing shades, though these were, in fact, real specs, and a stop watch in his hand presumably timing the numbers. What he had to time the numbers for, I just didn't know.

I had discovered Grant's scene by now. He was their personal manager, doing for them what Nigel had done for the Satin Odyssey. He hustled about on gigs making sure they got the right billing, collecting money, and keeping accounts. He was always very officious, and carried an expensive leather attaché case wherever he went. He was very difficult to get on with, being aggressive to the point of rudeness, not just to me, but to anyone he felt like. But I'd seen his charming side too, when he was buttering up promoters, and trying to get favours done. This used to make me giggle, because it seemed so out of character. I had to admit, though, that he did get things done, and always made sure that the group were together when there was work to do. Whenever he came across me at the house, or at gigs, he'd say, "Hello, here's the hippy". Apart from that he'd just ignore me, that is when he wasn't obstructing me by refusing to get Joe to come to the phone whenever I rang up.

Then I was contacted by this guy who manages The Other Kingdom. He's fired a whole lot of people for fiddling on the door and needs someone new to work on the door selling entrance tickets. I reckon that would be a cool job as it's on the scene.

This manager guy is called Jason Wylie. He's a young, charming hustler who's got himself a good position. He's what you'd call a groovy guy, with long hair and a Procol Harum moustache. Lots of chicks find him attractive, but I get rather negative vibrations from him myself. I have to work that night, as it's Friday, and soon get into the job, digging my new position.

CHAPTER EIGHT

Joe had given me the key to his room while he way away up north with the group. He must have had an idea of the uncertainty I was feeling about being in Theo's pad because I still hadn't got my own room yet. But also I'm sure he wanted me to wash his things and generally clean his room up. Joe was very lazy about things like that. So two nights after he'd gone I went over there straight from work and took all his things to the Speed Queen launderette and went through the whole domestic scene. I was just about to go to bed when I heard someone coming into the house, so I went into the hall and bumped into Wank. He said hello – saying hello in that house is like a reflex action, it's as if they're perpetually surprised to find each other. I said hello, and Wank, grinning, asked me if I was alone. He knew I was, and followed me into Joe's room. Although he had been fired for various misdemeanours, he was still living in the house. He stood there, looking me up and down, a very assured grin pasted to his lumpy face. His hair is thin and flat, and so is his body.

"I'm busy," I said, sitting down and giving him what I thought was a hostile look.

His grin widened into something really evil. "Don't give me that." His eyes darted about the room looking for somewhere to fix. "Besides, I'm looking for something."

Right, I thought. And I know what it is, you ratfaced git. "What do you want?"

Wank pointed to Joe's lampshade. "That's mine for a start. Joe pinched it out of my room."

"I wouldn't know about that," I said.

"I wonder what else he's nicked," Wank said, and started examining the mantelpiece and going through Joe's pockets. I kept a silent and disapproving watch as he searched. I didn't say anything, I thought maybe this was usual procedure. Also I was a bit frightened of Wank. I had sussed him out as one of those unpredictable freaks who really *don't* care what they do. Wank pulled a biro triumphantly out of the pockets and shouted: "Aha, my biro!" Then he fell silent and stared at me, making me more scared and uptight.

"Well what are *you* doing?" he said meaningfully.

"I'm going to bed."

"Alone?" he asked nasally.

"Yes, I'm tired."

He laughed. "Don't give me that."

"I mean it."

"Chicks never mean what they say," Wank said.

"Well, I do."

"I don't want anything from you," he said.

"You won't get anything."

"I just want to do something for you," he said, grinning mindlessly. "Something groovy before you retire to bed."

"You have nothing that I want," I said, all icy and uptight.

Wank cocked his head sideways, which, with his long crooked nose, gave him the look of a demented vulture. He slapped his hands together, and although he was smiling there was a lot of tension about. "I just want to get my mouth around you," he said.

I was horrified. "I'll tell Joe."

I was beginning to feel really scared but trying not to let him know it.

"Joe won't mind," he said.

This immediately made me very paranoid about Joe's feelings for me.

"You want me to," Wank insisted, "go on, admit it."

"I've told you, I don't want anything from you." What was the matter with him, wasn't he getting the message? How was I going to get rid of him?

"Of course you do. Why don't chicks admit things? You want to do things that you don't usually do with your boy-friends. You want your clothes ripped off and your face punched. You want me to scratch away your feelings because feelings are a drag. And feelings are a drag because they interfere with sensations, and deep inside chicks are all sensations. So how about being honest and admitting it?"

Wank was really worked up now, his body was twitching, and it seemed to be getting closer. He's mad, I thought.

"Get out," I said.

He gave me a sinister look. "I could have you. I could do anything I want to you because nobody would care, not Joe, not the others, not even you."

"We'll see what Joe says when he comes back," I said, trying to appear nonchalant.

"Anyway," he said, decisively, "I don't want to really. It's just as groovy for me to *talk* about it and watch your reactions, you see."

"Get out," I said, hating him.

He went, and I sat there listening to him crashing all over the house, my mind an icy blank. Did he really believe the things he had said? How could he think like that? What he'd said about chicks really wanting those things to happen to them might be true for some, but not for me. I dug feelings for people more than sensation; at least I had always thought so, and in any case I certainly wasn't going to find out from him, ugly bastard.

I had left my handbag down in the basement, so I crept out to get it. As I was slipping upstairs again, Wank suddenly came rushing out of Spike's room shouting things at me. I accelerated, and stubbed my toe on something, but dared not stop until I was inside Joe's room with the door locked behind me. I extracted what looked like a broken plectrum. I then started getting undressed, but froze when there was a knock at the door. It was him again.

"Hello," he shouted. "Let me in. I've left my cigarettes in there."

I couldn't see them, so I shouted that he hadn't.

"Let me in to see," he yelled.

"You haven't left any bloody cigarettes in here, I tell you." I was determined not to let him in again, because maybe he had had second thoughts about talking being just as groovy and was really going to have a go at me this time.

"Well, give me some of yours," he shouted.

I glanced at my packet of gold-tipped menthols. "I've only got two left," I said loudly.

"Give me one, then."

I took one out of the packet and slipped it through the keyhole.

"Open up," he said, all aggrieved.

"I've told you, I'm going to bed."

"You're just a slag," he shouted, going away. "Just like the rest of them. And if I get my hands on you, you'll soon find out."

I sat thinking about it before I got into bed. Do all the chicks who come to this house have to go through the same scenes? Or was it just my luck?

* * *

All in all that was a pretty grim week while Joe was away. There were problems at The Other Kingdom because the licence expired soon and Jason, the manager, didn't reckon on getting it renewed, what with the premises being busted for drugs earlier in the year and all the complaints from the Covent Garden authorities. The fuzz just didn't like us, and wanted us out. But there didn't seem to be anywhere to go, and to do our thing properly we needed our own premises. I got on well with Jason, but I didn't want a scene with him; I don't like sleeping with guys who pay my wage.

The day after the bad scene with Wank he took me and Lenny, the pretty DJ from the Kingdom, out to eat. We had to go to the Macrobiotic Restaurant, because that's all Lenny will eat. After that we went back to Jason's pad and got stoned. I thought that he was going to make a really determined effort to pull me; all the indications were there and he was staring at me, and leaning against me. I rather dug all this, and let him think it was all going his way. But I was going to show him I wasn't like all the other chicks he found so easy to pull, and split with Lenny, who was so pretty I just had to have him.

Lenny had a groovy little room in Fulham full of star charts and cosmological prints. He's one of those guys who is very hung up on UFO's and chases off to Ireland with lots of similar groovers at propitious moments, to trip and watch the sky for omens. We got into bed and he started telling me about Messagés. These Messages are in the form of topographical contours, and ancient monuments like the Pyramids, Stonehenge and Glastonbury are some form of instructions to super-groovy UFO voyagers, he said, and would be acted upon in due course. He reckoned that there were about a million like himself around the world who knew and believed in all this, and that they were the Select. When it was time for the instructions to be carried out, the UFOs would land and cart off the Select to some place he simply called "There", while the rest of us, egged on by faultily coded genes, spun into our inevitable destruction cycle. He also warned me about asbestos, he was mortally afraid of it but wouldn't tell me why, and almost begged me not to press him too closely about it. I knew he was hung up on Macrobiotic food, but it brought me down when he started to talk about it, because that was a scene I went through last summer. However, I cooled it and listened to him, because Lenny is very sweet and only seventeen. He looked like an angel in National Health glasses, lying beside me with his straight dark hair cut exactly like mine, and his very white body was glowing in the shifting changes of his trip lighting. To change the subject I started stroking him, and he became alive and kissed me rather passionately, but he wasn't having an erection. I began to get very frustrated because nothing was happening, except he clutched me hard once or twice and groaned, but maybe that was just my teeth. Presently I gave it up and just lay beside him with my arms around his shoulder. He was very wry and embarrassed and seriously reckoned he was going through a sex change and was impotent because of it. But he didn't fancy guys either, so didn't really know what was happening. Anyway, he said he'd plate me if I wanted him to, not that he dug it all that much, but he liked me and thought I was groovy and that maybe I'd like him to. He was nice, and I said no, leave it, he didn't have to do anything. And that's how we slept, just touching, with no hang-ups or come-downs the following morning.

The next night we all had a frightening experience at The Other Kingdom. As part of the responsibility of making a lot of money from underground support we often give the use of The Other Kingdom free to put on benefits for the various interests which make up the underground. Everybody gets their chance sooner or later to make some bread. The underground press use us, the Diggers (those who have dropped out into rural bliss), the politicals, the anti-drug law people, all sorts of them, they all use us and get their whack. And the underground Legal Service gets a slice off the top of all our takings. Because the music scene is probably the most commercially successful aspect of the underground they all reckon we've got money to spare, which isn't always true because we have immense overheads; groups like the Satin Odyssey now costing £350 instead of £30. Anyway, tonight was the turn of the Oaxaquahatl

Peyote People known to their friends as the O.P.P., a community of bearded freaks who are trying to find themselves through the ritual of mystical expression. I personally find them squalid and messy, but went down to work because I got paid just the same. There they all were, in long robes, painted faces and full of stuck-on stars. Although I was outside in the box office it sounded very much as I had expected; a lot of chanting and wailing and ceremonious announcements. And reed pipers, finger cymbalists, temple bell ringers and bongos adding to the already incredible sound. About halfway through the evening a distraught grandmother came rushing down looking for her granddaughter. Apparently one of the People has a kid of eight who is a ward of court to the grandmother and this People freak has snatched the kid away to bring her to this scene. Granny didn't think the place or the company was right for the kid and tore inside looking for her. We followed her inside, and sure enough, there was the kid all decked out in headband and robes, really grooving with her Mum and the others. Granny made a grab for the kid, who ran off to hide. Granny and Mum stood screaming at each other, and the rest of the O.P.P., thinking this was all part of the ritual, joined in. Granny decided to go and get some help, and arrived back with a couple of fuzz. They decided reinforcements were necessary, and re-appeared with fifty more fuzz. But instead of being cool and talking to Jason and getting us to co-operate, they just roared in, stopping the whole show and making us turn on the house lights. They crashed around, knocking over equipment and giving the People horror visions. But when the People had readjusted their perspectives, they started getting uptight, especially when they found their Trip Machine had been smashed. So abuse and scuffling broke out, until, after an ugly half hour, the child was found hidden under the stage. She was carried out, followed by screaming Mum and grim Granny, and irate chanters. When they'd all finally gone we started to close up; there were about half-a-dozen of the Other Kingdom staff left around, including Jason and Lenny. I was in the office counting money when this persistent hammering started at the front doors, and one of our doormen came rushing into the office, saying there were thousands of Covent Garden lorry drivers outside, with hammers and bars, trying to get in. We didn't have time to wonder why, because there was Jason shouting "Everyone out!"

I swept all the money off the table and locked it in the safe. I wondered whether everyone had already split as I ran. I looked back as I reached the exit, and there were all these overalled savages spilling into the hall, shouting "Get the bearded nits!" I couldn't close the back door from the outside, so just ran up a side street until I found some of the others. After a while we decided to go back and see what was happening. We went inside very cautiously; there seemed to be quite a bit of damage done, cigarette machines kicked in, projectors and lighting equipment smashed, and the telephone ripped off the wall. Jason and Lenny had locked themselves in the office after I had run off, and put an armchair against the door while they phoned for the police. It had taken three calls before any appeared, and then it was only two constables. They claimed to have been too busy to send any more. I wondered what had happened to the fifty that had appeared so eagerly an hour earlier?

When things had calmed down a bit, we discovered the cause of the lorry drivers' freak-out. Apparently someone (a fuzz?) had told them that we were holding a child sacrifice. They had held a quick union meeting and decided to sort us out. Eventually we managed to explain to them what had really happened and they grumbled off. I was still shaking when I got back to Theo's, but nobody there wanted to listen to my story because there was a bigger drama in process.

Mark had discovered homosexual tendencies within himself and had fallen in love with Jerome Charles, a friend of Theo's, who had been coming round to see him a lot lately and doing all sorts of research and taking masses of notes which seemed to have boiled down to a page of typing. Jerome is about twenty-four and slender and his dark hair is already going grey. He wears those little round, steel-rimmed glasses, and his face is handsome in a desperate sort of way.

Jerome had apparently indicated similar feelings to Mark, and had left him sitting on the floor of the bathroom to sort himself out. Theo was all in favour of him consummating the relationship, reckoning it would either put Mark right off any physical scene with a guy, or show him where he was really at. Blonde Giant was being loving and sympathetic; she knew Mark's dramatic personality and sussed the whole thing would calm down in a day or so – anyway, they were due to leave for the States in a couple of weeks. But Mark was shaking his head and saying, "All I want to do is be with Jerome and hold him". I talked with him alone for a while; he was staring into my eyes like a lost soul, but I'd seen that look before. Suddenly he grabbed me and kissed me violently and said in a broken voice that I was good. Then he downed a few Mandies and Blonde Giant hustled him off to bed. Theo came striding into the room, looking important. I tried to tell him about the attack of the lorry drivers, but he found Mark's dilemma far more titillating and started going through all the possible behaviour patterns that Mark should adopt. But it was no big drama really, Theo said, because everybody has homosexual tendencies. "Except me," he added, "I'm asexual."

"But that's because you're on speed," I told him. Theo has been at the methedrine because he has to meet a deadline with the script he's doing.

"Perhaps. But I rarely put myself out to do my best for any chick. I just haven't met any that turn me on enough. Except one, and that was a long time ago." Then he started talking about himself, and the sort of chick he might marry. He reckoned he'd never find physical perfection, so he'd either have to marry for money and looks, or preferably someone well-known, either an actress or a successful career woman; anyway, it all boiled down to someone that would add to his image. He wants people to say, "Theo's got a groovy wife". He went on and on about himself, asking me questions like did I think he was a reasonable guy (I didn't), and was he good in bed, and did I like his script. I find that Theo needs constant confirmation that he is an OK guy, and now he was on speed the paranoid fantasies were really beginning. I was quite bored with him by the time I escaped to bed.

CHAPTER NINE

When Joe came back he had to appear in court for his drug charge. He pleaded guilty and got off with a £30 fine and a warning from his manager. The group decided not to take any chances in the future and appointed Ruby, the new junior roadie from Newcastle, to be stash man, so that if the house got raided again none of the musicians would get busted. It would be a terrible drag if one of the group got put inside.

I mentioned the Wank incident to Joe, but he was so cool and indifferent about it that I flared up. "You don't care what I do, Joe, do you? I don't think you care, and I don't dig that at all."

"Well, did you let him?"

"Of course I didn't," I shouted indignantly. "Did you think I would . . . with *him* . . .?"

"I don't know, do I?"

"Do you really think I would?" I insisted.

"There was nothing stopping you," Joe said, matter-of-factly.

I felt really injured that Joe should think that I might sleep with one of his friends while I was his chick. And it really insulted my pride that he should think I'd let someone like Wank pull me.

"I mean," he went on, "if you wanted to, why not?"

If I had been reasonable I would have admitted that there was a lot of truth in what he said. I mean, if Wank was not such an evil-faced, screwed-up drag with no status at all, my scene with him might have taken a different turn and added a spicy twist to my whole relationship with Joe. But I hadn't because I dug Joe and felt rather faithful to him – I mean, Lenny was something else, another scene that didn't matter. So I didn't feel like being reasonable and cool about Joe's non-reaction, and thought, oh, you're too cool Joe, and maybe I'm right in thinking that you don't dig me so much. I started brooding about this, which is bad, because when I brood I become sulky and even more clinging.

However, when we were at The Star things seemed to be a bit better. Relation had been there rehearsing all afternoon and Joe had left my name at the door. I'd just scored some incredible black trousers with gold embroidery from Theo Porter, and had my hair straightened to its limit by Gavin. Inside The Star the first person I see is Grant, tearing about with his attaché case.

"Hello, where's Joe?" I ask.

Grant pulls a disgusted face and heaves me in the direction of a red and white striped door. I open it cautiously and there they all are, in various stages of undress. Hello, hello, they all say, which is a groove, and makes me feel easier already. I'd hate to feel they didn't like having me around, but they are always very friendly and always chatter away to me, especially when Joe wanders off, which he frequently does, sitting in corners with other guys from groups. He knows it makes me uptight, but doesn't seem to worry about it very much. I challenged him about this once, and he looked at me thoughtfully and said, "I suppose you want me to sit and hold your hand all evening". I told him not to exaggerate, but it would be nice if he could demonstrate some affection. "Well, you know I'm not like that; if you want to go out with me you'll just have to put up with things the way they are. Maybe you've got the wrong guy". I said I hadn't got the wrong guy and fell into a doomy sulk.

Anyway, there I was sitting in The Star dressing room, which is very narrow with a bright naked bulb and the walls all covered with obscene graffiti, when Relation's manager Roland Johns, comes in. I've seen him around, so I recognise him, but I've never met him. He sits down beside Joe, and Joe introduces me. He gives me a curt nod, which immediately makes me uptight because I think he doesn't like me, or rather he doesn't like me being in a dressing room with his group.

I go out outside to watch them play and I'm grooving away to their music when someone touches my shoulder. I look round and there's Max from Jubal Early Blowback. This is the first time I've seen him since the night he disappeared from Theo's. He seems too stoned to remember all that, and just asks me if I've come to see Relation. I say yes, I've come with Joe.

After the first set Joe, Spike, Max and I go to a pub for a drink, and I'm sitting squashed between them, fully aware of all the glances they are getting from the chicks there. A blonde comes up and accosts Max and we all giggle when he plays a little indecisive game of to pull or not to pull with her. Finally he doesn't pull, and we go back for the second set. Max must realise by now that I'm having a scene with Joe, but he's very cool and says to come round for a smoke some time. I decide he's a good guy. Then we all go down to The Joint for a meal, and it's good to be the only chick going in with them all. I have to go through more paranoia as Joe loons off to talk to other musicians; his coolness is really aggravating me.

I bring the subject up again as we are walking home, and I'm really feeling that I'm loosing my grip on things, having to break my cool like this. My complaints must have brought him down, because he started grumbling that chicks shouldn't come on gigs anyway, it's a drag having someone sitting in a corner watching you with a possessive glint in her eye.

"OK, I'll wait at home," I said, desperate to please.

"Is that what you want to do, sit at home playing little mother, warming the bed and darning my socks?"

"Yes, I suppose I do."

"Well, that's very nice, but it's not really my scene. It's too domestic, and I'd feel tied down."

"Oh, you needn't feel that," I said. "But do you like me, Joe?"

"Yes, of course I do. But it's getting rather *involved.*"

"You're so cool, I really think you don't care."

"I'm not one for showing feelings. You just have to suss them out."

"Well, I can't," I said. "What do you feel for me?"

"You're a groove in bed." What an answer, I thought.

"Do you like screwing all that much?"

"I'm easy," said Joe. "I make out with you all right."

"Just about," I said bitterly. "And that's only because I work so hard at it."

"That's what you're there for."

"Is that all?" I felt really brought down.

"Look, Katie," he said with finality. "It doesn't matter to me whether a chick screws or not. What is important is how she screws. Now you're a groove in bed, and I dig that very much, but don't start asking me for deep meanings or reasons, I honestly don't know anything beyond what I've told you. I don't look for anything in my scenes with chicks, it either is or isn't. Now let's forget it."

I wanted to have it out with him, but he seemed so non-committal either way that I didn't seem to be getting anywhere. And I'm cowardly about show-down scenes, so I shut up, but I was dissatisfied with things the way they were.

We got in about four-thirty and I had to go through the usual acrobatics to get into the narrow little bed. Our recent scene must have put an edge to Joe's responses because he was much better that night and actually seemed to enjoy what we did. After we had made it a couple of times Joe fell asleep, but I couldn't, and feeling the need to pee, I tried to clamber out of bed. I barely made it without disturbing him, but when I tried to get back I lost my footing and grabbed at the bookshelf, and the whole thing came away from the wall, showering Joe with all the books and things that were on it. His eyes blinked open in surprise. I pretended I had just woken up too, and said falsely, Oh, look the shelf has fallen down. What do you mean, he said grumpily, just fallen down. Do you mean it just fell down on its own? It must have done, I said, and foolishly started picking up the things off the bed. He shrugged his shoulders and went back to sleep. Got away with that one, I thought. I didn't want Joe to get annoyed and think it was a nuisance having me there.

* * *

I was shattered the next morning. I hadn't had enough sleep, and felt grotty; sleeping so close to Joe in that tiny bed, I woke up smelling of him and feeling sticky; even though it was summer he wouldn't reduce the number of blankets. I certainly didn't feel like coping with Grant when I found him getting onto the same bus as me. We went on top and sat down together. I kept an uneasy silence, not wanting to say something and have him put me down, with me feeling so fragile. Then amazingly Grant launched into what I suppose was some kind of explanation about the aggressive side of his personality.

After speaking about his aggro, as he called it, he shot me an accusing look and said: "You think I'm flash, don't you? Well, that's the way to be. People take notice of you if you're flash. The trouble is, I'm not *really* flash because I can't carry it right through like with chicks, for instance. I'm flash with them, but I can't pull them. I'm really waiting for one to come up and wrap herself around me and take me home to bed."

The idea of some chick raving up to Grant, oozing motherly instinct and leading him off to bed just like that was too hysterical to even think about. I kept quiet and he went on: "It never seems to happen, you know. Chicks aren't like that. You have to go through all kinds of hustles to pull them and who needs them *that* much."

That Grant was revealing a vulnerable streak made him more human to me, in fact I almost liked him. We chatted about Group Members having more pulling power than Personal Managers. He said that there were three different scenes, GMs, PMs and RMs. I was on a GM scene, explaining that it stood for Group Member, and the next two categories were Personal Managers and Road Managers. Group members got the best chicks, and these chicks had to keep the status thing going by not dropping into one of the other categories. They're all slags, anyway, Grant concluded.

"It's really just coincidence that Joe's a Group Member," I said defensively, though I knew in my heart it did have added attraction.

"And Max too?"

"Yes," I said, knowing my case was lost. Before Grant could bring me down further, his attaché case fell onto the floor and all his little chitties and football pools flew everywhere. I had to laugh at him crawling around gathering them up. When everything was in order again he launched into another attack, criticising me for being far too possessive about Joe. This rather annoyed me, because I thought I was being cooler with him than I had been with Davey. However cool I reckoned I was, it obviously wasn't cool enough by Grant's standards. I wondered whether I'd become so hung up on the status thing that group members were the only guys I could dig, and that I couldn't appreciate a guy for himself, only for what he stood for. Was I on an ego-trip? I knew that I had rather launched myself in a direction that had meant changing my priorities, and there was a certain position to be reached before I could sit back and sort things out like that. I just hoped this position could be reached before the whole thing I was into twisted me like Roxanna, making me blind to the false values that I was accepting as the real thing and unable to come down off my ego-trip. Anyway, I was glad I'd had a talk with Grant, and grateful in a way that he had pointed out to me what was happening, so that I could brood about it. And maybe he'd be nicer to me on the phone now.

* * *

A few days later it's my birthday, and I'm hustling Joe to take me to The Joint with them, where they're playing. I'm having a bit of trouble with him, because he's been saying I go on too many gigs with them, and really chicks shouldn't come – bad for the image, I suppose. Even Grant was starting to say, Oh, you again, whenever I turned up to watch them play, though he hadn't been so rude on the phone recently. And you don't want to get in Grant's bad books, because he'll start putting you down behind your back and turn you into a joke. So I knew I had to cool it, but I badly wanted to come on this gig, so I stuck at it, laying it on about it being my birthday. He finally gave in, and rather huffily agreed for me to come round later. But he rings me up later at Theo's and says he's got to meet some guys first, and will leave my name at the door. I don't like that arrangement, but it has to do and I set out for The Joint.

I find all of Relation sitting at a table, and there's no room beside Joe, so I sit at the other end with Grant, Wyatt and Paul. After about half-an-hour I get acute paranoia because Joe hasn't made any attempt to speak to me or anything. They all go into the dressing room – the dressing room at The Joint is even worse than The Star – there's hardly anywhere to sit and it's full of discarded pianos and tubas. Bill, the roadie, buys me a drink, and I'm rapidly losing my cool, because I start bleating at him that everyone treats me better than Joe, and it's not fair. He nods his head wisely, but doesn't offer much consolation. He is plump and sweet with an interesting face and a very soft voice, so it is hard to hear him when he *does* speak. They start playing, and I sit at the table watching, feeling very brought down.

Towards the end of the second set Spike starts freaking around with his microphone, kicking it off stage and throwing it around. He decided that this has quite a good effect and he's going to do it more often. I watch Grant chatting up some spade chick; they're both being very flashy, and I wonder whether he's trying to get it together to pull her. When the group finish Joe comes and sits opposite me and eats a steak sandwich rather gloomily. They all gradually appear, and then Joe disappears, but I keep my cool and talk to the others, until they too wander off. So I walk around, and come across Grant, standing in his multi-coloured striped leather jacket, watching the roadies clear the equipment.

"Where's Joe?" I demanded.

"How should I know," he replies, not looking at me.

"You don't think he's gone, do you?" I feel I'm losing my cool again.

"He might have done," says Grant, unhelpfully.

"Oh, that's a drag, that's really a nuisance," I said, because although I could easily sleep at Theo's, I'd given my bed to some American chick, reckoning on staying with Joe. Besides, I *wanted* to stay with Joe.

"Why, do you need somewhere to sleep?" asks Grant, still not looking at me.

"Well it's not that, exactly, it's just a drag." I didn't really know what to say.

"Well, if you need somewhere to sleep, you can stay in *my* room." And as Grant's room consists entirely of mattresses, that meant his bed. With him, I supposed. I couldn't believe he was just being kind.

"That's very kind of you," I said. "But I'm not quite sure what to do."

"Well, like I said, if you need somewhere to sleep . . ."

This presented a new twist which I didn't know how to meet. I didn't really want to sleep with Grant, but on the other hand I wanted to go back with them, and it would serve Joe right for going without me if I slept with Grant. On the other hand if I slept with Grant, maybe Joe would consider that was that and wouldn't take me back. It hadn't really occurred to me that Grant was trying to pull me, which was an interesting situation on it's own. Anyway, I said, "Thank you, Grant, I might just do that".

"Yes," he said, "You do that – stick around, I'll help them load the gear so we can get off faster," and he put his leather jacket round my shoulders. Well, I thought, that's really something, Grant never touches the equipment, and here he was rushing around with speakers on his back, and humping amplifiers and things. But I was feeling a bit dubious about the whole change of events, and still wishing I could find Joe. I decide to go into the dressing room; Grant's jacket must have given me confidence. And there's Joe, and

I feel all glad and rush over to him and put my arms round him, and he says "Hey, what's all this", and I say, "I thought you'd gone without me".

"Well, I haven't," he said, "And what's that?" indicating Grant's jacket.

"Oh, that's Grant's jacket," I said, and throw it onto a chair, thinking, good, I won't have to sleep with Grant now. Then Grant comes through the dressing room with some equipment and Joe says "What yer doing, Grant?" and Grant says he's loading the van because Bill and Ruby are so slow and I giggle because I know the real reason. He snatches his jacket and tells us to hurry up. Joe and I sit in the back of the van and hold hands, and the others get in and there's this chick in a knitted dress who can't make up her mind whether to come with us or not; she seems to be somebody Wyatt knows, and Grant's being aggressive to her, telling her to get in if she's coming because we're going. She says she'll only come if there's no funny business, and Grant tells her to get in and shut up. She has to sit next to him in the front, and he sticks his nose in the air and maintains a disdainful silence. Back at the house we all disperse into our various rooms, but I feel I should say something to Grant before going to bed. So I go up to the landing and knock on his door. He asks who it is and I say Katie. The door opens and there's Grant without any trousers on. It hits me suddenly that maybe he thinks I am going to sleep with him after all, so I quickly say "I wanted to thank you for being nice".

"Oh, that's all right."

"Well, goodnight," I said and rushed back downstairs.

CHAPTER TEN

Next day Relation went off to the provinces for a few days. I hadn't
stayed at Theo's for three days, and when I got there I found him
sitting alone in the big front room, with the sounds and the light
machine switched off, and a tense white look on his face. Since he
had started his script, Theo was up on speed all the time now. He had
rapidly begun to lose weight, and he was behaving more erratically
than usual. When he wasn't uptight and aggressively silent he was
garrulous and full of obsessive fantasies about his life, work and
friends. As the others had their problems too, everyone was having
a difficult time. The quiet in the flat was unnatural. Theo didn't
speak and hardly moved when I went into the room. I sat down
beside him.

"Johnny's gone," he said abruptly.

"Where?" I asked.

"I threw him out," Theo said grimly.

"What happened?" I asked. I wasn't surprised really.

"They're all gone," he said, "Johnny, Mark, Blonde Giant . . . the
freaks in the kitchen . . . I threw them all out."

"But Mark and Blonde Giant went to America," I said.

"Yes, I *made* them go." Theo turned and gave me a frozen snarl
which I suppose was just a very uptight grin. "A clean sweep, I
decided, was the best for all concerned."

"But they're your friends," I said.

"I don't have any friends," he said. "Correction, I can't afford
friends . . ."

I sat silently, digesting all this.

"What about me?" I said finally.

"A clean sweep is what I said."

"You mean you want me to go too?" I asked.

"I'm not telling you to go. I just want everyone out."

69

"OK," I said, and went out of the room. I left Theo sitting as still as a statue on the sofa.

I moved back into my old room in Bayswater with no trouble and a sense of profound relief. It was all very trendy and sceney at Theo's and a groove when things were going all right, but I wanted a place I could call my own.

Joe had been back a couple of days by the time I got things sorted out. I rang him up as soon as I thought it was cool to do so, and he didn't sound very pleased to hear from me. He was very down and depressed, and said he was busy; could I ring him in a day or two. This would have made me extremely uptight if I hadn't been so busy moving my things and settling back into my old flat. But, when that was done, I decided that he would just have to see me whether he like it or not, so I rang again.

Grant answers the phone and is surprisingly helpful when he discovers it is me. He tells me Joe isn't in yet, but will be back soon because they all have to go to this reception in an hour. Taking advantage of a pleasant Grant for once, I suggested that if I came round now I would catch Joe before they left. Grant said OK, and if Joe hadn't come back by the time I arrived I was to go up and see him. OK, I said, and set off from work feeling quite cheerful.

Grant answered the door for me and as I followed him into the house I noticed that Joe's room was locked, and presumed he had not come back yet. I followed Grant up to his funny little room on the landing. It's quite convenient in his room; you can see everything that is happening on the ground floor where Joe lives and also the first floor above us. You can hear telephone conversations as well, because the phone is on the landing outside Grant's door. And even with the door closed you can still see what is going on because Grant has strategically made a spyhole, which he peers through whenever he wants to be certain about things.

I sat there listening to the radio while Grant dodged about putting on his business gear. He wore a dark purple collarless shirt, a terrible grey suit with braces, and white plimsolls. I gave his suit some very doubtful looks and he aggressively asked me what I was making faces at. I told him his suit was awful, and he snapped back that along with his attaché case it was a vital part of his image. "But it's an awful suit," I said.

"I don't want no hippy telling me what to wear," he muttered.

"You don't expect me to dress like one of the group, do you? That's not the image I want."

"But you could get something better than that. I mean, it's a good shirt and the suit spoils it."

"Well, that's too bad," he said, and proceeded to go through the contents of his attaché case, throwing scraps of paper out of the window.

I sat there listening for the front door to open and Joe to come back. I wanted to see him, but was suddenly scared of facing him, in case he thought it presumptuous of me to come round just like this. Suddenly Spike darted up the stairs and said hello in a surprised voice when he saw me in Grant's room.

"Joe's in the basement," he remarked, and nodded his head a couple of times before disappearing upstairs. I gave Grant a suspicious look and wondered if he had known all the time that Joe was down there.

"It's nothing to do with me," he said airily, when he saw me looking at him. I really didn't know what to do. Obviously I should go down and announce my presence to Joe, but I was scared he was going to be all cool and disinterested. I was sure he was going to drop me, and couldn't face that, knowing the way he'd do it to me, leaving me all stranded and neutral in the house, while he went through a long withdrawn moody on me. As I thought about this the panic built up inside me, and I considered that I might be cooler to switch to Grant before Joe got his message across. That might be better for my ego rather than being dropped and picked up again. At least it would *appear* to have been my decision. But the hangup was that I still dug Joe so much. I sat there silent and incapable of deciding anything. When Spike went past again I stopped him and told him to tell Joe that I was in Grant's room, thinking that he would come up if he really wanted to see me. Spike's eyes jiggled about and he said yes, OK, but he couldn't understand why I just don't go down myself. When he went off I realised that as Joe didn't know I'd telephoned for him, and also didn't know that I'd thought he was out, it might seem as if I'd come over specially to see Grant. Oh, balls.

They weren't playing at this reception, just going to promote themselves and meet people. Grant started to hustle me about my movements later in the evening, but I couldn't decide; I wanted to see Joe, but the longer I sat there, the more impossible it became to go down into the basement. What I wanted to say to Joe was quite simply, Do you want me or not, because if you don't, I'll go with Grant even though I like you best. But I knew I'd never get that together. Grant suggested that I wait until they all came back. I said I wanted to speak to Joe. "I'm not stopping you," he snapped.

"Will you go down and ask him to come up and speak to me," I asked.

"I'm not having anything to do with it," he said.

"But I want to explain," I said. "Please tell him to come up."

"There's nothing to explain," said Grant, matter-of-factly. "You're building your scene with Joe into something more important than it actually is."

That surprised me. "Am I?" I asked. "Do you think I should just drop it?"

"Don't ask *me* questions like that. I don't want to get involved in your affairs."

"You bloody well have," I raised my voice at him. "You got me to come up here in the first place."

"You didn't have to, you know."

"Well, what shall I do now that I have?"

"That's up to you. I'm not going to make any decisions for you. But I'll tell you something – *I* dig you." Meaning, I thought, that Joe didn't.

"Yes," I said, because I'd sussed that anyway. "But I'm still not sure what to do. I'd like to have a word with Joe."

"Do what you like."

"I'm not waiting here for hours until you come back. Ring me at Theo's. That's where I'm going to be later on, because I've got some records to pick up. I'll have decided by then." I knew I was only putting the decision off for a while, but that was all I could do right then.

"Right," said Grant, gathering up his attaché case. "See you later."

I sat there fuming, my mind spinning with worries, hearing them all clattering out of the house.

I get myself together to go round to Theo's, and am going down the stairs when the front door opens and it's Joe coming back in for something. I leap back into Grant's room; I don't want to see him, though in fact this was an opportunity to have it out with him,

72

except there wasn't really time. Anyway, I'm a coward, and let instinct take over and cower in Grant's room until I hear him go out again. I set off cautiously this time and have just reached the hall when I hear a voice from the basement stairs saying, "Hello, who's there?" and Bill and Ruby appear with cups of coffee. I'd forgotten that there was no need for the roadies to go along as the group weren't playing. They look surprised to see me furtively sneaking off, and ask me up for coffee in Bill's room. I go up because I want to ask Bill's advice. In his very untidy room I tell him what's happening, but he's reluctant to pass comment, and sits there smiling enigmatically while he rolls a joint. "It's up to you," is all he says. "Do what you think is best."

"But I don't know what's best, I want to know what you think; do you reckon I'd like Grant?"

I knew that was a silly question as soon as I'd asked it. How can somebody know who somebody else would like. But I was half hoping that Bill would say yes, Grant is groovier than Joe, I'd go for Grant if I was you. But all he suggested was that I find out by trying him. He wasn't really any help at all, so I sort of dismiss Grant and Joe by telling them my *real* boyfriend is in the States. Bill asks me who he is, and I tell him it's Davey in The Dream Battery and Bill knows him and says Grant does too and that they used to spend a lot of time looning about with Zach Franks. So we sit there talking and smoking. I'm digging Bill because he's quiet and wise. Ruby doesn't say anything, but he's new and hardly counts, he's only a second roadie and totally unattractive anyway, with mangy hair and a low-slung bottom. He's called Ruby because he has these huge red lips that pout outwards at you, and everyone laughs at his Newcastle accent.

Before I know what has happened the front door bursts open and the others are back again, and with them my problems. I haven't got any kind of decision together, and vaguely wonder what will happen. I'm a bit stoned, and decide to let circumstances take over. Bill and Ruby are watching me to see what I'm going to do. I know I still want to see Joe, but can't think how to get to him, because I'll have to pass Grant on the landing. And then I hear Grant making a phone call, and I realise he's calling me at Theo's, and I'm still sitting here. And I think, this is ridiculous, I have retreated from the ground floor to the top of the house all in one day. I've hidden from Joe in Grant's room and now I'm hiding from Grant in Bill's room, and there's Grant phoning me and I'm still here. So I stand up – I've obviously got to speak to him and I'll probably end up in bed with him. I put my head out of Bill's door and called "Here I am, I'm still here", and then darted down past Grant into his cubby hole, still not wanting Joe to see me. He came in and wedged his door shut, and I thought, right, done it. I can't back out now. I tell him how I bumped into Bill and Ruby and didn't seem to get round to Theo's. He doesn't say anything, he reckons he's scored me now, and starts rolling a joint. I listen to all the different sounds coming out of the other rooms and wonder what Joe's doing and whether Grant has told him I was here earlier. I'll never be able to face Joe again, and I start thinking about how I dig him, and here I am sitting in Grant's room, I've committed myself. We smoke the joint in silence, and then someone comes marching up the stairs and a familiar voice says "Grant?" and Grant raises his eyebrows and smiles. "Hello, it seems to be Joe," he says casually, and I think oh, God, no, this is really it. I try to make myself millimetres small and hiss dramatically, "Don't open that door", but Grant takes no notice and pushes it open, leaning across me to do so. I hang my head so that my hair completely covers my face, which I can feel blushing, and Joe leans in. "Hello", he said, quite cheerfully, though a little surprised. I squirm and say nothing. He asks Grant for a sixpence for the phone, but Grant says he hasn't got any, so he asks me. I can't answer, but glance up through my hair and there's his face all lit up in Grant's orange light which shines upwards from the floor. I wish he'd go away.

"What's the matter? Aren't you talking to me?" asks Joe.

I don't reply.

"Yes, what's the matter with you?" Grant says.

I just give him a filthy look.

After a pause Joe disappears, and I can breathe again, but I feel very shaken. Grant demands to know what's the matter, as if he didn't know, but I'm bloody well not going to tell him; I just tell him to shut up and leave me alone. But now he's really won, and he sits there looking all smug and triumphant, and he's not as groovy as Joe, and anyway Joe is a group member, but I'll have to make do with him, I think, as he starts to kiss me. And I'm surprised, because I would never have thought he could kiss in such a nice affectionate way.

After a bit we undress and go to bed, and it's weird. The only place to move about on is the mattress, and I have to stuff my clothes in the hole at the end of the bed. I tell him to put the light out, I'm not having *him* looking at me. In bed he starts kissing me again, and after a bit we start making it, and even though I'm thinking about Joe, I notice that he's very good, much better than Joe. He's really got it together, vigorously changing positions and all that, and this goes on for quite a while until it turns me on in spite of myself, and we have this wild scene which is totally satisfactory. After that I plate him; I want to show him I'm good too, and he really likes it, becoming all tender and affectionate while I'm down between his legs. We don't say anything afterwards, my body is slackjointed and curiously light and my mind is churning out corny thoughts like "my body is on the landing, but my heart is on the ground floor" but it's groovy feeling so sad without being uptight.

Next morning Grant is up early, bashing at doors and telling them to be ready to leave by lunch time. He comes back into this room muttering that things will have to change, like he always does. I watch from a corner of the bed while he shaves and gets himself together. He's really got his room worked out, making use of every corner and wall. When he's ready to go to the office he tells me to padlock the door when I go. I nod and then he says this thing which blows my mind: "You can phone me next week", and leans over and picks up his attaché case.

"But . . ." I open my mouth to protest because I thought he'd want to see me before that.

"No buts," he said. "If you want a relationship with me, my girl, you do as *I* say. That's what went wrong with you and Joe. You've got to learn to be cool. None of this phoning up and holding hands all the time, none of that. You phone when I tell you and not before. I'm not going to bullied like you bullied Joe; it doesn't matter what *you* want, it's what *I* decide that counts."

I just said all right, but I was thinking that I hadn't bargained for anything like this. I had thought that I would have been able to do what I wanted with him, and that he'd be glad to have a chick, but here he was telling *me* what to do. Who did he think he was with his uneducated accent laying down the law for *me* when I can pull GMs and he only a PM. I was really taken aback. Maybe there was more to him than I thought.

While I was getting up, Spike appears, and, with eyes bulging, he tells me that he's had a black bomber and can't sleep and needs someone to talk to while he's writing a song he's had an idea for, and would I come down. I say, OK, and made the bed and lock up. Spike is fiddling about with his electric piano and guitar, which he can't play very well, and humming the tune he is working on. For a bit I try to help, but my mind keeps wandering over what has happened and I still want to talk to Joe. I get bored with Spike's song, and wonder whether Joe will appear before I have to go. Suddenly I interrupt Spike, who's forgotten I was there, and ask him if Joe is awake. He looks a bit alarmed, and says he doesn't know.

"Please go and wake him for me," I plead. "I've got to speak to him."

Spike goes and comes back, saying Joe is still asleep, and that he wouldn't wake him up if he were me because Joe's always bad-tempered in the morning. I said that I hadn't noticed Joe being bad-tempered when I'd been with him, and Spike said, "Well, you'd slept with him then. This time you didn't, did you?"

"I'm going," I said decisively, and went and stood outside Joe's room. I wondered whether to knock, but that meant he would have to get up and unlock the door, and maybe he wouldn't want to see me anyway, and maybe it was cooler just to split and let him wonder why I'd done it. It was easier to do that than to confront him about it – I might have come off rather badly – so that's what I did, I just split.

CHAPTER ELEVEN

I went to Gavin to have my fringe cut; I could hardly see because it was so long. I came out with my hair all spiky and wispy and streaked with grey. Gavin had said, after flicking my hair disparagingly, that I'd had my Brian Jones cut long enough and should change my hair image more frequently. As usual he had his way, but I wondered what Grant would say when he saw me, because I was meeting him at the Kingdom that night; Relation were playing there. This would be the first time I'd seen him since I'd slept with him. I had rung him, but because I'd broken my cool, as he put it, he wouldn't have time to see me until Saturday.

Sitting in the box-office that night, Grant suddenly appeared. He stared at my hair, and then nodded his approval. He even ruffled it, saying yes, it was an improvement on the other rubbish. He'd got his multi-striped leather jacket on and of course was carrying the attaché case. It was a groove having Grant so nice to me, and, just before he swung off on a business circuit of the club, I grabbed him arm and asked him if I was coming back with him that night. He considered for a moment and then gave me a grudging nod. Much later, when Relation had done their set, he came into the office to collect the bread, and made a big show, all for my benefit, I thought, of counting it into piles of singles and storing it away into the confines of his case. That finished, he told me to be ready to leave very shortly, and went off to supervise the loading of the gear. He came back into the office about half an hour later and summoned me out with a nod of his head. We picked up a cab and the Sunday papers – that really started his aggro going because I bought the *Observer* and he got the *News of the World* and *People* – and went back to his pad and got into bed, still arguing. We'd already read the papers and made it when the others started pouring in. I heard this chick's voice which sounded familiar and recognised it as Wendy's, the chick who shares my flat. I knew she fancied Spike and reckoned that she had pulled him. I vaguely wondered what Joe was doing. At least, I thought, as I curled up beside Grant, it was easier to sleep here than in Joe's room; more bed and less noise.

Grant crashing around on the mattress woke me up at twelve the following morning. He was already dressed, and bent down in a corner pulling piles of shirts and socks, as if by magic, out of seemingly invisible holes and corners, all with frantic energy.

"What are you doing?" I complained.

"None of your business, you," he said, not at all nicely.

"Thank you, Grant," I said. I was learning how to cope with him by now.

He twisted round and said, "If you must know, Sunday is washing day. *Some* people are not too groovy to let things like their washing slip, you know. Some people can groove and still be clean, some people can."

"I'm not dirty," I said, thinking he was having a go at me.

"Maybe you're not. But this room smells."

"Well, if it does, it's your smell, and you and your dirty washing are smelling."

"You know what to do if you don't like it," he retorted, twisting the whole issue round. I didn't answer, and he reached over and took a pill out of a bottle and swallowed it dramatically.

"What's that?" I asked.

"A leaper," he said, and gathering up his dirty clothes he stomped down the stairs, making a lot of unnecessary noise. Everyone else was asleep, and I dozed off again. It seemed ages later when he came back in and woke me up to say that it was very strange but he was having incredible difficulty staying awake over his washing. With that he fell down on the bed. I asked him to describe the kind of pill he had taken, and realised from the description that he had taken a downer instead of a keep-awake. He had in fact taken a Mandy, which is a sleeper, not a barbiturate, but strong nevertheless. I told him about the Mandy kick, that you're supposed to fight off the initial sleepiness until you can groove on the feeling that floors have turned to cotton wool and your body to fluff. You zig-zag about bumping into things, and it's all very hilarious. Grant dug this idea, and looned about all afternoon like a sleepy bear. He instructed me to get him some more, and then launched into another lecture of cool. He said I was uncool, I'd already phoned him up, and it didn't do to let people know I liked them. As for being possessive, well, he wasn't having any of that, and definitely no affection in front of other people. Anyway, he was going to teach me. I'd have to learn to wait until he phoned me, because I was only to see him when he decided. I protested that when I like someone I sometimes phone them just on impulse, and what was so wrong with being a bit uncool?

"Well, you'll have to watch your impulses, won't you?" he said. "And I tell you something else: every time you're uncool I'm going to give you a black mark. Enough black marks and I'll punish you. Nothing physical, more psychological; yes, that's the kind of punishment I favour. But if you're cool and do as you're told I might let you come and see me as a reward."

I realised that he had been reading my copy of *Catch 22* that I had left behind last time. I wanted to tell him that all these games of being cool were really a drag, at least taken to this extent they were. I mean, maybe it's really uncool to be so cool; I wouldn't know. But I seriously considered what he said, and thought it was a groove to be cool and careless and not get hung up on emotions. But I couldn't say any of this to Grant because he had passed out. The Mandy had got him.

I'm only a beginner, and when it comes to Wednesday I feel I want to talk to Grant. I sit and argue with myself. Look, I've got to be cool. I don't want to get a black mark, especially with this concert at the Albert Hall coming up that I want him to take me to. But why shouldn't I phone him? Why can't I break my cool, whatever that is. Is it so cool to be cool? So I phone him and he blisters my ear with shouted taunts and insults. But I think he is really pleased that I'm so weak, it puts him one up and he likes that. "I just phoned to say hello," I protest, when he pauses. "I'm not after anything."

"Yes you are," he retorts. "Else you wouldn't have phoned. What did I tell you. I try to teach you and look what happens."

I said I didn't see anything wrong in phoning to say hello, but he has me sussed out. "I suppose you want to come over," he says, all silkily, "don't you?"

"Well, what if I do, what's so wrong in that, you're not busy, are you?"

"I'm too busy to see *you*, that's for sure. So you can't come," he said.

"But I want to see you, why can't I come?" I felt extremely peeved.

"Because I say so," he paused for a moment. "Tell you what, I'll ring you Sunday." I give up, he rings off, and that's that.

And so the game progresses. I am getting very involved in it, really trying to suss Grant out, to discover why he is so aggressive to talk to and yet so tender and groovy in bed. And our bed scene is getting better all the time. Grant works very hard at making it good for me, and he really appreciates my skill at plating. He's started making me plate him the morning after, if I'm still there when he comes back from the office towards midday. Although I still get a bit uptight when I bump into Joe, and haven't spoken to him except for hellos, Grant is almost totally absorbing me. Another thing is that Grant always rings when he says he will – although he's forever aggressive on the phone, demanding that I get there immediately, and reeling off lists of things he wants me to take over to him. I always go, because I can't bear to miss a single game.

Wendy and I are given tickets for the concert Relation are doing with a big American folk singer at the Albert Hall. Wendy has had no luck with Spike, so she has switched to Bill, the roadie, which is fair enough if that's her scene. We get to the dressing room and Grant stops to chat to me, muttering something about having a lot of aggro to cope with and dashes off like a demented speed freak. I talk to Paul, the drummer, and he calls me a schmock.

The rest of the group are in there as well. It's a really classy dressing room, not like most of the dressing rooms and with lots of armchairs and tables and glasses and champagne. I furtively watch Joe struggling with the zip on a new pair of tight, white trousers. I want to go and help him, but I'm not that presumptuous. I really want to speak to Joe about what I did, but never seem to find the chance. They've all had their hair done for the occasion, and Joe's hasn't come out too groovy. I make a sarcastic remark about his hair to Bill, who only turns to Joe and says "Katie thinks your hair looks like a suburban housewife's".

Joe's face goes very tight and he pauses before saying rather bitterly, "So now I know what you really think of me".

I can't say much to that, and I can feel myself blushing. I seem to blush very easily, and it's a real drag and a disadvantage. I get Wendy to come and find our seats because it's about to start.

Our seats are not all that good; they're a bit too far back. Wendy seems a bit pissed, and she's behaving very strangely. She sits there looking moody and fed-up, and cracking her knuckles; I reckon she's still hung up on Spike. The hall is reasonably full, and I peer about recognising faces and getting waves from several unidentified people. Then Relation start and they are bad, well, what I mean is, they're different, not the same as on gigs in clubs, they sound too far away and you can't get into the music. Spike doesn't look right in brown, and we can't see them properly anyway. They also have this backing orchestra all dressed up in DJs, who stand up every so often and blow, which makes me giggle. Wendy is really looking rather distraught, shaking her head in despair, and then she suddenly blurts out, "Oh, it's not fair! I dig Spike so much". I think help, she's going to freak out. But she doesn't, she just sits there making clucking noises and trying to get a cigarette together. I see Grant sitting motionless at the back of the stage with earphones on, and wonder what that's all about. When their last number comes up we split to the loo to tidy up and then make our way back to the dressing room. But we get lost along the way, it's so huge and there are all these passageways, and it's really a bad scene, with Wendy getting more and more hung up, and I'm annoyed because we're missing all the happenings in the dressing room.

Finally we get there and have to hustle ourselves in past some security guy. It's a real drag and bad for the ego when you can't get past doormen and the like. We drink champagne and there are a lot of people filling up the room. Roland Johns, their manager, is there, in a frilly white shirt, and I'm sure he gives me a hostile stare, so I keep out of his way. Grant is still finding it necessary to dash about doing things, so I leave him to it. Joe sits down beside me and takes one of my gold-banded menthol cigarettes, just like he used to when I was with him, and this made me feel all sentimental and sorry. He looked a bit brought down, which is usual for him after playing, so I don't say anything. When the folk-singer comes on, we all go and watch from backstage, but I don't dig him as much as his records. He's sick and looks it, and has to work hard at staying on his feet. There are some doubts as to whether he can make the tour, which is bad for Relation; as it turned out, he had a relapse later that night, and the tour had to be called off.

When I got back to the dressing room the crowd has thinned out and just the group are there. Wendy seems to have been through some crying scene with Bill, and although she is red-eyed she has calmed down.

Paul comes up to me and says, "Hey Kate, don't you think I look like Paul McCartney?" I tell him he must be joking, he looks nothing like Paul McCartney. He gets very offended because apparently he really does think he looks like Paul McCartney, but he's small, plump and blond, with a baby face, and couldn't possibly look like Paul McCartney. However, I manage to console him by telling him he doesn't want to look like Paul McCartney because Paul McCartney is a drag, and I say maybe he looks more like Clint Eastwood. He says, "Do you think so?" and leaps up to study himself in the mirror.

"Yes, I suppose I do a bit," he says coyly.

He's very strange, I decided, as I watch him practising thin and wolfish faces.

Then suddenly Grant makes a very dramatic entrance and sits on a stool in the middle of the room. Everyone looks at him expectantly, and he says, very loudly, "I've got VD."

And I think, what, what's this? Then everyone looks at me and I say, "Well, I haven't got VD". The others switch their heads round to Grant, and he says, "Well, I've got *something* wrong with me."

"You didn't catch it from me," I say.

"Well, I've got it," he says. The others are looking at me now. They are waiting for me to suss out that Grant must have caught something from someone, and if it's not from me then it must be someone else. But I don't twig and say, rather annoyed, "I shan't be very pleased if I've caught something from *you*".

Grant grumbles on about not knowing what's the matter with him; his hair is falling out, he's going to die before thirty, and now he's got VD. The others have lost interest; apparently he's always going on about his health, and they've heard it all before. I don't say anything more, maybe it was cool not to ask where he'd got it from – though if I'd though about it I would probably have asked all sorts of questions and got all sorts of nasty answers.

When we got home and into bed, Grant started pulling out his hair, and he was right, it came out in little handfuls from his head, from under his arms, his chest and even his pubic hair came out. It didn't seem to get any thinner, but it definitely came out. I told him to stop it, but he said he couldn't, and this went on for about an hour. When he started the preliminaries to making it, I asked him about his VD.

He said he didn't have VD.

And what about the scene in the dressing room?

He had thought it was VD *then*, but now he wasn't so sure.

What did he have if it wasn't VD?

Posteritis.

What on earth was that?

Too difficult to explain.

Was it a form of VD?

No, it was nothing to do with VD, it only *looked* like VD.

Did he have a dictionary?

What for?

To see what posteritis meant.

It wasn't in the dictionary.

Then what did posteritis mean?

It meant what he'd got.

How did he know he'd got it? Had he had it before?

No, but he recognised it.

How could he recognise it if he didn't know what it meant and hadn't had it before?

He just did, and I was stupid.

Let me have a look.

What at?

This posteritis.

Why?

To see what it looks like.

See what?

His cock.

Grant sat up and turned on the orange light. I examined him.

"It looks all right," I said. "Just a bit orange in this light." But then I didn't know what I was looking for.

"Well, I've got it," he said, and lay back as I began to plate him.

Next morning Grant made everyone very uptight by turning them out of bed very early and making them autograph the back of 500 group photos for their fan club. After that, when everyone else had gone back to bed, he found he had some time and must see a doctor. I take it easy about getting up and make myself some coffee. Joe appears in the kitchen and asks me to make him some too. I take it up to his room, he's fiddling with his cello, and I place it on the floor beside him. There's a pause while I stand there, then suddenly I start to tell him why I let Grant pull me. I blurt out that I hadn't felt like being rejected and had moved on before he had dropped me, which I had felt sure he was going to do. He was most unhelpful, and kept on fiddling with the cello without saying anything. I went on, telling him how I had felt I had been hanging him up. He stared at me in an expressionless way as though he didn't know what I was talking about.

There was an awkward silence in which I wished I'd never opened my mouth, and then he said that although he hadn't been trying to drop me, he had found me rather overwhelming. Before we could go any further, Ruby walks in grandly, and he's only dressed in identical clothes to Joe. Joe looks a bit put out, he doesn't dig the idea of the second roadie wearing the same gear as him, and tells Ruby huffily not to wear those clothes when he, Joe, was around. Ruby starts complaining, and I retreat back to Grant's room, thinking what a mess I had made of all that, and it would have been cooler not to have said anything at all.

Grant comes back shortly afterwards from the doctors, but the explanations he hands me are senseless. He still claims that he has posteritis, and we go through the whole scene of me trying to find out what it is, and if it is catching and so on, but I can't get any sense out of him. He announces that the doctor told him not to have sex for a month, but then adds that it will be cool to make it in three days. He's really trying to screw my mind up, and I'm very annoyed with him when I leave, not really knowing what's going on.

CHAPTER TWELVE

John, this guy from my flat who does light-shows and environmental freak-outs, has finished his plastic dome for the deb dance, and I got myself taken along to the party as part of the light show. We smoked a lot of joints on the way down in a hired taxi that didn't seem to have any brakes. When we arrived at the country place where it was all happening, some guy in plus-fours at the gate asked us if we were the group, and when we replied, no, we're the light show, he didn't know quite what to do. Anyway, we parked by some haystack and walked towards the house. It was a groovy summer's evening, with the sun low, everything green, and nobody uptight, except perhaps John, who was running round in his spangled waist-coat with great tubes of polythene. I was dressed to show the debs who think they've got groovy clothes where it's really *at*, and I was looking forward to meeting The Elevation and The Shadow Cabinet who were playing there. The Elevation are big, very big. They have just returned from America, and are banned from The Albert Hall for controversial behaviour on stage. Although the underground digs them, they have a very heavy teeny-bopper following. Anyway, it's cool to meet these guys, the more you are seen around with them the more you are accepted and can say "hi" to everyone.

The first person I see is Bert, The Elevation's roadie, setting up the equipment. He knows me, and says hello. Then we are shown into this big room at the back of the house that says "Groups – Private"; and it's an incredible group room, with TV, and a large table set for dinner, and lots of champagne in buckets. So I sit there and wait for the groups to arrive while the others set their projectors up. I'm on my own except for the odd gliding maid or butler. The Elevation are the first to turn up and I suss them out. Jim Edwards, the organist and star of the group, is with a blonde chick; he's always in love with blonde chicks, so I leave him alone, and turn my attention to the other three who are on their own. I wouldn't even blink my eyes at Les Williams – he's one of your group members who reckons he's the works, and scores chicks and drops them before they know what's hit them. Shady, the drummer, is rather nice, but it's the lead guitarist I reckon on. He's called Andy, and he's young and shy, with a weak face and lots of dark curls. Though I don't know whether I would have liked him if he hadn't been one of The Elevation, I decide to see if I can pull him, because his group are very big. So I sit next to him at dinner and we have a quiet little talk while all the others are behaving very badly, getting pissed and doing their aggressive non-educated bit. And I'm thinking, really, aren't these guys animals. They were being so rude to the butlers and maids who were serving us all this delicious food, and I wondered why I dug people like this. They are really spoilt little monsters abusing their ridiculous prestige. But Andy, he's not like them because he is so quiet, and I dig him for not throwing bread rolls around.

After dinner we all go to see the light show in the Dome, and then we wander off to look at all the people. Nobody speaks to us very much, but maybe they are just being cool, pretending to be as groovy as we are. But I get the impression that they are giving us the eye quite a lot, sussing out our clothes and behaviour. The Shadow Cabinet are late, which is a drag, because they've got a groovy organist. So The Elevation have to play first. I sit and watch them from the side and they are great. I smile at Andy, who doesn't move around the stage at all, not like Les Williams, who prances and leers all the time. When we get back to the group room, The Shadow Cabinet have arrived and are very uptight because we have eaten all the food. Andy and I go and watch them play and they are very good, too. They have these two great singers and all their numbers have a mind-splitting throb to them.

But trouble starts when both groups get together in the group room later. The Elevation, being the main group, were supposed to have played the second spot in each set, but because Shadow were late they did the first stop, and now reckon on doing the first spot in the second set, so that they can get home first. Shadow don't like this at all and say they were booked to do the first spot, and Elevation say, well, you shouldn't have turned up late. But Shadow say that they weren't late and Elevation shouldn't have gone on first, and they are getting very uptight, while this breakfast food is being

86

served – liver and sausages at four in the morning! Then the roadies leapt up and started grabbing each other, and Bert went bright red and, picking up a chair, hurled it at The Shadow's roadie, who ducked, and it crashed through the panelled door. Then they fell against the table and the food and crockery smashed and scattered all over the floor. It was bedlam, with maids screaming, and the other guys trying to pull the roadies apart. When things are a bit under control I suggest to The Shadow guys that they take their bread and split, and they thought this was a good idea, and that's what they did, while The Elevation rushed on to play. And I never did get to talk to the organist.

When we get back to the group room there is a very disapproving atmosphere, with servant people clearing up the mess, and while Andy's packing his guitar away, he asks me how I'm getting back to London. I say I'm OK, because I can go with the light show people, and then he asks me if I'd like to have breakfast outside in the marquee. We sit at a table with Les Williams, who's scored two deb chicks, and press knees. After a bit he asks me if I am sure I can get back to London because they've got a car and I can go with them. So I say, yes, I'll do that then, it will save me hanging about until everything's finished.

So we all go and pile into a large saloon. We sit in the back with Jim Edwards and his blonde, and Andy starts getting all passionate and kissing me. I'm looking forward to making it with him. Grant has been more than a drag lately with his weird disease, which is posteritis one day, pertussis the next and steaming whistle whenever he feels crude. I mean, I never know what I'm going to catch when I'm with Grant these days. So imagine my fury when we really start getting down to things in bed and Andy winces, takes my hand away and says, "It hurts, you'd better not touch me."

"What's the matter?" I ask.

"I've got something to tell you," Andy says, in a slightly strangled voice.

"Tell me," I say, a horrible suspicion beginning to mushroom inside my head.

After an awkward pause he says, "I'm under medical supervision." And I think, oh bloody hell no.

"I've got VD," he says.

That's all I needed. "Why didn't you tell me before?" I'm a bit uptight with him.

"Because I thought you wouldn't come back with me," he says, all hopeless and young.

So I feel sorry for him and gently manipulate him to a climax with my finger and thumb. There wasn't much else I could do. What a drag all these diseases were becoming.

I woke up much too early and couldn't get back to sleep. I lay there wishing I was with Grant because I was used to it there, and slept OK. Here the bed dipped and the room smelt, and it was really grotty. I wondered what one of The Elevation was doing in a place like this. There was a lot of noise from the rest of the house, and I started feeling very grumpy. Then Andy woke up and demanded more action from my hands and I felt really pissed off, but rather than go through a scene I obliged. Then I got up to make toast and coffee in the kitchen, after washing my hands.

Andy was taking me to the park that day, to one of the free concerts that had just started in Hyde Park, and which Nigel Bishop was helping to organise. I took a long time getting myself together and when I'd finished Andy made me sew and press some trousers for him. I was feeling a bit resentful now, but cheered myself up with the prospect of being seen by thousands of people with The Elevation. And when we got there, talk about people, there must have been about twenty thousand stuck to the grass like flies to flypaper. Little groups of people strolled around looking cool and groovy, stopping now and then to chat to other little groups, and then passing on. People walked about eating ice-creams, and kids and dogs raced around upsetting the groovers who were staring at the sky or reading their underground publications, which were doing a roaring trade. Lots of foreigners stood around the peri-meters, slack-jawed and immobile, or else prancing about using up camera film, not believing their eyes. Here and there discreet pairs of fuzz patrolled around, keeping a wary eye open for pot smokers, but they never have much luck at scenes like this. The fuzz, I'm sure, must have doubts about letting Hyde Park be used for some-thing like this, expecting anything from obscenity to revolution, but seeing so many of us together all at once, being so appreciative and well-behaved, must have daunted them somewhat. The groups give their services free at these scenes, and the best and the worst turned up that day, but it didn't really matter, because the sounds all seemed good, floating upwards until they got lost.

However, *I* didn't really feel all that good, because my eyes hurt and I didn't have any shades. Also I was in the same clothes from the night before, and I don't like that. I suppose I look fairly OK, perhaps a bit over-dressed, but all these people coming up to me and saying hi made me want to run away. Then I got paranoid that Relation were going to turn up, because I didn't want Grant to see what I was up to, and I was tired and felt confused. After The Elevation played and everyone said how great they were Andy and I wandered around hand in hand, which looked good. But Andy had to split for a gig up north, so I went with them and they dropped me off at my pad.

I phoned Grant up later just to reassure myself and he was incredibly rude and I got angry. I reckoned he didn't know how lucky he was I still dug him. I'll drop him, I vowed, I'll show him. And, still angry with Grant, I accepted Andy's invitation to the cinema a few days later. It was weird standing in the queue. I somehow felt that famous pop musicians shouldn't be subjected to hang-ups like this. Several chicks came up to Andy and said they'd dug The Elevation in the park, or else they liked the group's latest single, and this made him smile in a shy gratified way, though he didn't really know what to say to them. But I wasn't grooving to him; he sent out shy vibrations, and I had to work hard to keep him at his ease, which was a drag. Also he is into Gurdjieff and the reincarnation thing – all lead guitarists' minds seem to hook onto the same preoccupations. But I've heard it all before, and he's not as together in his reasoning as Davey was, and anyway, it's all rather boring the second time around.

We went back to my place because I couldn't stand the idea of another night at that pad of his. We lay around eating bananas and playing records, though clearly all he wanted was to screw me. I asked him how his VD was and he said OK now, that he'd been for a final check-up. He got very impatient, but I didn't let him make me until he'd promised several times that he was really clear. I reckoned that if he'd been straight the first time, telling me and all that, then he would be straight now, so I let him go ahead. He was rather frantic, coming lots of times, but, as he hadn't had a chick for a month, I suppose it wasn't surprising. I just hoped it wasn't catching either.

* * *

The Other Kingdom had finally been pressured out of Covent Garden, the authorities refusing to re-issue the licence. It's a nuisance, because club premises the size we need are very hard to come by in London. But we make some long-standing arrangement with The Big Tower to hire it on Saturday nights. The Big Tower is a large building that used to be a railway hangar, and is being got together to put on plays, concerts, or used for filming. It holds nearly 2,000 people, and is ideal for us, being so high and large.

Jason was giving me a lift home that evening, and after telling me all the financial troubles The Other Kingdom had, he suddenly said, "What's wrong with me?"

"I don't know," I said, not really understanding.

"I mean, I'm not bad looking, I've got a groovy job, I've got wheels, why can't I find a chick I dig?"

"Maybe you go to the wrong places," I suggested. "Unless the sort of chicks you meet at The Joint are the ones you like."

He said he loathed the type of chicks that went down to The Joint, and wanted to know where all the nice chicks were. I said they were probably sitting at home or grooving around with friends.

"Well, why don't I meet any?" he complained. "What I want is a nice chick to love me, and to cook for me. Then I could stay at home in the evenings, not go spending all my money in places like The Joint. I only go there because I've got nothing else to do."

I felt sorry for him, but didn't have any suggestions.

"You're a nice chick, you've got a great personality and I dig your body. Why don't you like me?"

This was awkward. I tried to explain that it wasn't that I didn't like him, it was just that I was sort of involved elsewhere.

"That's always the way," he grumbled. He stopped outside my flat and asked if he could come in. I said I'd have liked to ask him in, but I had to get ready to go out, because I didn't feel like going through a parrying scene with him. "There you go," he said, and drove off.

I haven't spoken to Grant for a week now, not since he was rude to me on the phone, but tonight Relation are playing at The Big Tower, and I want to go home with him. I don't really want to see the guy from The Elevation anymore. I really dig Grant too much to get involved in anything else. I'm working at the box office as usual when Grant comes scowling in, and announces he's full of aggro and hates everyone. He is looking very ferocious, threatening to sack Ruby for something, and I suss that I'm going to have a hard time getting him to take me back with him. Anyway, I ask, and he growls, "Dunno yet, can't decide. Very uptight I am. Ask me later." So I go into the dressing room after they've played and sit beside him and kiss him. He looks suspicious and asks me what I want.

"To come back with you tonight," I say.

Grant immediately says no, and I have to decide fast what to do. I know I'll never get my way by playing Grant's game back at him. I mean, if I was cool, I'd say, OK and walk away, and that would be that. But I know he digs it when I humble myself, and I can do that, I'll do anything to get what I want. So I go through this pleading routine, and he's digging it, and tells me I'll get a medal for perseverance if nothing else. He still hasn't said yes, and I start to bribe him. I offer him a Yellow first, but he says he doesn't need a Yellow. Then I offer him a Blue, but he doesn't want that either. I next offer him some tincture, but he doesn't trust that. Finally, I offer him my doomsday weapon, which is a Mandy, and he relents a bit and says he'll accept one as a present with no strings attached, and a chill of defeat blows through me. I think that maybe I'm going to lose tonight.

Eventually Grant stands up and picks up his attaché case, which means that it's time for off, and he still hasn't said anything to me and I'm feeling very brought down. He turns to me and says, as though he has only just noticed my presence, "What are you doing here?"

"Waiting for you," I say, and he smiles grandly. "In that case, follow me, and don't say a word or I'll hit you on the head."

Groovy, I think, and rush into the office to say that I'm splitting.

There's an incredible hustle getting everyone into the van, and then we can't get it started. Grant is having to drive because Bill is having licence hang-ups, and that's a bad scene when a roadie has no driving licence. We've all eaten hot dogs, and the air is polluted with oniony breath. I have to sit on Wyatt's knee, and his head keeps dropping onto my breast; he seems to be really exhausted and falling asleep or something. Grant told me later it was his way of trying to pull me.

When we are in bed I'm wondering whether Grant will keep up his game and not make it with me. But no, he pulls me towards him, and becomes the different Grant, the bed Grant, who's tender and kisses me like he really means it. Full of love, or perhaps it's relief, I give him the Mandy and we sail off to sleep after making it.

In the morning he's grumbling and demanding breakfast. He wants six boiled eggs, but I finally get him to accept them scrambled because I'm good at scrambling eggs. After washing up lots of plates stuck full of ancient spaghetti, I produce a really good scrambled egg. I want to show him that I can get things like that together. Soon everyone was up, and Spike appeared in his flapping sandals which look as though they are going to fall off but never do. They have recorded a session for a pop radio programme and they all crowd into Grant's room to hear it.

When they have all dispersed again, Grant and I start one of our getting nowhere conversations. Like I'm trying to prove he's not like he is, and he proves me wrong by being more like he is than ever. He laughs at me trying to get round him, trying to get him to commit himself in some way, and as I wasn't getting anywhere I plated him. He liked that, and it put him in a good humour. We lay around exchanging gentle insults until it was time for them all to split for rehearsal. I become furious when I find my battered velvet hat is missing, and Grant goes round demanding to know who's taken it. Finally, he gives me his funny straw hat to be going on with. Feeling quite pleased with myself, I rush up the Kings Road to have supper with Reginald.

CHAPTER THIRTEEN

I get the horrors when I find I have a discharge and I'm all tender in the groin. It's getting worse, too, and as I'm going to some sort of underground party that night, I dash off to Casualty for help. The doctor there suspects VD and says I've got to go straight down to the Special Clinic. What an ultimate drag! I can hardly believe that it's happened to me. I bet it's that bastard from The Elevation.

So I furtively go down to the VD clinic, which is in the basement, and I get given a green card with a number. Some doctor questions me about my sex habits and I confess all. Then I have to go into a cubicle, strip to the waist, and hang my legs in these stirrups. I feel like a lump of discarded beef while the doctor and his assistants probe and discuss me and my complaint in a weird, impersonal way. Then they take some bloody painful tests, and of course I've got it. They unstrap me and shoot two whooping great penicillin injections into my backside and tell me to come back tomorrow for more of the same, and, of course, no sex. They also give me these slips of paper to give everyone I've slept with in the last month. Apart from the culprit, there's only Grant – I haven't slept with Reginald since going with Andy. But I decide to freak him out just the same, so I give him the slip of paper and watch his face crease in annoyance. "Oh God," he says. "Does this mean I've got to go for a blood test or something?" I kid him along for a bit, but tell him he's OK in the end. He passes a few disparaging remarks about pox stars, and laughs at his joke. Next I phone Andy, and tear him off a strip. He keeps saying that he went for his final check up, and what a drag it must be for me, and he's very sorry. I discover that he goes to the same clinic that I do and decide to check his story out tomorrow. He ends up by asking me to go to the Windsor Jazz Festival, where they're playing, but I can't go, it's a Saturday and I'm working. So I tell him he must be joking.

I'm not relishing the thought of breaking the news to Grant. He's bound to abuse me and call me a slag or something and never see me again. Having slept with him since I made it with Andy, he's sure to have it. But if I don't tell him, and get cured, and then sleep with him again, and he's still got it, then I get it back again. Anyway, I know I've got to tell him, so I phone and he answers, which is a drag, I'd hoped he'd be out so I could put it off. "Hello Grant," I said, not quite knowing how to put it.

"Oh hello you. What do *you* want?"

"I've got something to tell you."

"Well, get on with it then. I'm busy."

"Can I come and see you?" I asked, "I mean not to *see* you, it's something personal I've got to tell you."

"Tell me now, come on, tell me," he insisted impatiently.

"All right then," I said, "I've got VD."

Instead of the expected explosion there was an odd pause.

"Does that mean that *I've* got VD?" he said, in an unusually quiet voice.

"I don't know what you've got. And I don't think you know either." I was grabbing the initiative.

"Well," he said heavily, "I haven't got VD, I've got posteritis."

"You told everyone at the Albert Hall you had VD," I said. He hadn't asked me who I'd got it from yet. I wondered if he thought he'd given *me* something.

"Well I haven't."

"Anyway," I said, "I've got a piece of paper for you which says that you are to go to the clinic for a check-up."

"All right, you can give it to me tonight." And he even said goodbye. I was amazed, no tantrums, no abuse, a very quiet reception from Grant. But maybe he'd be back on form by tonight, so I was still not looking forward to facing him.

* * *

Round about midnight Relation made their noisy entrance into the foyer, and I nodded at the doormen to let them through. But Grant came straight up to my desk and demanded the piece of paper. I told him I was busy getting customers in, so he sat on the desk and waited, with his nose in the air and swinging his legs. Suddenly he said in a loud voice "I've been thinking." People started looking at him. "I want to know who you got it from."

I began to blush, and tried to hustle the customers though quickly.

"Shut up," I hissed.

"Go on," he prompted mirthlessly, "tell us how you picked up this horrible condition."

I told him it was none of his business and I'd talk to him later.

"Is it someone I know?" he asked.

"Probably," I said.

"Tell me," he insisted.

"No."

"Tell me, or I'll knock you down the stairs."

"You'd never find out then, would you Grant," I said. I was beginning to enjoy this, it wasn't often I had Grant wanting things from me, though he was always pumping me about the running of The Other Kingdom, how much we paid groups and so on. But that was business talk and this was a different experience. However, I wasn't going to tell him. Grant knew I was on the group scene, so it was important that I didn't sound like a groupie boasting. And Grant would be able to squash any boast I made, so I reckoned it was cooler to keep him guessing.

"I can find out if I want to," he asserted. "And anyway, I've got posteritis. You'll see." And he went inside.

I went in later to watch Traffic, and saw Grant standing with the rest of Relation. I went up and touched him, and he took me aside and started hustling me again for the piece of paper. I handed it to him, saying sorry for being a hang-up. He didn't reply, and looked at it closely.

"I don't know when I'm going to find the time to get along there," he said. "But I suppose I'll fit it in sometime." And I felt such a drag, causing him all this trouble and wasting his time, all because I had insisted on going back with him last weekend.

When Traffic had finished Grant said they all had to split because they were leaving for some gig in Wales in the morning. "Yes," I said, thinking this was goodbye, see-you-around-sometime. But surprisingly he said "I'll ring you soon," and when I stared at him trying to understand what he was up to now, he added, "You can ring *me* if you like," I said yes, and then put on a doleful expression. He came up to me and kissed me, telling me not to go getting

95

uptight, and that everything would be OK. This knocked me out and made me think how nice he really was. He'd taken it much better than I'd expected and I thought he was going to use it as a real excuse to excel in nastiness.

*   *   *

After about a week of confinement I go to this intelligentsia party I was invited to by Thea Porter, who has a shop in Soho which specialises in beautiful materials from the East. The party is at her Mayfair house, and I decide to take Reginald along. It's going to be the sort of thing where everyone will know him and it looks cool to arrive with someone like him. Jane, my friend from the glossy magazine and John from the flat came as well. I took a lot of pills and tincture to make me super and I put on the hat I've l got to replace the one stolen from Relation's place. I've suitably battered it, and tied a pink chiffon scarf around the crown with the ends hanging down. I had lots of silver white under my eyes and was wearing my black semi-transparent top with all the little coloured beads sewn on it. And of course my Thea Porter trousers. Jane, John and I ate at The Drug Store which is made out of bendy aluminium and distorts reflections, making it very difficult to manoeuvre when you are stoned. I was feeling pretty highly strung and dying to make an impression on all the trendy straight people I was sure were going to be at the party. We picked Reginald up and he was wearing typical Reginald clothes plus the inevitable dark glasses. He was all darling and witty and fondled me in the back of the car which impressed Jane. She thinks I have made a catch with Reginald, and that I am very clever to have kept going out with him for so long. All sorts of ridiculous girls chase after him, because he is relatively rich and famous, and his father is a Lord or something. But Reginald digs me because I'm different to them and he even looks down on them because he's so straight and aristocratic. I'm always telling him that he's not my scene, which makes him uptight and he says "But darling, I'm on every scene. I was on your scene before you left school." But then I tell him that only proves how old he is, although he's only just gone thirty, and I accuse him of not being able to understand our scene, being so old and that. I say these things to make him uptight and he always finds things to tease me back with. But I dig him. He makes an interesting change from the non-too-intellectual group members. And he's clever and successful, so I like to be seen out with Reginald, it extends my image.

When we get there, Thea kisses me and that looks good. There are all these well-kept looking people in bits of her clothes wandering about, and she takes me around, introducing me. They all ask what I do. When I say that I work at The Other Kingdom their eyes light up and they get excited, asking me what psychedelic means and have I ever taken LSD. They really don't know anything about my scene and it's a real groove talking to people like that. You can say all kinds of things and sort of blow their minds a bit, thought it would have been very difficult to have blown the minds that were around me that night. It's not that they were stupid or anything, it's just that most of them suffer from a form of mental tetanus that locks their minds into rigid forms of thought and attitude, and it makes it very difficult to get into them in any meaningful way. I think most people could do with a massive dose of acid at least once in their lives, and I say the sooner the better, because then at least they could start from scratch again with a better chance of understanding.

Of course, it's always the same with very straight people, we're nothing more than freaks to them. So when a couple are thrown into their midst they cluster around to probe and examine, not to really get fresh insight into different life plans, but merely to confirm their prejudices. A lot of them have skimmed about the edges of our life and half-understand, and identify with our beliefs and ideals when it suits them. Others think we're a waste of time and even possibly dangerous, but they still question us so that they can compare notes and convince themselves that they are right. But the nice ones are those who just dig us for what we are, they don't want to be like us, they don't want to change us, but they find us groovy to talk to and we can laugh a lot together, and dig each others' different minds. Thea's like that, she's got a very turned-on mind that has nothing to do with drugs and that's why I came to her party.

I really enjoyed it there, having some incredible conversations and enjoying Reginald, the way he pushed me into groups of people as his freaky little discovery, and then standing back to watch me dealing with them. It was a beautiful house with super rare furniture, and lots of champagne and party type food in the kitchen – though

I didn't drink as it's not cool to mix alcohol and tincture. Reginald started getting a bit jolly as he slowly got pissed, and knocked over a glass of red wine. "Oh God, is it blood?" I said, and everyone thought that was hilarious. See what I mean?

Jane leaves early, but we virtually stay to the end, and then John drives us home. He's been really freaked-out by all the straights, but anything will freak him out because that's how he wants to be. I sit on Reginald's lap. His hands are going all over the place. but I've decided not to sleep with him in case I'm not clear yet. So we drop him off, and I kiss him tenderly and say I'll see him soon "*Very* soon," he says, and our outstretched hands part in an exaggerated romantic gesture.

Back in the car John went on about how he couldn't believe it when he saw Reginald. Sure he was intelligent and successful, but that I should have him for a boyfriend just didn't seem to be my scene. I explained to John that Reginald was my scene because his difference made him my scene. He couldn't entirely appreciate this. Straight people aren't the only ones with locked minds.

CHAPTER FOURTEEN

I was sitting in bed eating a buttered bun and reading *Darkness at Noon* when John burst into my room and said Grant was on the phone, demanding to speak to me immediately. And I thought, too much, *him* phoning *me* – even though I had sent him a little note a few days ago to tell him I was better. So I say, "Hello, what do *you* want?" like he usually says to me.

"What are you doing?" he demands.

"I'm in bed. Why?"

"Never mind why," Grant says, "what have you got?"

"What do you want?"

"Drugs, pills, sex-books . . . the lot," he says, "bring them all with you and come over here immediately."

I protested a bit. "But Grant, it's one in the morning, and I've got a terrible cold . . . and I'm in bed."

"You've got every fucking thing, my girl, but get over here just the same." So I said OK, because it was worth it, even though I did have a cold and was in bed. I tried to make myself look not too awful and got various books and bottles together. I thought, I'm going to freak them out, I'm going to keep my nightdress on and just put my long coat and boots on. I took clothes for the next day with me, and taxied over there. The front door bell seemed to have disappeared. There were just two naked wires sticking out with a message under them saying: Cross wires to ring. I managed that, and heard Grant flopping down the stairs in his slippers.

There are a lot of people sitting in Bill's room experimenting with Wendy's tincture in cigarettes – she's got the kind without syrup and it's difficult to drink because it's so full of raw medical spirits. I always get my prescription made up with a syrup into what this groovy chemist I know calls a Cannabis Cocktail. Wendy and I managed to hustle ourselves onto prescription after the flat was raided again – they didn't get anything, but it was a good excuse to go along to a doctor in London who is sympathetic to pot-smokers and explain why we wanted to be on prescription. Anyway, tincture is such groovy stuff, it's a higher high than smoking and less trouble.

I empty my bags onto Grant's bed. There is a bottle of Mandies, a bottle of leapers which haven't got an amphetamine base, and my bottle of tincture and two heavy green sleepers that my doctor gave me in an emergency one night when I swallowed too many leapers. I tell Grant that he could have the Mandies and the green sleepers and a few leapers, but not many as I needed them. While he's fiddling about with the bottles, he tells me to give him some tincture. I pour him out a slight overdose, and tell him to drink it down in one. He looks at it a bit suspiciously, and grimaces at the taste. While all this is going on Spike leaps down the stairs, and seeing so much mind food all at the same time his eyes started darting about with amazing rapidity.

"Hello, hello," he says, in a breathy, distended voice. "What you got there, what is it . . ." he looks pretty smashed already.

"Cannabis," says Grant officiously.

"Oh cannabis, cannabis," Spike echoes all in a rush.

"Yeah, cannabis."

"Can I have . . . can I have . . ." he can't quite finish the sentence, he's so worked up. Grant tells him it's mine, and he looks at me hopefully. I pour out some for him, not as much as I gave Grant, and he swallows it.

"Look out there," Grant warns. "Here he comes . . . he can smell drugs a mile away."

"Hello," says Joe, pushing his face into the room. "What's all this?"

"It's trincture of callabis," Spike says so fast that he misses the words.

"Christ, pull yourself together, you," Grant admonishes him. "It's cannabis."

"Ah . . . cannabis linctus," Joe says foolishly, smacking his lips.

"Tincture," I say.

"It's linctus . . . I know it is," Joe argues. "What does it do?"

I explained and his eyes lit up. "Can I have some?" he asked. Spike was chatting away to Grant, asking him when the effects started, and Grant was telling him to shut up and wait. I poured some out for Joe, more than Spike, but not quite as much as Grant.

They are all demanding to know when something will happen, and I tell them to wait about half-an-hour. So they turn their attention to the pills that Grant is sorting out into bottles with prescription labels on so that he won't get busted. They all want some, but Grant is being very dictatorial and telling them he's in charge of all pills. Joe wants to take a downer, but we won't give him one, it's silly to take a downer with tincture. We can't make up our minds where to hide the bottles, so Grant stuffs them under the mattress for the time being, and starts to play some records. He's very fond of old soul and blue beat, and insists on playing them at full volume. Spike disappears, muttering that nothing's happening yet, and Joe says the same and can he have another spoonful. I give him one, though he doesn't really need it because the tincture hasn't begun to hit him yet. People from Bill's room are complaining about Grant's choice of records, but Grant just roars back, "I'm disc jockey tonight, so you'll get what you're given".

I dramatically take off my coat and reveal my nightgown, but neither Grant nor Joe seem surprised to see it. I take a couple of swigs from my bottle because of the cold, and I'm sure tincture is good for colds. Then I take a few more swigs for luck and because I want to get smashed. Grant and Joe are complaining that they still haven't felt anything yet, and I try to explain that you don't really notice it coming on you until suddenly you know you're stoned, and after an hour or two, you start getting these strange physical things happening as well, if you have taken enough. Joe asks if it's trippy, and I tell him that it is a bit. Grant's ears prick up when I say this and he shouts "I'm not having any of that . . ."

"It's too late now, Grant," I say.

"I'll fight it," he says confidently.

"Do what you like," I reply, because I know.

There we are. Joe is sitting against one wall, Grant is sitting against the other and I'm sitting between them. Grant decides that he is going to give us a light show, which means that he takes out his orange bulb and puts in a blue and red one. Then he starts going through all his old singles, and putting on these really ancient soul records, and Joe is supposed to guess which club in Nottingham each one reminds him of. Grant used to be Nottingham's top DJ, and was called Sir Grant. Joe managed to identify the Oodle Boodle Club in Grampton Street, and he and Grant start giggling and reminiscing. We're all giggling now and I ask Joe if anything is happening and he says yeah, his face and voice one big smile. Grant springs up again and shows us how they used to dance when Relation were a real old thumping soul group, but there's not much room on the mattress and he keeps tripping over our legs. Finally he can't do it any more, and he flops down on the bed. I ask him if he is feeling anything, but he won't admit it. Then he jerks up and gives us both a weird look.

"What's the matter with him?" I ask Joe.

"She wants to know what's wrong, Grant," Joe says.

"I've got to check something," Grant is almost speaking to himself.

"Check what?" I ask Joe.

"I've got to check Bill's room," Grant says.

"Why?" I ask.

"Because he's a bloody fire hazard, that's why." Grant struggled to the door and looked back. "And he has to be watched . . . *constantly.*" He tore off up the stairs shouting out Bill's name. Joe and I turned off the sounds and listened. Grant banged on Bill's door very vigorously, and, getting no answer, he called out "Bill . . . Bill . . . answer me immediately!"

"I'm down here, Grant," we heard Bill's quiet voice answer from the basement.

"Down *where?*" Grant shouts furiously.

"In Spike's room. We're all down here now."

"And I'm up *here,*" Grant roared.

"What's wrong, Grant?"

"The bloody door is locked, and for all we know your room is in ashes."

"My room . . ." Bill's voice grew closer and somewhat panicky, "what's wrong with my room?" Bill is always setting fire to mattresses and having books burned. He has a horror of going up in flames one night. Spike's frantic voice poked it's way in. "What's up, what's up, what's happening?"

"I can smell smoke," Bill cried, and we heard him clambering up the stairs.

"Get up here and open this door before we all go up in flames." Grant began rattling the door handle futilely, the panic beginning to grip them all. Up they came, stumbling and falling, and Spike

102

giving out little yelps of excitement. We hear them open the door after a lot of fumbling, and go inside. The muffled voices resonate as they stumble about checking Bill's room, and we lose interest.

I felt a bit funny being alone with Joe. I still like him, but no more than I like Grant, so that's cool. Joe has gone into a deep reverie, and when Grant returns, apparently satisfied that Bill's room is OK, Joe suddenly says he's decided that Grant will be the face of 1970, in fact, he adds emphatically, he *knows* Grant will be the face of 1970, because Grant has it in him to make it. And I have a sudden shattering thought that, wow, maybe Joe's right. He's such a way-out creature he might really be something. Then Grant, after a deep mini-think, says decisively, "I'm only being me. Though, of course, it's not the underneath me I'm being, it's the external me." He pauses and considers this statement. "Though if that's how I act, it must be the underneath me that's making me act the external me," and then he goes into this long thing about his external me and his underneath me. Joe nods wisely and says he has sussed him out. Then he puts his hand on my leg and says he has sussed me out as well. Grant says he'd sussed Joe out long ago, and that he'd sussed me out as well. And I think, this is terrible, because I haven't sussed anyone out. Here were these crazy uneducated guys who reckon they have sussed everyone out, and here was I, not presuming to have sussed anyone out. Grant told me to shut up and get back into my corner, though I hadn't moved or spoken.

Grant had put an LP on, and after a while I noticed that Grant's and Joe's legs met and it was like I was sitting in a triangle, and that's what it was anyway, with Joe the past and Grant in the present. I was seeing things a bit differently now, but kept getting disturbed by both of them. Every time Joe spoke to me he put his hand on my leg, and Grant was having difficulty keeping upright and kept flopping across me. It was like the time was confused and I couldn't remember who I was supposed to be with. Then Wendy appeared like a phantom in the doorway and asked if anyone had any change. This took a few minutes to sink in, though Grant said no immediately, because he says it's always easier to say no. She drifted off, and like what seemed almost immediately, she returned. Apparently the meter was running out. Grant and Joe made no effort to help, so I had to lean right across Joe to get my purse. Then I had to lean right across Grant to see in the light what was in it. I found something she wanted, and had to lean over Joe again to put my purse back. Joe was just lying there, digging the record, and I sat back and watched him through my fringe and wondered if I still fancied him, and found I did. Then I examined Grant and found that I dug him too, and I thought about this situation, but it wasn't hanging me up or anything, it was just so groovy being stoned with two people I liked so much.

The record ended, and nobody could say anything until Joe decided to put another one on. He didn't really know what he was putting on, and when he came to sit down again he sort of misjudged, and instead of sitting on the bed he disappeared through the curtain onto the floor. He sat there with his legs sticking out until the curtain fell on top of him. We all had to get the curtain up again, and we did, somehow we managed to pin it back to the ceiling and flopped back down on the mattress in relief. Then the record stopped and Grant had to lean across to put another one on. The volume was still turned up, and people from Spike's room were still shouting abuse at the records, but their complaints were getting weaker now; they must have been as stoned as us. This time it's a Dionne Warwick LP, which I wouldn't normally dig so much, but listening to these great rolling drums I was drawn in. Spike broke it up by sticking his head through the door and saying he was starving and he was going to cook. Joe said he was hungry too, but made no effort to move. I lay back on my pillow, and Grant put his head on my shoulder. With my legs outstretched I found that one of my big toes was touching Joe's leg. Somehow I couldn't move it, though I wanted to, and after a bit it really started burning, like it was getting bigger and filling up with liquid fire. I wondered if Joe's leg was burning from my toe, and tried to pull my toe away. But I thought it might look a bit suggestive if I started wiggling my toe against his leg, so I left it there, flaming away. Joe was trying to read the cover of the Dionne Warwick LP but the light was so dim. Whatever position he moved into he couldn't see, and finally fell back defeated. Then his nose started twitching, he could smell Spike's cooking. After a few minutes it became too much for him, and he scrambled across our legs and down the stairs, to crash into Spike, whose eyes were right out on two little sticks now, and he was babbling something about two fuzz cars being outside the house. We thought about all the drugs lying around, but our paranoia only reaches the suggestion stage – no action to hide things can be made, we're so smashed. Joe goes off on reconnaissance and comes back saying that Spike must be hallucinating, because he can't see any fuzz cars. They both descend to the kitchen, still arguing about it.

CHAPTER FIFTEEN

I'm finding I can hardly talk now. I'm all inside my mind, which has taken over my body. Grant must be feeling the same because he hasn't spoken for a long time. He's just sitting there with his eyes propped wide open; listening to the sounds or maybe listening to his thoughts. And I start wondering whether Grant thinks like he behaves, or whether he works out how he will behave in his thoughts, and I'm not really working anything out when he pulls me over and starts kissing me. But my cold is so bad that I can't breathe properly, I have to snort and gasp for air out of the corner of my mouth. But I do my best because it's groovy, and we're getting very involved with our tongues when we realise the door is open. I get up and go for a pee, and when I come back and lock the door I find Grant is already in bed. As I've already got my nightgown on I don't have to go through the scene of arranging my clothes at the end of the bed, and as I get straight into bed I'm vaguely wondering what will happen. I mean with all our various afflictions and medical orders to abstain we should really discuss the matter and make an effort to be sensible. We start kissing again, and then Grant's hand wanders down my leg, and I'm wondering whether he's going to touch me *there*, and I also wonder if he's wondering if I've still got what I had, but anyway I get hold of *him*, and I wonder if he's still got what he had, whatever it was. But nobody says anything, and after a while it becomes so groovy that I stop wondering anything. It doesn't matter who's got what, I couldn't blow a scene like this apart with a reasonable discussion on whether we should or shouldn't. He doesn't seem to be wondering anything anyway, he's got his hand right inside me, and then we're making it properly. We're leaping about doing this and that and really getting into it when the radio falls off the wall on top of us. It comes as an incredible surprise, because we're in another world, and it could have spoilt everything. I'm told it's my fault and abused in the usual manner as Grant struggles to get

106

it back into position. It looks very precarious and crooked, and I say "I won't be able to sleep with that up there".

"Serves you right if it falls on you," says Grant, grabbing me again. He seems to be able to turn sex on and off at will. Everything becomes instant groovy again. I'm on top of him and he makes the first remark he's ever made while having it with me. He says, "Not too fast", and I think, does he mean he's going to come too soon, or that he's enjoying it too much to let it finish. So we start doing all these slow motion things that seem to go on for hours. Suddenly I'm flung on my back and he's on top of me and he's really going at it now. Then something unusual happens. Normally when I'm making it with Grant he goes to great lengths to satisfy me, but he always makes me plate him until he comes, either because he's being careful (we've never discussed whether I take the pill) or because he digs being plated. He only came inside me once and that was the first time we made it, and I didn't really notice because I was thinking of Joe. So I'm not sure what's going to happen this time until it happens; he comes right inside me, which at that moment was groovy, and I felt I had scored a victory. But when he rolled off and my mind cleared a bit, it really hit me what had happened. As I wasn't supposed to make it this month on account of the clap, I had decided to stop taking the pill as an extra deterrent. But, being so stoned, I had completely and utterly forgotten, I'd been so hung up on what I was going to catch, and what he was going to catch, I'd just forgotten, I'm so used to taking the pill all the time. So I lie there thinking oh, fucking hell, and then I have to tell him, because I have to tell people things after making love. I said, "Oh . . ."

"What is it *now?*" Grant says, resuming instant aggression. This is the way he is after being virtually a normal lover, though with him it's normality with a difference because it's *Grant* being normal, and it's so unusual for Grant to be normal it's abnormal, if you see what I mean. Maybe I'm privileged to have him like this, though I've no idea what he's like with other chicks.

"I've got something to tell you," I announce.

"What have you given me this time?" he snaps.

"It's more what you have given *me* . . ."

"What's this?" He gets very suspicious, up on his elbow glaring at me.

"It's nothing to do with diseases," I say. "It's just that this is the worst time of the month."

"So?"

"So I haven't been taking the pill this month. I didn't think there was any point, did I?"

"And what does that mean?" Ominously this time.

"Possibly and quite probably, it means that I might be pregnant."

The response was much as I expected. "I don't want to know. Don't tell me things like that, I just don't want to know," all of it roared in a single breath.

"At least I can tell you, can't I, Grant?"

"No you bloody well can't. It's entirely your own fault. I've got enough problems."

"You can't mean that," I said, egging him on.

"I bloody well do. And the sooner you believe me the better."

"You're not like that." I wondered what all these problems were that Grant seemed to be burdened with.

"Yes I am. You just get rid of it and don't bother me. And it's no use running to me in six months with a fat belly. I don't want to know," he warned.

So I dropped it for the moment. It wasn't hanging me up, because I didn't know if anything was going to happen yet. I changed my tack.

"Will you take me to the park on Saturday, Grant?" Relation were playing at one of the free concerts, and I rather wanted to go with him.

"No," he barked immediately. Obviously I had chalked up a few black marks.

"Why not?" I asked.

"Because I'm taking another young lady, that's why?"

Now that did blow my mind. Any other reasons for not taking me I would have accepted, but another chick ... no, no, I couldn't believe it. "Who are you going with?" I demanded furiously.

"I'm taking Patty." Patty is Roland Johns' secretary.

"Why are you taking *her*?"

"Because she asked me to ... and that's not all," he added smugly. "That's not the whole of it." He was really making me squirm with jealousy.

"What's not all?" I asked.

"I'm going away with her to the country afterwards." He waited with satisfaction for my reaction.

"Why?" I asked, sulkily and very uptight.

"I'm taking her because she asked me to and I like her. I'm going to have an affair with her," he decided.

"I don't want you to go with her," I said dolefully.

Things were getting out of hand, this was really bringing me down. I insisted I was coming to the park with him, and he said:

"That hurt, didn't it?"

"Yes," I said.

"I know, because I could feel my words hitting you, pow, pow crashing into you like great rocks of pain. That'll teach you to make me uptight . . . now go and sulk."

I had retired in silence to the other side of the bed, trying to work out what was happening. Was Grant going to have a scene with this chick? It could be possible, he saw so much of her at the office. I wondered what she looked like. But I couldn't believe it; maybe he was making it up to hurt me – he liked watching me squirm.

"Aren't you crying yet?" he asked pitilessly. "You should be crying by now."

"No, I'm not crying," I said, in a disinterested voice.

"Well, you should be," he snapped.

"If you have a scene with her, I shan't come round here anymore."

"Good," he said.

Shit, I thought, I never get anywhere. Grant then launched into this great thing about his power scene. I couldn't tell if he was serious or not. I just don't know where I am with this guy most of the time.

"When I'm the face of 1970, I don't expect you'll be around," he rubbed in. "Though I suppose I might call you up sometime."

This last remark was a mistake. It was a hint that he hadn't meant any of the previous nastiness. I told him he was lying, which he denied furiously, though I don't think either of us knew what he was lying about. Then he said he never told the truth anyway, so where were we then? I couldn't cope, I just supposed that all I could do was to rely on Grant's actions, not his words. Then I told him that Wendy had repeated to me what he had said to her in the kitchen, about me being a drag because I was never rude to him when he's so rude to me.

"That's right," he said. "I knew it would get back to you and make you uptight. I like making you uptight, but why don't you get rude? You're never rude, and that's a drag, because I'm rude, so that means we're incompatible. There you are, we're incompatible, it'll never work." He liked this deduction, and went over it several times.

"Well, stop saying things to Wendy, because she tells me, and I don't want to know if they're nasty."

"That's why I do it."

"But why? Aren't you nasty enough to me, without other people telling me what you think?"

"I just want to keep reminding you, in case you get too sure of yourself. It's good for you to be uptight, and it amuses me. So there. Keep me amused and you're all right."

Is that the only reason he likes me, because my moods and efforts to get him to like me amuse him?

"You're a bastard," I said.

"Yes, I am, aren't I," he agreed. "Some of us are made to be nice, others are all nastiness . . . that's me, all nastiness. It's easier to be nice than nasty. But it's the nasty ones who make it, and if I'm going to be the face of 1970 then I've got a lot of nastiness to fit in."

"You're out of your mind," I said, but did I mean it?

"Good," he said. "Keep thinking like that."

"You don't want me to think that you're all nasty, do you, Grant?"

"Course I do. Knowing me to be nasty you expect me to be nasty, and I have to be nasty if I'm going to be the face of 1970. Anyway, I'm going to die in eighteen months, so what's there to be nice about?"

"You're lying," I said, but I wasn't sure what he was doing.

"Of course I am," he said. "I lie all the time."

"Are you lying now?"

"Yes."

"Is that a lie?"

"Yes"

"Were you lying about Patty?"

"Yes."

"Oh, thank you Grant," I said, falling into false security. "I knew you didn't mean it."

"I don't mean anything."

"Well, I do, and that means a lot to me."

"Anything to keep you happy."

"Thank you Grant."

"Anything to bring you up."

"That's nice," I said. "And can I come to the park?"

"Of course you can."

"Thank you Grant."

"But you can't come with *me*. I'm taking Patty. But I'm not stopping you coming, am I?"

"But I thought . . ."

"I know what you thought, and I wanted you to think that, I watched your mind falling into the trap. You'll never learn, will you?" And he looked at me triumphantly.

I couldn't take any more. I was defeated again, and couldn't cope with all this skirmishing. I hadn't got anywhere, and my head felt like a huge zeppelin ready to take off. I lay back to sleep and got involved in this weird physical thing. My legs felt as if they were suspended two feet above my body, and my chest felt like an iron box. Wondering if I was going to be able to keep on breathing, I fell asleep. There was only one interruption during the remainder of the night. That was when Grant's cardboard pussycat fell down on top of us. It woke us up and we peered at it, peered at each other suspiciously, and then went back to sleep.

CHAPTER SIXTEEN

We woke up at 10.30. At least that was the time when Grant prodded me awake and made me go outside and ring TIM. Ruby had Grant's alarm clock because he had a lot to do this morning. I got back into bed as Grant stomped about getting dressed. I'm never very hilarious in the mornings and always wait until Grant is out of the way before getting up. I have an appointment with my solicitor at half-past-eleven – it's about a £250 phone bill from the Rome Festival days, calls to America and Europe, that I have been lumbered with – and I don't think I'm going to make it. I'll phone him later with an excuse, I decide.

I lie and watch Grant getting dressed. He's wearing cord levis, a navy shirt and a short sleeveless pullover this morning. He goes in for mini-jumpers quite a bit, they make him look very boyish. He has a brass chain around his waist with his keys hanging from it, like a jailer. He puts on his battered white gymshoes which I saw him in the first time, only now I see they are in fact baseball boots. He's very proud of them and polishes them lovingly. Then he stands up and says, "See you" and goes out. I don't answer. It takes another half-hour before he finally leaves the house. Ruby has overslept and Grant's shouting at him and having to re-arrange the morning's assignments. Bill has to be woken up and I hear a lot of arguing about who's going to go to Sound City. Finally Grant departs, announcing to anyone who's interested that he's going to have a bath at the office because he might catch bugs from the bath here. I lie there for a while. I still feel stoned this morning, but in a different way; I feel far away from everything that's happened and yet I'm still thinking about it. I think my mind has been a bit blown by last night's conversations and I find it hard to believe they actually took place. But I know they did, and thinking about them I just lie there shaking my head in wonderment at the things that go on inside Grant's head. Would I ever work him out? Was he like this with other chicks? But there were no chicks around that he'd pulled for me to check with, and the others in the group wouldn't be any help because they'd known him so long that his eccentricities didn't strike them as anything unusual.

I noticed there was a writing pad on his table and decided to check out his letters for clues. I started to look through it and gathered quite a few together. The first was a letter from his mum. It read: "Dear Grant, Here are the things you asked for. I couldn't send a tin of soup through the post, so I've sent a packet. It comes out just the same if you follow the instructions carefully. Make sure your saucepan is clean because I'm sure there is a lot of food poisoning in London." And I thought, oh, isn't that sweet and mumlike. The rest of the letters were all written on small sheets of blue notepaper in this really childish handwriting, and they all said the same sort of things, startling "Darling Grant, I do miss you so much, it was a pity you couldn't come and see me at the weekend. But I expect you are very busy. I long to be alone with you for just a few hours . . ." And, "Darling Grant, I wonder if you will be coming to see me next weekend. I do love you. I love you very much. I can't forget the lovely times we spent together before you went away, and I'm sure you can't either . . ." And, "Darling Grant, I do wish I could come to London to be with you, just for a little while. You would, of course, have to send me the money, but wouldn't it be nice to stay together for a bit, we never seem to have more than a few hours together." And one said, "Darling Grant, I'm sorry to hear about your illness. I wonder what it could be? (I wonder too, darling) Is there anything else wrong, darling. Your letters seem to have changed lately. If anything is bothering you, please tell me darling, you know I would do anything for you . . ." Christ, I thought, what is *this*? There were various references to a child called Derek, but nothing that pointed to Grant being the father. She was obviously keen to get to London, but didn't seem to be having much luck. I couldn't believe what I was reading, these letters were so bad and uncool, and the spelling was all wrong. Grant indulging illiterate and pubescent love letters? What's happening? He wouldn't stand any mushy talk from me, yet here was all this drooling nonsense from some provincial chick called Susan. Did he really dig her? Love her even? How could he stand all the mindless rubbish, and what was he writing back to her? Maybe she's fantastic to look at, but anyone who writes letters like that couldn't be, they wouldn't have the mind to get it together to look groovy. Perhaps that's the type of chick Grant really likes, and I remember his criticism of my "hippy" clothes. It fascinated me, and I lay there for about an hour trying to work it all out. Someone came down the stairs and started making a telephone call. It was Wyatt, calling up Kettering or somewhere, and he says, "Hello, Mrs Roberts, it's Wyatt here . . . how's Dad?" and he kept having to push sixpences in.

"Hello, Mrs Roberts, it's Wyatt," he says again.

"No, *Wyatt*, Mrs Roberts . . ."

"No, Mrs Roberts (patiently) it's Malcolm, only my name is Wyatt now . . ."

"Yes, Mrs Roberts, Malcolm Richard, Mrs Roberts . . ." and the sixpences kept pouring in. He seems to have sorted Mrs Roberts out and continues:

"I've seen these shirts in a shop on the corner here, they're only twenty-five bob each, and I'm wondering if Dad would like a couple."

Mrs Roberts must have said yes, Dad would like a couple, because Wyatt says "OK, I'll get a couple and bring them up as soon as I can." Then he rings off and pads quietly back to his room. Too much, I thought, intimate confession day for the groovy pop people. Then I hear Bill announcing that there's coffee for anyone who comes up to his room. I decide to blow work out today, and phone to say I'm overcome by my cold. Then, still in my nightgown, I go up to Bill's room. I've got to consult Wendy about these letters. She doesn't seem surprised, and points out to me that the type of people Relation would have known before coming to London would all be like Susan in varying degrees. I supposed so, and looked at Bill to see how he was taking this. But his eyes were studiously blank, he was being cool. I hadn't suspected that Grant might have a chick in the provinces. That he might be a totally different person to a chick less groovier than me, a chick he confided in, confessed to, and was affectionate with, really intrigued me. I asked Bill if he had seen this chick of Grant's.

"I don't know anything about her," he said defensively.

"I don't want to know the details," I explained. "I just want to know what she looks like. Is she pretty, is she groovy, is she clever (she couldn't be, but anyway), is she funny, you know, things like that. You can tell me, surely."

"Look," Bill said. "Honestly, none of us have seen her. I saw her once, very briefly, about two years ago, but I can't remember what she looked like at all."

What a drag it was not being able to find out about this home-town chick. Perhaps Grant kept her locked away somewhere. All the same, I wasn't too pleased at the thought of competition from a chick like this, and if this was really Grant's scene, what was I doing around? Or was London beginning to change his standards and did I fit in with his new scene? He can't have met anyone like me in Nottingham, and maybe he found me a novelty. That was cool, as long as the novelty didn't wear off. I don't have much to contribute to the breakfast conversation, I'm too busy with questions and answers inside my head. Then the front door slams, it's Grant coming back, and I'm not dressed or anything. I hear him going into his room and, finding it still a shambles, he comes up to Bill's room to investigate. He looks in disapprovingly and announces that if Ruby hasn't got it together by next week he'll have to go. We all nod dumbly in agreement and he goes out again. A minute later there is a roar from the landing:

"Come down here immediately and tidy this room!" Wendy and Bill giggle as I obediently disappear. I get chastised for not being dressed and not having the room tidied for his return. "I didn't know you were coming back, did I?" I complained, as I scrambled about straightening out the bed. Then I get dressed and Grant flops down and starts going through today's chitties.

"Can't sanction all these taxi fares of Joe's," he mutters.

That done, he starts reading *Billy Liar*, turning the pages over so quickly I can't believe he's actually read them. Looking up, he sees that I am about to go, and says, "You're a good bed maker, I'll give you that."

"Thank you, Grant."

"You'd better go now," he said quickly.

"Why?" It was obvious I was going anyway.

"Because if you're going . . . go . . ."

"Why?" I insisted.

"Because I'm feeling sexy," and he picked up his book again. Grant has been going in for afternoon plating scenes, it's becoming a sort of ritual.

"Well, I'm going," I said.

"Go on then," he said, not looking up.

I lean over to kiss him goodbye thinking shall I or shan't I and decide I shall because he puts his arms round me and kisses me. I'm still having problems with my breathing, so I have to hold my breath. Grant gets up and shuts the door. It wouldn't do for anyone to see him being affectionate with me, all they see of our relationship if Grant being aggressive and domineering, and they probably think I sleep on top of the television or something.

After I plate him, Grant lies there making satisfied sounds and I move up for a verbal skirmish. I ask him to take me to the park again, and this time he's all mellow and reasonable and explains that he really can't because he is taking Patty from the office because she asked him to.

"And are you going away with her for the weekend?" I ask.

"No," he says. "How can I? We're playing in Sunderland on Sunday."

"But you said . . . Why did you say you were?"

"That was to punish you."

"Punish me for what?"

"Blowing my mind like that." He gave me a hostile look. "You're never to say things like that again."

Blown Grant's mind? When did that happen, I wondered.

"What did I say?" I asked.

"I just don't want to know," he went on, not really hearing me.

"What are you talking about, Grant?"

"All that about you not taking the pill, that's what I'm on about. Sitting up in bed the minute after we've made it and saying that you're pregnant . . . you can't pull that one on me." He was getting all worked up again. He's really hung up about it, I thought, it's really annoyed him or something. And he went on about having enough problems and not wanting any more responsibilities. However, if I went ahead and had the kid, he'd like to see it – but no money, mind you. He was talking as though I really was pregnant. As though the hint had become fact.

"I'm saving up to run away," he announced suddenly, "I'm going to live in the middle of the Gobi Desert until all my hang-ups have blown away and then I'll come back and sneer at all you losers and tell you that you don't know where anything is at."

I asked him how he was going to be the face of 1970 living in the middle of the Gobi Desert, and he said he'd fit that in as well. Then I told him he had a conscience and that he was only being aggressive to cover it up. This he denied furiously. He kept telling me to get rid of "it", but "it" didn't really exist yet, except in his head as another hangup to be dealt with. When he questioned me about what I was going to do about "it" I gave vague unsatisfactory replies, enjoying his display of guilty bad humour.

"You bring me nothing but bloody trouble," he grumbled.

"You can't get out of it by saying things like that," I said.

"Why weren't you taking the pill, anyway?"

"Well, I wasn't supposed to have sex this month, was I?"

"I don't know. It's not my fault."

"Who got me to come over here?" I asked.

He ignored my question. "You're not still dosed up, are you?"

"I don't think so. I should be cured . . . they say I am, but they keep telling me no sex. That's why I didn't bother with the pill this month."

"So we've both got VD again . . . is that it?"

"I know what I had . . ." I said, "but I never did find out what *your* complaint was."

"I have something wrong with my bladder," Grant said, and I thought how unromantic. "It's called posteritis." Here was my old friend posteritis again. I got a bit of an explanation this time. Apparently it's something to do with the liver, and Grant was told not to drink alcohol or coffee, and not to make love because it would send up his blood pressure which in turn would strain his kidneys. All very strange, but at least it wasn't venereal.

I put the bottle of tincture into my bag, because I'm really going now. "And don't bring that stuff round again," Grant says. "I turn on and end up catching VD and becoming a father. Don't bring that poison round here again; it's nothing but trouble."

"So I'm going," I said.

"Yes, get out."

He followed me down the stairs and out of the front door. I asked him where he was going and he said to have a sausage sarnie. I asked him what a sarnie was and he said didn't I know anything, and, sticking his nose in the air with an exaggerated gesture, he went off down the road to the cafe on the corner.

CHAPTER SEVENTEEN

It is a week since I last saw Grant. Maybe he thinks I'm being cool by not calling him or anything, but in fact we have been very busy at The Other Kingdom getting ready for The Doors and Jefferson Airplane, two big West Coast groups who are coming over to do a couple of concerts at The Big Tower for us. It's to be their only appearance in England, so there'll be a lot of press coverage as well as television, and everyone on the pop scene will be there.

Although I haven't seen Grant, I know what he's been doing because Wendy keeps me informed. Grant has been getting at me. He's really hung up about me being pregnant, and keeps cornering Wendy in the kitchen and asking her all kinds of probing questions about my age, my men, and how long I've been pregnant. She has told him about Davey being in the States, and how I write to him, but she won't tell him who I go out with on the side and denies that I am pregnant, which just infuriates him. He has announced that he is not going to speak to me again and has rubbed my telephone number off the wall by the phone. Then he rang me up and dramatically told me that my number was off the wall and out of his life. It would be a long time before he called *me* again. He slammed the phone down.

I wondered how I was supposed to react to this, and then decided not to react at all. Grant's wild statements didn't really mean anything, he just seemed to throw them at me because I expected them. Anyway, I am incredibly busy with the concert. The hangups are terrific – tickets late from the printers and a lot of concentrated publicity to be done. This chick, Liza Bellamy, and I are in charge of the press and guest list, and the numbers of people trying to hustle free tickets is unbelievable. Liza doesn't work for the Kingdom, she organises relief schemes for the underground and paints enormous pictures in her spare time. She is very groovy to look at and is frighteningly together and articulate.

In getting the concerts together I was meeting lots of important people and talking to newspapers and things. When the Jefferson arrived I went along with Jason to the reception with my best gear on, and some photographer stopped me at the door to take pictures, saying my outfit was the best they had seen yet. This impressed Jason, and gave me an ego-boost into the bargain. Inside there were a lot of people I knew and more that I didn't, so I circulated, and people I didn't recognise but felt I ought to kept coming up to me and trying to con free tickets to the concerts. Reginald was there, though I couldn't think why, and we spoke for about ten minutes, but I was up on him because this was my scene and he was really only a spectator. I didn't want to get involved with him, because I don't like mixing the scenes; he wouldn't stand a chance with me if he was on this scene. I dig him because he's involved in different things that I know little about. So I move on and bump into Harold Grimes, a young intense-looking reporter I've met before. He's an alcohol head and specialises in underground groups and folk music, and writes for Hit Maker, your actual pop paper. He's a bit pissed and he grabs me – it was obvious what he was after. As I couldn't see anything else of status to pull I decided it would be cool, I mean although he's not groovy to look at, he is Harold Grimes. So I let him talk me into going back into his Earl's Court pad, which is rather respectable and shared with the manager of a big blues group.

I was disappointed to find that he didn't have a groovy sound system, just a useless little record player, and all those *incredible* free records! So we sat and watched the television with this manager guy just sitting there while Harold went in for a lot of pre-making-it fondling and noisy kissing. Every time this other guy left the room Harold had me virtually undressed, and when the guy came back in we stopped gyrating and sat there as though nothing was happening at all. But I was finding it all a bit irritating – and besides, I was interested in the Chicago riots which were showing on the TV. So I said mind my trousers and did anyone want any tincture? They said no thank you, which surprised me, and then they said they never touched the stuff, which surprised me even more. So I got stoned alone, which made me feel rather foolish. They kept making ribald jokes and laughing knowingly at my condition, which I thought I was concealing rather well. Except I was laughing at things that they weren't which made them laugh at me. Finally, this other guy, Phil, went to bed, and I was alone with Harold. He dived for me, and rather than go through another clothing struggle I said "Lets go to bed", and he said, all jolly, "Just like a woman to be practical".

"Yes, well, it's my clothes I'm thinking about," I said, and laid the strained objects on the back of the sofa. Interesting face he may have had, but stripped to his pot belly he caused me a lot of doubts. He was enthusiastic in bed, and kept asking me if I'd come. I told him I never answered that question, but not to worry. Looking into his green eyes made me forget his silly body.

Next day I went to the free concert the Jefferson gave in Parliament Hill Fields. It was nice except it rained. Later I joined up with Harold and went to the Doors reception at the ICA. He was hustling around trying to interview Jim Morrison, who is the singer and main attraction of the group. He's a tall blackleathered beauty, a sort of updated Elvis. It was gruesome the way the cameras followed him around. He was like a worm on the end of a pin, wriggling this way and that, trying to avoid the scene as much as possible, and his eyes were as dead as ashes. I was a bit taken aback by it all, and the fact that it was taking place in the middle of this Cybernetic Serendipity exhibition – squeaking machinery and weird machines moving about – didn't help.

As soon as that was over I split with Harold and Phil and two others to a terrible little club called The Case which is always full of musicians and their managers, and chicks and pop people on the make. It was a drinking scene, no music or dancing, and everyone stood pressed against each other talking business or being crude and getting pissed. I was getting a bit dubious about my image, being seen around with Harold Grimes. OK, so he was influential and known on the pop scene, but he was plump and wore straight clothes, and not even good straight clothes. And he did very uncool things like play football for the *Hit Maker* against the Show Biz eleven. As a person I was beginning to find his mind dragged heavily with lower class hangups, and that he strongly disapproved of hippies and drugs and made a lot of nasty remarks about the underground which seemed directed against me personally. He considered I was representative of "that way of life" and kept bugging me with explanations about why we saturated our minds with drugs and didn't go to work. This made me extremely annoyed, because I find these type of people a complete waste of time – and for this stupid little Cockney git to class me with them was just being unreasonable and narrow-minded. I don't really consider myself a hippy at all, not if it means that I go around with bare feet and matted hair. I have my boots hand-made and go to one of the most expensive hair salons in London. I turn on to groove, not to escape the way some people do, especially alcohol heads like him. Saturation point is when one trip is like another and you can't remember how many you've had. I can remember all my trips clearly, and I don't lie on my back saying wow, too much, and freaking over clouds in the sky – although I did cry in Regents Park once because it looked so beautiful, and tears came instead of words. I work, and consider I have a sort of career, and to have a career you have to be together, hippy or not, and I'm together because I can get things done. I told him all this patiently, but he couldn't seem to grasp any distinction between people on the scene. A hippy is a hippy is a hippy was his formula and his mind was clamped to it tighter than a limpet. He told me about Uncle Bert and what a hard time his family had had in the margarine forties. Then he'd had all these hustles getting out of the ledger clerk scene and working for Hit Maker. I admired him for this, I just wished his mind had come along too.

Anyway, there I was at The Case really hating it, and Phil, the flatmate, was going on about birds being slags. He said that if he liked a bird he never slept with her the first night he took her out. I said it was nonsense to say that if a girl slept with you on the first night she was automatically a slag. And anyway, what was a slag? He said he could tell a slag, and that I wasn't a slag and not to get him wrong. For example, if he took me home with him and slept with me he wouldn't think I was a slag; some were, others weren't. What sort of line was this? Come and sleep with me – I won't think badly of you. I told him that he'd better open his eyes and look about, because chicks these days didn't have to put up with scenes like that anymore, not unless they were clearly mindless. There were enough men around who realised that chicks had minds, bodies, needs and roles to play just like them, even though there would always be idiots like him with small minds who'd put down chicks who enjoyed being screwed without any guilt to hang them up. I told him we could do without guys like this because they didn't know where anything was at, and he got all offended. I wasn't enjoying myself at all, so I split without saying anything to Harold.

I next saw him when I was sitting at the Press Desk with Liza on the night of the second concert. He came capering up wearing some baggy cord jeans and a windcheater and he had a cowboy hat on – he thought it made him look funny. After making a lot of beery jokes he went inside, and I felt quite relieved. Liza suddenly started asking me questions about him, she knew I was having a scene with him because things like that get around. When she said she considered me such a groovy chick and anyone I went out with must be groovy too, my mind was somewhat blown. I had always considered her the most impressive person on the scene, and for her to say anyone I go out with was groovy was a weird and unexpected compliment. What she was really saying was that she dug my guys and now she wanted Harold. I was amazed, because if he wasn't my scene he could hardly be hers. Though on second thoughts she might enjoy turning Harold away from alcohol because she digs the crusade bit. But that was no reason for wanting him. Maybe she wanted him because I had had him and she wanted to suss out my scene at close quarters. But why choose him? I had so many better people, though I certainly wouldn't have liked it if she had gone after someone I really liked, because Liza is just about the strongest competition you can have. Anyway, I told her to go ahead, I'd blown him out, and that's what she did.

I read in *Hit Maker* the following week that Harold Grimes had spent a very busy week interviewing the groups and reporting on the concerts, and I had to smile. Starting with me at a reception and ending up fondling Liza on the balcony of The Big Tower, he can't have known what hit him. But it was all a good write-up for the club, and other things worked out too. As I was watching Liza charm the slightly bewildered Harold, a brusque Grant appeared out of the blue and told me I was going back with him tonight. I was glad to be with Grant again, full of familiar aggro, whose body was brown and hard. I didn't argue, but I couldn't help wondering how Liza was faring under the pot belly.

CHAPTER EIGHTEEN

Some weeks later I had a letter from Grant, and that's the first time it has ever happened. He's up North with the group, and will be away for another three days. He is having a lot of aggro with promoters and Ruby hasn't been getting it together and is going to be abandoned in Pitlochry if he doesn't improve. Grant is also troubled about his hair, which is still falling out, and there is a lot of tension between him and Joe, who keeps trying to put him down. Apart from that, the weather is giving him indigestion, the chicks are all slags and they are starved of drugs. I am to have it all together for his coming back. No mush, no tenderness in his letter, yet it read like a poem addressed to me personally. He'd thought of me while he was away, and I intended to confront him with this when he came back. He would have to explain himself. The thought of Grant coming back soon set me up for the day.

That night I had nothing to do and went over to Theo's pad. It was a long time since I'd been there and I was curious to see what had happened since the big bust up. Johnny, Mark and Blonde Giant were gone. Johnny was living in some hole in Kilburn and getting a book together. Mark and Blonde Giant were in California where horrible things were happening to them and they were breaking up – Mark had telephoned everyone around on reverse charges, yelping help and wanting his fare home raised. The wire genius had split, leaving his computer unfinished. He believed that M.I.5 were after him because of the things he could do with telephones and he was now hiding somewhere up north. His deadly enemy the Hobbit guy who built light machines, had been taken over by some American merchant bankers and he was now busily engaged in making another fortune for them, or so they believed. That had left Theo all alone with his bread, his pad, and his paranoia; and the horror it all, plus the pressures on him to finish his film script, had driven him onto methedrine and the needle in a dangerous way. The last time I'd been round there had been terrible. He phoned me up one evening and asked me over to help him. He wanted me to read through his script from the audience's point of view and suss out things that might not be clear and suggest the necessary changes. He offered me a fiver for my trouble, so I said yes, I'd do it. When I got there the usual groover types were lying about the front room, stoned and hypnotised by the light machine, and all alone in the study Theo was shooting up an amp of meths. I don't know how much he'd had before I arrived, but he was quite high, pacing about and talking a lot. I settled down to read the script and it soon became obvious that it had been written by a speed freak, and needed some sorting out. I wrote down my suggestions as I went along, but he kept interrupting me, because every time he saw me noting something down he demanded to know what was wrong. So I'd point out to him what I didn't think was clear, but he couldn't concentrate and kept letting himself get diverted onto other subjects, like showing me his paranoia chart and making me read extracts from books on midget submarine warfare. This was all connected to a thing he called his power chart, because when his present commitment was finished he intended to write and produce a film about submarines which would make him rich enough to possess his own midget submarine and this would automatically get him into Box 22 on his power chart. Box 22 is a good Box. It means immunity through fame – like the Beatles and Greta Garbo, that sort of scene. It was all very freaky listening to him explain it, but it seemed to make sense as I got into it, and I really admired Theo's mind for working it all out. He got quite carried away and we had wasted several hours before I reminded him that we were supposed to be working. So he took another shot of methedrine and we started to re-write a scene. This went on until ten in the morning, with continuous interruptions as Theo insisted on showing me something, or making me listen to some boring tapes by some Major guy talking about his experience with the subs.

"Did you hear *that?*" he would say, pointing a finger at me accusingly. "Do you realise what *that* means?" And as I didn't he would launch into yet another explanation about the chaotic tragedy of the midget submarine situation. It struck me how differently Theo and Reginald approached their work. Reginald worked sensibly all day in a coherent condition, while Theo never started work before midnight, and had to fill himself with drugs to cope with the pressure of work he'd let pile up. While Reginald treated his writing as a job, Theo seemed to regard it as a traumatic experience. He must have taken four shots of meths, and once he spiked some cereal I was eating by squirting some on while I wasn't looking. I didn't realise what he'd done until he asked me how it was affecting me, but I didn't notice any drastic change, probably because I was pilled up anyway. However, I was very cross at what he'd done and told him not to do it again without telling me because I didn't like what meths did to people, and he'd better get off it too, because meths was a killer and if he went on like this he wouldn't be able to keep his sanity together, never mind finishing his film script. At the rate he'd been taking it that night – and from the state of his arms – he'd obviously been pumping the stuff into himself for quite a time. Apart from the feathery tracer lines of needle marks down the length of the veins, he was also pitted with thousands of other holes, for, as you can't eat on speed, he had also been shooting pure vitamins into himself. There were so many holes in him that Theo was almost breathing intravenously. He pooh-poohed my lecture, because, like all speed freaks, he reckoned he had it all under control, even though he admitted that it was the thrill of the needle he was hung up on almost as much as the stuff he was shooting up. He accepted the fact that his brain cells were being burned up by the billion, but he'd worked out the figures for his renewal theory on brain cells, and reckoned that it would be cool for him to go on using meths for the length of time it took to finish the script. I never argue with people who have got it all worked out by numbers; I just hoped he knew what he was doing.

Anyway, Theo was becoming incoherent by now and over-writing – when he could get his mind to focus on what he was supposed to be doing. I suggested that we stopped, feeling physically shattered myself and coming down from the Blues. But he insisted on going on, even though what he was putting out was useless. Then his mind went skidding off in all directions, and he started telephoning people and pouring all these wild ideas out as fast as his mouth could flush them from his mind. Nobody really wanted to know at that time of the morning, and he eventually abandoned the phone and went back to the typewriter. It was strange, because in spite of all the stuff inside him he was actually beginning to fall asleep. He was going into frozen reveries with his fingers poised rock still in mid-air above the keyboard. I had to keep poking him with my pencil, until finally I stood up and said I was going to work. After a minute he turned and stared at me unseeingly. Then he said accusingly "We don't seem to have done very much work". Well, thanks, I thought, and shrugged my shoulders. We had only managed to re-write one scene, and it was still too long. I didn't ask for my fiver. He'd fallen back in the chair into another trance, his mind was racing on though his body had given out, and I didn't feel like disturbing him. If that's what meths did for his script, and if that's what it was doing to him, I reckoned it was a waste of time. I was shocked at the state he was in. He'd become as thin as a rake, hooked on needles, and was obviously in trouble with his script. I hoped he'd get himself together soon. As for me, I went home to sleep. I certainly wasn't in any state to go to work after *that*.

That was six weeks ago, and today I'd phoned Theo and he'd told me to come on round. He'd got new people to live with him and he wanted me to meet them. When I got there and rang the bell, it took ages before the door to the flat opened. When it finally did, I was let in by this very suspicious sandy-haired guy I didn't know. I saw why it had taken him so long to let me in; Theo had fitted two extra Ingersoll locks, which, together with the original one and the chain bolt, was really more than one person could manage. I told this guy who I was and who I'd come to see and he grudgingly let me in. He told me his name was Robin and added that Theo was watching telly in the little room. I said fine and followed him into the big front room to suss out the scene in there first. The place was incredibly clean. The gold carpet looked as if it had just been shampooed and the glass and perspex table shone dull and spotless with nothing on it but a large ashtray and an almost full bottle of tincture. There were five people sitting around on the velvet sofas, talking and listening to the sounds, which were very low. There was only one chick there and she was sitting between two of the guys on the large sofa. The guy who had let me in, Robin, introduced me by simply reeling off five names very quickly, and then telling them I was Katie. The chick was called Gisela and looked foreign. One of the guys handed me a joint, and, after I had passed it on, he handed me the bottle of tincture. "Ever had this before?" he asked knowingly and before I could answer he said, "take a tablespoon". I said thanks and emptied just a little into my mouth. It was tincture without syrup, and I don't fancy it too much like that because it's evil stuff to swallow in its raw state. When I put the bottle down, the guy I had sat beside, who had a thin rabbity face, floppy black hair and straight clothes, leaned nearer to me. "I don't feel anything yet," he confided.

"You haven't had it before, that's why," Robin told him.

"How much did you take?" I asked.

"I told you you hadn't taken enough, Paddy," one of the other guys said.

"I think I am stone also," said Gisela, and her voice sounded very foreign.

Paddy looked at her intently for a moment, and then swiftly grabbed the bottle and lowered three great swallows. His face went through all kinds of anguished distortions as it burned its way down. I looked at the others and they seemed only mildly interested in what Paddy had done. For a guy who hadn't had it before, he'd taken a lot. In fact, I had never seen anyone take that amount all at once.

"That's a lot," was all I said.

"Paddy wants to drop out," Robin told me seriously. "He's never turned on before."

Drop out, I thought, he'll be lucky not to drop dead with all that inside him.

"I'm going to see Theo," I announced, and went down the passage to the telly room. Theo was sitting, staring morosely at it. There was a Hollywood musical on, and the colour looked all unreal and washed out in the brightly lit room. I sat down beside him and we spoke. He looked haggard and jumpy, and seemed very low. He told me how he was coming down off speed now his script was finished. When it came back from being printed, he would be handing it in to the studio and waiting for their reaction; he didn't expect they would have many changes for him to make. After that, he'd go the States and get his submarine scene together. I said I hoped it worked out for him, but privately I had my doubts. If the script he was handing in was anything like the way it was when I'd seen it, then he was in for a shock and lot of re-writing.

He asked me if I'd met his new people living in the flat. I said yes, and asked him who they were. Robin was a bum who could drive – Theo was letting him live there in return for chauffeuring services; being up on speed he hadn't been able to manage the Bentley, and so Robin was driving him about. Gisela was a German waif who had appeared one night and slept on the sofa. She was staying on condition that she kept the flat clean, made tea, and massaged him whenever he was uptight. Niall and Keith were odd-jobmen. Niall was building Theo a huge working table in his study. The table would run the whole length of the room and would have shelves for his charts, maps and pictures. Parts of it would raise up and swivel round as drawing boards, and generally do all sorts of interesting things. Theo had designed the table himself, and the only time he became animated was when he spoke about it. Keith was Niall's mate and helped him with the carpentry. He also did errands, hid the gear and was general dogsbody around the place.

"I don't like it round here anymore, Theodore," I said, "it's not the same."

"I know it's not the *same*," he admitted, "but people like *those*," he nodded contemptuously in the direction of the main room, "people like those are necessary, don't you see?"

"No, I don't see," I decided to let him have it. "What are you doing with them? They're not your friends. You despise them, and they're afraid of you and probably don't even like you. You walk about like a stranger in your own pad."

"I don't have friends anymore. They all left when things got rough. They didn't even *try* to understand my condition." He sounded bitter.

"Don't talk so bloody foolish, Theodore." These were typical Theo hangups coming out.

"Well, that's the way it is now," Theo said, all dark and broody. "I've done a lot of thinking. I don't need friends anymore. My friends were dragging me down, holding me back. Now that's finished. Where I'm going I can't take friends . . . in fact, there's nobody I want to take along. Meanwhile, I'll keep people like those around, because I need people to bounce my ideas off, and, of course, I don't like being alone. I don't need *them* . . ." he paused, "I need their presence. There are no hangups about motives, I know what *they* want, and it's easier to refuse them than friends. There won't be any guilt, and competition, don't you see, nothing like that *now.*"

"You've gone wrong somewhere," I said.

He smiled for the first time. "We're in a very cynical mood tonight."

"I just can't agree with how you're thinking. It's sad that you can't have friends."

"Well, I don't mind being wrong and rich," Theo said, sounding pleased with his discovery.

"Maybe you're wrong about that too," I said.

"About what?" The tinted specs were turned on me.

"About being rich."

"We'll see," he promised.

"Anyhow, how are you?" I asked. "Are you really off speed?"

He hesitated and then said, almost confidentially, "Almost."

"What does almost mean?"

"I tell you it's not a problem." He was a trifle impatient. "That's all under control."

"Good for you," I said.

He was going to say something, but it never came out. The scream cut him off. It was a high-pitched scream of naked horror and it had lanced all the way down from the front room, down the passage and into the TV room. Theo went white, took me by the arm, and bundled me out of the door.

"Tell them they must be *quiet*," he said, locking the door behind me and turning up the volume of the television to full pitch.

129

CHAPTER NINETEEN

I didn't stay around very long when I discovered what was happening. I didn't know what to do and I didn't want to know, either. The state Paddy was in frightened me, and I could see real trouble if it wasn't handled properly. Hospitals, doctors, questions and fuzz flashed through my mind. Paddy was having a bad and very weird attack of the horrors. I went up to the front room and found him standing in the centre of the room, his body rigid and shoulders hunched and unnaturally raised. He was staring straight ahead without seeing anything. I looked around the room and saw Gisela crouched in a corner, trembling and watching him with her mouth wide open. The others had all disappeared into their various rooms and had swallowed tranquillizers in order to still the panic Paddy's scream had caused. I went up to Paddy and touched him. His body was all tensed and felt rock hard. I said hello, but he didn't seem to hear me. I'm not staying in here, I decided, and nobody else seemed to be helping, so I split.

I found out later how they coped. Theo told me about it on the phone, although he hadn't been much use because he'd refused to come out of the telly room until it was all over. When the tranquillizers had taken effect, the others had held a little conference about what they should do with Paddy. The overdose of tincture was affecting him in an unknown way. He was going into these rocklike trances for a period of about ten minutes and then coming to with ear-splitting screams, and then abruptly subsiding into a trance again. Everybody was pretty freaked out by it all, and the German chick had to be put to bed and given a heavy green sleeper to knock her out. The others decided Paddy must be got rid of. They thought the screams would be heard and that fuzz might appear. Two of them took him by the elbows and manoeuvred him out of the flat and down in the lift and out in the street. Then they half lifted him across the road and propped him up inside a shop doorway and fled back to the pad before he started a screaming fit again. They could see the shop doorway from the flat, and kept a nervous eye on him. They also tried to tell Theo what they had done, but he refused to open the door or turn the volume of the telly down. Then Paddy screamed again as he came to in the shop doorway, and even though the flat was across the street and two storeys up they still heard it. They all crowded round the window and watched as Paddy screamed and flailed his arms until he sank back into his stony silence. They saw someone come across the road and stop and say something to Paddy. Getting no response, the man looked about him indecisively and then made off quickly. Then they decided it wasn't very cool to leave Paddy out there, so they all trooped out again and brought Paddy back inside, and locked him in one of the big cupboards. The screams, muffled now, but no escaping them, still came through, periodically followed by the unusual silences. Then, after a long time, there weren't any more screams, so they went to investigate. Paddy was standing there, looking quite normal, when they unlocked the door. "Hello," he said. "Why am I locked in here?" Then he screamed again and collapsed. They put him on one of the sofas and tried to decide what to do next. He would have to be knocked out, and they debated what to give him. It wouldn't do to give him any barbiturates because there is a lot of raw alcohol in tincture, so they finally gave him two of the green sleepers. Paddy had started talking about his horrors, and it sounded like he was reeling off verbatim a report in a Sunday newspaper by someone who had experienced a bad "Heaven and Hell" scene on acid. They gave him a bath, and by the time they had finished Paddy's voice had become very weak, and his mind had become about as fertile as a cabbage. He passed out before they got him into a bed, and didn't function again for fifteen hours. I was well away from that kind of thing, but maybe I should have stayed, because when I got home we only got busted again.

I mean, living in a flat with hip people it was hardly surprising that the drug squad should raid us again. I was sitting in Wendy's room telling her about the Paddy scene at Theo's and John was somewhere sawing up perspex for one of his new light machines, and Ted was out rehearsing his group. I told Wendy that I felt a bit guilty about leaving the guy in that state, but it wasn't all that much to do with me, and anyway, he'd been uncool with all his talk about "dropping out" and "tuning in" and his big hero act of taking so much of a drug he knew nothing about. Wendy reckoned it served him right and maybe he wouldn't be so uncool from now on. We were swapping old horror scenes, sitting cross-legged on the floor in front of the fire, with an ash-tray between us. I had on my long white jellaba and looked like a casual flower child. Then there was this loud knocking on the front door. We thought it was the landlord come to harass us again. He's always complaining about the noise and accusing us of stealing light bulbs from the landings. He gets very worked up because we can never make any sense out of what he says, the reason being he's foreign and his disjointed English and perpetual anger manage to reduce us to helpless giggles. So we didn't answer, even though the banging on the door got more insistent. Then there was an almighty crash, and the door burst open, and there they all were, my friends from the Drug Squad. "Hello, Katie," the leader of the gang said, smugly waving a warrant.

"Hello," I said weakly.

"You know what we've come for, don't you?" he said, and the others filed in behind him and spread out.

"I can't imagine," I replied, but my knees had turned to water at the thought of a box of Blues on the table beside my typewriter. I'm told to go into my room while one of them searches it.

"Yes, of course," I said, in co-operative tones.

He started scrabbling in my underwear drawer as soon as he got inside the room.

"Where's the charge, then?" he said.

"I've given it up, after last time," I said, placing myself between him and the box of pills. He moved on to the bed, lifting the mattress at the corners and putting his hand in the pillow cases.

"It'll be quicker if you tell me where it is, because you know we'll find it," he said reasonably.

"But there isn't anything to find," I protested.

"But we know you're carrying."

"Who told you that?" I asked, but I wasn't convinced, because this is a favourite trick of theirs. To make you paranoid they try to make you think they know all about you, insinuating that they have people watching you, people like yourself, who are on the scene. Although there are a few people who do give information to fuzz in return for immunity and bread, I don't think there are many and they usually get sussed out before they can do much damage. I was pretty convinced that this was only a routine bust on convicted heads which perhaps works on a sort of rota system, and in comparison to the last one this was only a half strength bust, they didn't even have any dogs to sniff it out or women fuzz to search us on the spot. But I knew I couldn't do with another conviction, and I had to get rid of my box of pills. He'd moved round to another chest of drawers, and I knew I had to act.

"Is it OK if I smoke?" I asked.

"Let's have a look," and he held out his hand for my packet of cigarettes. "Flash," he said, observing the gold band round the tip. "OK, go ahead." So I lit one, and went and sat down by the table with the pills on it.

"Who's that?" he asked, pointing to a picture of Davey I had on the wall.

"I don't think you'd know him," I said.

As he peered more closely I casually leant my hand with the cigarette in it on the table.

"Don't be too sure," he grinned. "We know more than you think."

"Anyway, he's in America." I transferred my cigarette to the other hand and put my hand back on the table. He continued to stare at the row of pictures I had of me with guys I'd been with, and I closed my hand over the box and moved it down by my side. Then he turned to look at me.

"Are you stoned?" he asked abruptly, looking at me piercingly.

"No," I said, and wondered why he asked; I didn't know they used words like stoned.

"We can tell by the eyes, you know."

"Tell what?" I wished he'd get on with his searching.

"It's the eyes. I can tell you're stoned by the way your pupils are contracted."

"No, no, you're onto the wrong drug," I said. "Pot doesn't do that."

"Look at your pupils," he said, "I know."

By now I had opened the box and spilled the pills into my hand. I think there were seven, but I didn't dare look.

"It's the bright light in here," I explained.

"Is it?" he asked. "Are you sure?" He smiled knowingly and then resumed his searching.

"What's wrong with my pupils?" I demanded. "Let me have a look." And I got up and went over to the mirror. "They look all right to me."

"Never mind," he said, busy reading some letters. I pretended to study my eyes in the mirror and poked at them with the hand that was holding the pills. As I dropped my hand I popped the pills into my mouth and swallowed the lot. They seemed to fill my mouth completely and I never thought I'd swallow them, they tasted incredibly bitter. After I'd forced them down I started to choke.

"I must have a drink of water," I said, not caring at the indiscretion, and rushed for the kitchen, coughing. There was another fuzz going through the food cupboard, and after I'd got a glass of water I asked him if he'd had any luck.

"Well, now what do you think *this* is?" he asked triumphantly. He'd got hold of a jar of Lapsong Soushang tea, which he'd mistaken for grass.

"Oh, you'll never get promoted for that," I said cheekily. "That's drinking tea some macrobiotics left behind." He unscrewed the lid and sniffed at it suspiciously.

"Yes, I suppose it is," he admitted. "Oh well."

I went back to my room, feeling slightly hysterical at my success. I wanted to laugh and tell them what I'd done, but I knew that wouldn't be cool. I wondered how my pupils were doing now. Then another guy came in; I'd only got it together just in time. He started going through my things as well.

"What's the matter, don't you trust your friend?" I asked. I couldn't help being cheeky, the relief and effect of the pills was beginning to make me feel high.

"It doesn't hurt to double check," he said ponderously.

"You're wasting your time."

"That's for us to decide." He turned to the table and found the empty pill box I'd put back there. I watched eagerly as he picked it up and shook it. Then he opened it and looked inside. I was having to suppress the giggles inside me at their futile efforts to bust me. After patting all the posters on the wall to make sure there was nothing lodged behind them, they stood in the middle of the room and thought for a minute.

"This room's clear," one said.

"You've had a lucky escape," the other told me.

"I tell you, I don't take drugs." I felt very innocent. Then we all trooped outside to see what was happening in the other rooms. John was safe; he's on prescription for tincture like me, but whereas I throw my bottles away, his room is littered with them, and he sticks labels on them like "sweet dreams" and "dangerous drugs". They took one of his especially artistic bottles away with them "as a souvenir". But Wendy wasn't so lucky. They'd found a tiny bit of hash in her make-up bag, which they pounced on, their faces beaming with vindication. They all examined it, and weighed it in their hands; it could only have been enough for a couple of joints. Anyway, that was it for Wendy. She was already on a conditional discharge for a wretched ampule of speed, and they said because of this they wouldn't be able to release her on bail that night. So she had to go with them and spend the night at the police station. Feeling sorry for Wendy made me realise how lucky I was, and it was really this selfish relief that was uppermost in my mind. I still couldn't get over how I'd managed to trick them, and I stood high and trembling and exchanging witty remarks with these guys from the Squad who seemed quite pleased that their time hadn't been wasted.

"Give my love to Detective Sergeant Phillips," I said, as I let them out. When they had gone we rushed into John's room to exchange experiences, and try to figure out a way to help Wendy. We got a straight friend to attend court the next morning to give her bail, and she was told she had to live at home with her parents because my pad was a bad influence.

After the raid I didn't sleep for twenty four hours and felt really ill; I wasn't used to so many uppers all at once. But I finally collapsed and when I came to, Wendy was moving all her stuff out. It wouldn't be the same without her around.

CHAPTER TWENTY

I was pleased when Grant rang me up as soon as he got back. I told him about the bust and he said it served me right. But he sounded a bit subdued, and asked me to get some food together and come over. I told him I'd be there at nine and arrived at ten. He didn't seem to mind; he was in a rather mellow mood, alone watching the TV. "Oh hello," he said, and I went over and kissed him.

"None of that now, what have you brought to eat?"

"Chicken and things."

"Come on, come on, get it together," he said, investigating the contents of my bag.

"But I've only just got here," I protested.

"I'm hungry," he said.

Grant looked tired and hungry; maybe it was all the travelling. I was pleased to be doing things for him, and it was nice to be back in his tiny room. I made him a chicken salad, and took what was over up to Bill, who was lying on his bed tripping, and mournfully playing his harmonica. He already knew about Wendy, and I didn't want to bring him down by talking about it. When I returned to Grant's room I found him knocking the food back like a famished wolf. He paused briefly to tell me to get into bed and then went back to his meal. I brought out my new bottle of tincture which I had scored that day and swallowed some.

"Give it here," Grant said, and I passed the bottle to him. He washed down the salad with a good mouthful of tincture and smacked his lips. Then he put some sounds on and got into bed. We lay side by side watching the telly with the volume turned off. Then we started making it and for the first time we kept the lights on so that Grant could watch me. He plated me which he'd never done before and it all got pretty ecstatic. Things seemed to be different tonight with Grant; new vibrations were coming from him. I'm sure I could sense it and I wasn't just stoned. But I didn't try to analyse it or interpret, nothing like that, it was enough to be lying beside him without him pushing me away and our thoughts rambling but happy. Well, mine were anyway.

We were lying around naked when the door opened and there was Joe. He was all dressed up to go out and looked great. I started to cover myself but thought, why bother, it's only Joe and he's seen it all before. So I lay there.

"Hello," Joe said, "having it away on the sly?"

I could feel him looking at me, but kept my eyes turned away. I suddenly thought, wouldn't it be groovy if we could all have a scene together. I was sure they would dig it, but in a nasty way. They were too provincial to do it in the right frame of mind. I liked them both and from my point of view I felt it would have worked out. But things weren't as easy as that. I could feel bad vibrations between them.

"What do *you* want?" Grant asked irritably.

"I have to go over to Hampstead. Can I have the car?" I imagined Joe didn't like having to ask Grant for permission.

"No, I can't sanction that," Grant answered shortly, busying himself with a cigarette.

The car was an enormous beat-up American limousine which was used to take the group on gigs. This meant they didn't all have to squash in the van and arrive with the equipment, which didn't look too good now they were getting bigger. Grant was responsible for it, and no one else was supposed to drive it. But Joe was always pestering him for it, and he often relented. But not this time, it seemed.

"Why not?" asked Joe, his face white.

"Because you're not allowed to. I'm responsible for it and I say no."

"Look," said Joe, very evenly, "the only reason I'm asking you is because I'm late. Now, don't be a prick, let me have it."

"That's not *my* fault," said Grant, sticking his nose up in the air.

Joe was really uptight. He kind of ground his teeth and there was a tremor in his voice.

"Who do you think *you* are?" he got out. "Whose car is it? You're not even a member of the group and you're coming on like Jesus Christ. You're just a glorified roadie, you know, nothing else . . . you're here to do what *we* want."

137

"All right," said Grant, as though he hadn't heard the insults. "If you want the car you had better get it in writing from Roland Johns. If he says you can have it, OK, but he won't, so nothing doing. Now get out!"

That was it. There was nothing Joe could do now. He knew as well as Grant that Roland Johns wouldn't hear of the group members grooving around in the car in their spare time. He stood there and stared at Grant.

"You think you know it all, don't you?" He shook his head. "But you stop bugging me, Grant, or there'll be trouble!"

"Oh, do get out, Joe," said Grant in a bored voice. Joe, looking very grim-faced, kicked the door shut behind him as he went back downstairs.

"Oh dear," I said. I'd never really heard them argue like that before, although I knew things hadn't been too good between them recently.

"He's really getting on my nerves," Grant said. "While we were away he tried putting me down in front of other groups. Like telling me, not even *asking* me, in front of Hendrix's roadie to carry his guitar case. He only did that to be flash, and to make people think he's more important than me. And there are other things as well, when I'm chatting up promoters and people, Joe will come up and tell me to stop talking and go and check the equipment, or something like that."

"But it's not your job to carry things and check equipment," I said.

"I know. And he knows too. But it's because he's competing with me. He's trying to prove something. You see, when I was a DJ and having it all my own way he was nowhere. Then Relation started getting somewhere and for a while he was on a better scene than I was, because when I came to London I didn't have a job. But now I've got this scene together and I'm making it, and I reckon I'm in a better position than he is. If this group doesn't make it, I know I'm OK for a job, because I'm good at what I do. So he'd better watch it. I don't need him, or the group. I can get my own things together now and I'll be doing just that if he doesn't stop annoying me."

I hadn't realised this undercover ego battle had been going on between Grant and Joe, and I found it pretty interesting. Then

138

Grant grabbed me again, and that make him forget his aggro for a while. Maybe he was trying to work it all out on me because he was rather violent and scratched me hard when he came which was quickly. We carried on and this time it was in slow motion, and he was very gentle, stroking my breasts and playing games because although we were tired, we were still stoned and sexy.

Afterwards we lay together and started to play our talking game. My part is to lure him into personal, and what he considers dangerous, conversations. His part is to divert me with squashing comments. For example, I reflect: "Why do I like you?"

And he says, "Don't answer that."

"All right, but why?" I insist.

"I don't want to know," he says.

"Why not?"

"It's a dangerous one, I can see red lights flashing with that question," he warns.

I have to persist in a roundabout way, changing from subject to subject, almost getting lost myself, but managing somehow to bring it back to the original question. This time it took me an hour and a half before I managed to tell him why I liked him. I only wanted to say I dug him because he was cool, and he never bored me, we grooved in bed and the longer I was with him the less I understood him and yet the more I wanted to know. I was continually intrigued by him and he kept me in check by somehow keeping me in a state of confused inferiority. Even in his tenderest moments he never bared his soul or confessed his feelings, and he didn't want me to, either. He seemed to distrust words that described feelings and allowed his actions to speak for themselves. He was rude without being malicious, and funny without even trying to be. I finished off by deciding that even if I didn't dig him in the way I did, I'd probably respect him because underneath the image he put out, he was OK.

Anyway, so that he didn't start taking me too much for granted, I split early the next morning without waking him up. Let him make the bed, I thought.

CHAPTER TWENTY-ONE

On Thursday afternoon I rang Grant up from work. I needed some information on a barring clause Relation have on one of their contracts.

Joe answers the phone in a squeaky falsetto voice and says Grant isn't there. I tell him to stop fooling about, and if Grant is refusing to speak to me he's just being childish and silly.

"Honest," says Joe, in normal tones, "he's not here."

I get a sort of instant flash back to the times Grant refused to let me speak to Joe.

"Well, where is he?" I ask, annoyed.

"I've no idea, anyway, what do you want *him* for?"

"Well, I want to speak to him."

"Speak to me . . . who needs *him*."

"I do," I say.

Joe paused for a moment and then asked me to come over. What? I thought.

"I don't think that's very cool, Joe. I really wasn't phoning Grant to ask him if I could come over, I just have a few things to talk to him about." I wasn't quite sure what Joe was up to.

"*I'm* asking you to come over, so it's got nothing to do with Grant."

"I don't want to get mixed up in your battles with Grant," I said. "And I normally never come over unless Grant asks me to. He might get uptight if I just appear."

"You've got a mind of your own, haven't you?" Joe persisted. "If I ask you to come over, you don't have to ask Grant's permission, do you? I mean, the house belongs to all of us, Grant's just one person here."

"Yes, I know, but I don't want to make Grant uptight."

"Listen, *I've* asked you over, and if Grant doesn't like it he can sort it out with *me*. And while you're here you can tell him what you've got to."

140

I suppose it sounded quite reasonable, the way Joe put it. There wasn't anything wrong in going to see Joe, I told myself. Then he asked me if I had a certain kind of cough mixture which people are using these days. I told him I had a bottle, and, as this gave me a good excuse to go over, I told him OK, I'd be there soon.

I felt a bit dubious of the outcome, and when I got there I went straight into Joe's room. He was in his tight white trousers and Kewpie Doll track top.

"Hello," he said, grinning.

Ruby was there, and then Wendy and Bill came in. She and Bill were still managing to keep their scene together although she had to split to her parents' house in the sticks every night. Wendy looked at me intently, wondering what I was doing in Joe's room. Joe wanted to go out to eat before he took the mixture, but I told him it was best to take it on an empty stomach, or else take the mixture and then eat very quickly before it hits you, because, when it does it freaks out taste sensations. You can feel what you are eating, but it is completely tasteless. It's very weird, I told him, bread and butter tastes like paper with something greasy on top.

There is enough in one bottle for two turn-ons, but Joe drinks more than his share, gravely watched by the rest of us. Just as I'm drinking the rest, complaining of Joe's greediness, Spike appears, his nose twitching.

"Hello," he says, anxiously. "Hello," we answer. The hello ritual is still going strong.

Spike is a bit petulant because there isn't any drug left for him. He stands there shuffling backwards and forwards. While they are all arguing about where to eat, I slip upstairs to Grant's room. I knock on the door and he says come in. I open the door and then freeze, because there on the mattress is Grant and he's got a chick with him.

"Hello," I say, because I've got to say something.

"Oh, hello," he says, at a loss for once.

My mind is blown, I went back to Joe's room and demanded to know who the large chick was in Grant's room. Nobody seemed to know there was a chick in Grant's room and they were all as amazed as me. They shook their heads in disbelief and said I'd been hallucinating and why didn't I try again. Joe, however, had a weird little grin on his face and in a flash of paranoia I believed that he'd

141

known about the chick with Grant. Right, I thought, I'll show that Grant. I'll sleep with Joe, and see how he likes *that*. I half wanted to anyway, and this gave me enough justification.

I went into Joe's room and lay down on the bed. I decided not to undress or get into bed in case that would have been uncool. My mind felt calm as I lay on my back in the darkened room. I felt no sense of anticipation as I waited for Joe. Sure I'd been mad at Grant, but that wasn't the reason I was here in Joe's room. I was also convinced that I wasn't hung up on Joe, although the fact that our scene had finished in such an unsatisfactory way might have been needling me deep down to work it out to some kind of belated conclusion. Though what kind of conclusion there could be, I just didn't know. If I felt it was going to be an unpleasant conclusion I wouldn't have faced it, because I'm that sort of coward. Yet I know it couldn't be entirely satisfactory because of the way I felt about Grant. The thought struck me that all I wanted to do was to reassure myself that I could still pull a groovy pop musician, although even that need was not as compelling or as necessary as it once had been to me.

It also occurred to me as I lay there that I had been taking a lot of drugs lately, especially since I'd come onto this scene with Relation. I knew that my attitude to people had been changing a lot over the past months, and I wasn't sure whether it was the drugs, the competitive power scene I worked on, Grant's influence, the natural course of events, or a combination of some of all of these things. I was ruder and less tolerant to people who didn't matter, and more at ease and confident with people who did. I had learned how to operate now, not perfectly, but successfully enough to get the things together that were important to my career. I knew how things worked on the scene. I knew how people made bread and how people got power, and I knew what power and bread meant and how they could be used. So, when the opportunity presented itself, I would recognise it and know what to do to turn it to my advantage. But I was not quite ready yet. There were still things to know and lessons to be learnt. That was the career part of me anyway, and I reckoned that, all in all, it was coming along very nicely. My emotional scene was lagging behind in progress. I had learned how to cool things, but I still made mistakes and I couldn't distinguish between what was good and what was necessary for me. At the moment it was still necessary to sleep with guys who were not good for me, guys like Harold Grimes, for example. But that would change because the need to do that would eventually disappear. Of course, I still needed to love and be loved, both physically and whatever other kind of way a person can be loved, but not in quite such a time-devouring manner. I would get that together too, because I was going to learn by my mistakes, and I was prepared to get hurt, be desolated and to totally open myself to whatever torment and nastiness came my way. Just as I had learned to suss things out which affected my career, so I was learning, at a slower pace, to suss out the kind of scenes and the types of men which suited me best.

Meanwhile, there was Grant upstairs, me down here, and Joe imminent. Then I thought about Grant and the chick in his room. I didn't care who she was, and I didn't feel threatened. Sure I'd been staggered to find her there with him and I'd been angry and jealous. I knew that I wasn't being rational about him having another chick – maybe he hadn't even made her. But she'd been there, and what's rational about anger and jealousy? Rationalisation is all in the head, whereas anger and jealousy are all in the genes, and I know I've got a good share, and there's no fighting them. If anyone told me that I wasn't being fair, I'd just laugh at them, because fairness is something you're told exists, like God, but the others, love, anger and jealousy and the like are things you *feel* exist. My mind coasted on and I think I went into a kind of trance. That mixture is too much, is the last thing I remember thinking.

Then Joe was tickling my feet. "Why aren't you properly in bed?" he asked.

"I only lay down temporarily," I said.

"Are you stoned?" he asked.

"Not really," I said, but I'm sure I was.

"Come on, get into bed."

And it was almost just like it was before. I got in on the outside and then remembered that my place was on the inside. I turned my back to Joe, waiting to see what he'd do. He told me to turn round, which I did, and he said "Hello".

"Hello," I said, and we both laughed and started making it. It was all right, but I didn't love him any more. I'd got over whatever love I'd had for him, so that was that. And anyway, he wasn't as good as Grant; we just didn't fit together so well. There wasn't much to say the next morning, except goodbye. He kissed me and said he'd ring me, but I didn't care, I was thinking about Grant. I could hear him moving about and dictating orders from the landing, and I didn't want him to see me. So, when he wasn't around, I sidled out of Joe's room and dashed for the front door. There would be more to this, I thought, as I safely made the street.

CHAPTER TWENTY-TWO

Feeling slightly tatty and used, I had four drugless days during which I slept a lot, cooked sensible food and read *Auto da Fe.*

At work, however, we're going well. I was right on top of the heap there, and the management knew it. Over the months I had gathered in most of the administrative strings and now anything that happened had to go through me. I was advising Jason which groups to book, and booking some of them myself. I was getting the club some good PR in the papers, as well as doing all the day-to-day things like getting the advertisements together and doing the books and working out groups' bread and knocking off percentages. I really knew how the place worked, and to test my value I started hinting at leaving. The result of this was an immediate rise in pay. OK, I thought, and stopped the hints, because now I knew where *they* were at.

Jason often gave me lifts home, and when we weren't talking business he would make languid attempts to pull me. But I was always very firm about that. He still rubbed me up the wrong way, and anyway, I was in enough trouble with my men scenes and didn't want to complicate an already over-complicated situation. Also, I was sure I would have more value if I remained unpulled, so I kept putting him down, but politely, because I didn't want him uptight with me.

Wendy rang me and said Grant had cornered her and demanded to know what I'd done the night I'd burst in on his scene with the other chick.

"She went home," Wendy had said, as she genuinely thought I had.

"But I heard her up in Bill's room later on. Why didn't she knock on my door?"

"Katie doesn't knock on doors twice," Wendy had told him.

"But I was alone by then," Grant had said grumpily.

"You weren't alone the first time."

"She was only a friend."

"Katie didn't know that," Wendy had replied.

"Well, I was alone, and she should have knocked," Grant insisted.

Then I told Wendy that I'd slept with Joe, and at first she didn't believe it, but when she did she wanted to know why. I didn't really want to go into all the complicated reasons, and tried to play it down.

"You still like Grant best, don't you?" she wanted to know.

"Of course I do," I said.

"Then why did you do it?"

"He was with another chick, wasn't he?"

"Chick or no chick, you wouldn't have done it if you really dug him," Wendy said, and sounded cross. "And why Joe? He's about the last one to go off with. I mean, he's such a creep, how could you do it?"

"Because I wanted to," I said, and got a bit uptight. Apart from the fact that I don't like people putting down guys I sleep with – whatever I feel – she was echoing the kind of doubts I myself had about the whole situation. But I didn't want to explain it. It was something that had to be done, and now I could only wait and see how it turned out. It worried me that Grant would find out, and it worried me that he wouldn't, and in between, the waiting for something to happen was a drag on my nerves. This was one of the reasons why I was off drugs for the moment, because drugs usually prodded my mind into thoughts I didn't want to face just yet. So working, sleeping and reading seemed a sensible way to occupy my time, and the only pills I was indulging in were vitamin pills.

"Well, I think you've been silly," Wendy continued, "and I hope Grant doesn't find out, because what will you do then?"

And then, while I was brooding about Wendy's criticisms, Grant rang up and said that he wanted me around there immediately. Nervously, I swallowed some tincture and hopped into a taxi. It was the same Grant who let me in, no special looks, no questions, just grumpy orders which I was relieved to obey. He always searched my bag to see if I had anything interesting in it, and when he found the tincture he gulped down a lot without measuring it, and then handed the bottle to me. Forgetting that I'd already had some, I drunk another lot, and then realised I'd probably had a massive overdose. Help, I thought, but I didn't say anything.

"Don't take your boots off," he ordered, "we're going to the pictures."

"What kind of film?" I asked.

A Roman war film, he told me.

It turned out to be *Oedipus the King*, which wasn't exactly a war film. I tried to explain this to Grant, but he insisted on going, so we did. By the time it got round to the main feature we were in trouble. It was very hard to follow the plot, especially with the dialogue being in this sort of Shakespearean English. Grant suddenly nudged me.

"See that guy there?" and he pointed at Oedipus. "He was in *The Sound of Music*. What's he doing in this thing?"

It was really freaking Grant out, and he kept laughing about it. I tried to concentrate, but I was getting frightened by the physical changes I was going through. I couldn't feel my body at all; it felt as though all my sensations were cramming themselves into my head and that it would explode. I had to change my position and shake myself a bit to bring my body back to life. I took a look at Grant to see how he was coping. He was sitting slumped in his seat with his mouth hanging open and his sunglasses on, and he kept shaking his head in bewilderment at the long speeches and flashbacks.

"I can't get this together at all," he was saying over and over again, "and where's all the fighting?"

Just as I started to get into it he said he wanted to leave. But I wouldn't.

"Why not?" he demanded loudly.

"Because I've got to work it out," I hissed at him.

I'd read the play, and I was hung up on trying to reconcile it with the film I was watching. It had all the same characters and the same plot, but somehow it all seemed to be happening back to front. I was trying to work out whether this was being done on purpose, and if so, why. Or maybe it was coming through all mixed up because I was over-stoned? When Oedipus finally stabbed out his eyes and kept making his pleadings to be banished I couldn't watch it anymore, it was too gruesome. I let my head rest on my knees to cut out the images for a change, and just let the dialogue filter through. But this was even more confusing, because of the long pauses and dramatic musical effects.

"Sit up," Grant ordered, "don't do that when you're in the cinema with *me*." And he kept prodding me until I finally righted myself.

Grant was still holding the full carton of ice cream which he'd bought in the interval and it had now totally melted. Not being able to bear the images on the screen, I watched him trying to finish it by drinking it straight from the carton. We both burst into giggles as it dribbled out of the corners of his mouth and made trails down the front of his jacket. Suddenly we were aware that lots of people were turning round and giving us stern disapproving looks, and this made us laugh instead of giggle. More people turned round, and we knew we were in serious danger of becoming hysterical, so we had to get up and leave. This caused another commotion because getting past all the people in the seats was almost impossible for us in the state we were in. Then, instead of making for the main exit, we somehow got ourselves caught in the emergency one, full of long passages, steps that didn't seem to lead anywhere, and prison-like doors which wouldn't open. Being alone in these passages made it even worse for us, and we both felt and communicated the small risings of panic which began to hit us. Back we came and into the auditorium again and Grant said, "You get us out", and immediately became hung up on the film again, standing and staring at the screen and shaking his head. I could see the exit lights as coloured blurs in the distance up a long hill, and grabbing him by the elbow I managed to move him in the direction of one of them. Feeling like the capital letters on a huge sandwich board, we made it up the long carpeted aisle, and I pushed him through the doors, and there we were in more passages. I began to think that we'd gone wrong again when suddenly we were in the Gents' loo. I had never been in a Gents' loo in a cinema before and I stared around me taking it all in. A guy at a pisspot stared over his shoulder at us, alarm and amazement chasing each other across his face. When he did up his flies in a hurry he must have damaged himself, for immediately his face creased into an expression of excruciating pain.

"He's caught his balls!" Grant roared in delight, and gave out a huge guffaw.

"Out!" I shouted, and we beat it, making for the next light, past the usherettes who stared, and finally we were outside.

After walking along for a bit, I felt we must be going the wrong way because I didn't recognise any of the shops. Neither did Grant. He said he didn't know where he was going, but it didn't matter anyway. We just ploughed on in silence until Grant announced that he was hungry. This meant we had to cross the road to get to the restaurant he'd spotted, and without waiting for me he dashed over at full speed. I wasn't so lucky; the continuous stream of oncoming cars seemed bent on preventing me personally from crossing. Twice I was out there in the middle of it all and twice I had to scuttle back to the wrong side. Grant was bellowing and gesticulating at me from the other side of the road, and my impatience reached panic proportions until finally I just walked out hoping for the best, fixing my eyes straight ahead. I made it, no horns blew, no cars stopped, the sound of them zipping past me was all I heard.

"Why didn't you wait?" I demanded of Grant.

"Oh, I'd never have made it if I'd waited, look what happened to you," he replied. "I just saw a gap and ran."

Then we were inside a seedy restaurant, and confronted with a menu which neither of us could read. I was scared to order a full meal in case the sight of it freaked me out, so I asked for some apple pie. It took Grant ages to decide what he wanted, and the waitress was hovering above us impatiently while Grant kept changing his mind. Finally he ordered something that sounded like breakfast to me. The noise from the other people was coming and going in waves. Sometimes it became so loud that I thought my head would burst, but it always receded before it became intolerable. I wanted to go for a pee, but Grant said he didn't want me to leave him alone. "You'll never make it," he warned. But I had to go, and told him I'd manage somehow. It seemed to take me ages to find the loo and go through all the processes, and when I returned Grant was staring in disbelief at the enormous plate of sausages, eggs, bacon and chips that had arrived in front of him. I managed my apple pie quite well, and we got up to pay as soon as we'd eaten. At the cash counter we found ourselves confronted by rows of glistening cakes and gateaux. Grant gasped, and his eyes widened at the sight of them.

"I've got to have one of those," he said.

"So have I." We took a long time choosing, and while the guy who was serving was putting one in a bag, he handed a knife to Grant to lift the piece of lemon meringue pie I had chosen.

"Oh . . . I can't get that together," said Grant, momentarily taken aback. "That's a woman's job."

He handed me the knife and stepped back to watch. Oh Christ, I thought, and started giggling. I examined the pie, which didn't look in very good shape. It was bound to break into pieces if I tried to lift it into the bag, but I had to try. Grant was falling about laughing at my efforts to slide the knife under the pie, and my hand was shaking. I managed to lift it up a little, but before I could get it anywhere near the bag I was holding in my other hand, the pie fell off and landed upside down on the plate. That started my giggles again, and the guy behind the counter was watching us both in amazement. I began to get paranoid about being obviously stoned, and knew I had to get out. So I picked it up bodily and it all squelched inside my hand. I stuffed it into the bag, though most of it stayed stuck to my hand, and Grant dropped some money onto the counter. We ran for the door, leaving lemon meringue all over the door handle.

Outside we collapsed, laughing helplessly, and then noticed it was raining. My hand was horribly sticky, and I seemed to be carrying too many things to manage to clean it. We set off again, and turned into the long road that leads to the house. We weren't saying anything now, both of us staring ahead to the end of the road which didn't seem to be getting any nearer. Grant increased his speed to get there quicker; he didn't want to admit what was happening. I quickened to keep pace with him. We kept up this swift walking for a time but it didn't seem to be making any appreciable difference. Grant broke into a run, and I ran after him, clutching the bags of cakes in my sticky hand. I managed to catch up with him, and we ran like that, with our hearts thumping and our eyes staring straight ahead, until with profound relief, we got there. We fell into his room, shedding our wet shoes, and kept telling each other how we couldn't believe it.

"We must have taken too much," I said, washing my hands.

"You're dead right we did," he agreed. "It's never been like this before. You know, I was really freaking out in the cinema. That's why I wanted to leave."

"Yes, but I had to stay to try and sort the story out."

"It was a bloody con," Grant growled, tearing the bag off his cake, "it wasn't even a war film."

Then he started stuffing the cake into his mouth while I looked at my disintegrated meringue pie and took a bite. It didn't taste as good as it had looked, and I threw it out of the window.

Grant started to put on his bluebeat records and sat grooving to them, hunched up on the edge of the mattress and rocking back and forth on his heels. I couldn't stay, the noise was too much for my head, which seemed to be full of incredible pressure. I went up to Bill's room to find a little sanity. Bill was in there with two guys I didn't know, and nothing much seemed to be happening, so I started explaining to them about the cinema and the cakes, but they just stared at me blankly. Maybe it wasn't so funny, I thought, but I was sure it was, and why weren't they laughing?

"What's the matter with you lot?" I asked anxiously. "Are you stoned? Is something hanging you up?"

No, they were tripping. That was all I needed. I went back to the claustrophobic beat that was throbbing relentlessly in Grant's minute area. He was still rocking backwards and forwards, and oblivious to everything except the music. I lay down. I wasn't digging all this. I felt I might scream in a minute because it was all becoming unbearable, and I didn't want to scream because that's very uncool. I decided I had to sleep it off, so I took my clothes off and got into bed. Without speaking to me, Grant turned down the volume a bit, and my mind began to wander off. He got into bed a bit later, and shook me from my meandering dreams. He wanted me awake. More, he wanted to make it with me. If it was going to be as groovy as the other stoned sex scene we had had, that suited me, and we set to. But this time I found everything was too intense. I could hardly stand him touching my clitoris without writhing, and when he went inside me I felt as if my body had gone into one intense orgasm which wouldn't stop. I was bursting all over, and then when he plated me my mind went blank. If it hadn't, I don't know where it would have gone.

Next morning all was sane again. After Grant had leapt off to the office with his usual alacrity, Joe came padding up the stairs and put his head in.

151

"Hello," he said. "I thought I heard you around last night. Why don't you make some coffee and come and talk to me?"

I mumbled that I'd do it in a few minutes and he went off. I got up and went to the kitchen. When I took him the coffee he was back in bed, reading a science fiction book. After talking a bit he patted the bed and told me to get in beside him. It was obvious the way his mind was working. He reckoned that he'd pulled me once and that he could pull me again, any time in fact. He believed that he was the one I really wanted, Grant being a weak second choice. By playing it this way behind Grant's back he could call the changes in our occasional confrontations, lay on the power and practise the domination bit, without the hangup of having to have me around him permanently. Also, as he was battling with Grant, this coloured his attitude and added little vicious refinements to the rather soft, uncaring Joe I'd originally gone for. I saw through him all right and rather despised him. However, by coming on like this, he was really playing my game. I didn't want Joe now, but I was interested in Grant finding out that Joe could pull me back. Grant's reactions were infinitely more interesting than Joe's company or body. So let him have me; it meant nothing to me.

"Just because I slept with you last time doesn't mean I'm going to make a habit of it," I said. I wasn't going to make it *too* easy for him.

"I'm sure you'd like to, though," Joe grinned. "That sort of thing appeals to you doesn't it, a three-handed scene. It does to me, anyway, it's sort of like Shules ate Shim."

"Not quite," I said, sarcastically. *Jules et Jim* seemed far removed from Grant and Joe.

"If you don't get in, I'll pull you in," Joe said, putting down his book.

"Shall I take my clothes off?" I asked rather inanely.

"You'll be hot in here if you don't," he said, expansive in his imagined victory. So I undressed yet again and slid in beside him.

CHAPTER TWENTY-THREE

My mind is taken off the whole things by this telephone call from *International Magazine* who have heard of me from somewhere and want to interview me about the underground and take my picture. I like the sound of that and spend a lot of time working out what I'm going to say, and deciding what to wear. Of course I have to go to the hairdressers, and Gavin and I decide another style change is due. Curls again, but this time nothing too freaky; and, as my hair has grown again, it comes out soft and floppy with my face framed halo-like by the curls. The interview isn't for another week or two, so I've got plenty of time to get myself prepared.

Also I've been getting the occasional letter from Davey in the States; apparently The Dream Battery have broken up and he's joined up with Zach Franks again to play with The Savage. So he's really hitting the big time now, because The Savage are incredibly popular in the States. In the last letter he intimated that he might be home soon, and that he was looking forward to seeing me, and all that. Nothing passionate, just a polite guarded letter like the rest, and typically Davey. It then occurred to me that I'd never really given much thought to meeting Davey again after all this time. I remembered how I had felt for him, and how his going away had strengthened my resolve not to merely drift along but to get something really concrete going for myself. I remembered that all right, and I'd always clung to it whenever the going got difficult. But the actual return of Davey with his physical presence right here in front of me, just hadn't entered my head at all. So I got out all his photographs and peered at them, trying to imbue them with a sort of life and reality. But it was impossible to know what to think or feel. Yes, he was pretty, and yes I had loved him, and yes, yes, he had hurt me and made me cry. But it all seemed frighteningly long ago. He'd find that I had progressed and got things together, though he had probably changed more than I; he was now in one of the biggest groups in the States, and would be rich and famous by English standards. And here he was, coming back and wanting to see me again. Hard as I examined his photos, and deep as I went into our thing together, the more I realised that I didn't care what he thought of me any more. Even the fact that he was a big name now didn't really impress me. It was enough to say I knew him. Yet he remained a bit of a question mark in my mind. I'd loved him deeply once, and if he hadn't changed, and looked the same, thought the same, behaved the same, then surely these qualities which had made me love him then, should work their same magic now. Yes, I thought, I want to see you, and tacked all of his pictures on the wall above my bed.

Meanwhile, there was another big American group appearing at The Big Tower. The New York Sound & Touch, they are called, and as this was their first time in England, they were having a reception. They are an East Coast group, about the oldest on the scene, and they are very political and socially conscious, way beyond the protest bit, using a crude and savage sense of humour to shock the message across, without relying too much on electronic bombardment. There are six on them, three performers who sing, read poems and tell stories, and three musicians.

Jason took me to the reception. He was still being very friendly to me these days, taking me places and talking to me about his chicks and his business. Once we got there I managed to lose him in the usual crowd which always turns up on these occasions. I sussed out The Sound & Touch from a distance. They were a weird looking bunch. The three poet performers were much older than the musicians. They all had this very long hair streaming down their backs and were dressed like hillbillies. I fancied two of the musicians and flopped down into an empty chair beside them and looked into the distance. People were thrusting past, and those who knew me would stop and examine my new head. Then someone called out: "Who's on at The Big Tower next weekend?" And I pretended to think for a minute. "Isn't it The Sound & Touch?" I said vaguely, and everybody laughed.

Then one of The Sound & Touch guys leant over and asked me if Jimi Hendrix was in town. Well, he wasn't but it started the conversation, and soon I was deep in discussion with this guy, comparing the scene over here to the States. He had very long dark hair which he kept off his rather serious face with an elastic band, and these really penetrating eyes that never seemed to leave me alone. Suddenly he paused, narrowed his eyes, and said "Gemini".

"How did you work that out?" I asked, intrigued because he had guessed right.

He grinned confidently. "Easy," he said, "I just related it to myself."

So he was a Gemini too, and I got all excited, because, although I don't know very much about the Zodiac scene, I'm sure there is a lot to it, and the kind of star symbol you go out with is supposed to have a great bearing on the outcome of relationships. In retrospect, for example, you say, "Well, he was a Leo, and I never get on with Leos, because I'm a Capricorn, and it's a well-known fact that Leos and Capricorns just don't mix". It's probably just an excuse for the scene not working out, but it's quite fun.

So there we were, two Geminis, four personalities, really hitting it off, though I'd have thought that two Geminis were a dangerous combination. As I'd arranged to go down to The Joint later I asked him if he would like to come along. He said yes, so we split alone. I have no hustle getting into places like The Joint now, and when they saw who I was with they really turned on all the smiles and hospitality. We sat in the restaurant and ate and talked. But talking against the noise of the group became a strain, and there seemed so much to say that we split back to my pad. He told me how relaxed it was over here in comparison to the States, where they were so intolerant of hippies and eccentrics, and with murderous cops continually uptight. He spoke in a positive, almost aggressive way, and so fast that I had difficulty understanding all he said.

"It's your accent, I just can't make out some of the words," I apologised, after the umpteenth "what's that?"

"I wish I spoke like you do," he said, "I just can't get over your voice."

"What about it?"

"It's the way you speak."

"What way?" I asked.

"Your accent. I've never heard anyone speak like that before. We only seem to get the Irish and Scots in New York. I mean it. Your voice knocks me out."

I couldn't believe there were only Irish and Scots in New York, and even so, I didn't think there was anything particularly inspiring about my voice. I consider I have an accentless accent; educated middle-class with hip slang thrown in. But it was nice to think he liked listening to me, and I wondered if he wanted to sleep with me. I didn't wonder for long, it simply didn't matter, it was just right as it was. When he took hold of my hand, his touch was light and cool, and his fingers moved around a lot in a very sexy way.

"Hey, you know I'm not a lechy musician type," he said. "I despise guys who pull just to show off."

"I know what you mean," I said.

"I like chicks I can talk to," he said, and I agreed with him. Then he let go of my hand. Cool, I thought.

Just then the phone rang. It was Joe. Had I got his message?

What message?

To come over.

No, I hadn't.

How about coming down to The Joint, then.

I've just come from The Joint.

Well, come over for a smoke.

I'm with some people.

Then we'll drive over to your place.

He put the phone down before I could say anything, and that was that. What a drag. I had tried to let him know I wasn't keen to see him. With guys like Joe, I was discovering, you had to sock it to them, quite literally, before you got your meaning across.

"Hey," I said, all false and jolly when I came back to my American Gemini, "the Relation are coming over."

I said it like it was a big thing, and I knew I was making a bad impression. So I tried to explain that Relation were old friends and always dropping round. But that sounded phoney too, so I stopped. I was cursing Joe for phoning, and hoping he wouldn't be alone. I was still too involved in my experiment to tell him bluntly to piss off, but it was becoming really inconvenient, and I hoped it wouldn't blow my American out because I was beginning to feel that I really liked him, apart from the fact that he was a pretty good pull. I'd never had an American group member before. On the other hand, I reasoned, no guy can expect to walk in on some chick and find no complications and involvements as if she hadn't existed before.

And as this seemed to be the season for tests and experiments, it would put him to a little test, too.

About ten minutes later they all stream into my room, and although I'm glad Joe isn't alone, I wasn't expecting quite so many people. Nearly all the group are there plus two others I don't know. I wasn't expecting Grant because it wasn't his scene to go visiting, and I was sure Joe wouldn't be so uncool as to take him along. The vibrations are a bit puzzled at first, but Joe sussed it out, and made a point of being over-familiar and kissing me hello as if to demonstrate a claim to me.

"Hello everyone," I said, "this is Larry from The Sound & Touch, they've just arrived in London." And I named the various faces out to Larry and they smiled and said hello to each other. Spike eagerly leapt over to him and they were soon talking music.

"Don't waste much time, do you?" Joe hissed in my ear.

"Shut up and count yourself lucky I let you come round at all." I felt really strung up, as if I was on pills.

Joe looked at me in surprise. "I'll go if you want," he said, and seemed a bit offended.

"That would be pointless now," I said, and went and sat on the bed. Bill was rolling a joint and somebody was putting on the sounds. My whole scene was being blown out and taken over. I felt very resentful as I sat there listening to them talking about groups and America. I watched Larry and wished I didn't have to go with Joe. I'd have to rethink this whole experiment thing if Grant didn't find out soon, I decided. Joe was hanging me up.

After a couple of hours Joe stood up and said he was going. "Are you coming?" he said to me.

"Yes," I said irritably, because he had made it so obvious. I turned to Larry and said we'd drop him off at his hotel.

"Can I see you tomorrow?" he asked me.

"Yes, I'd like that," I said, relieved he wasn't offended. I wrote my phone number down for him. On the way to his hotel I sat next to him, and when we dropped him off we just exchanged goodnights, and that was it.

When we were safely inside Joe's room, I asked him where Grant was.

"In bed asleep," Joe said, just as I had thought.

"Does he know about us?" I asked.

"I don't know. What does it matter, anyway?"

"What have you got against Grant?" I asked.

"Nothing in particular. He's just hanging me up, that's all." Joe was very guarded, and didn't seem to like being asked all these questions.

"Are you still not speaking to him?"

"Yeah, I'm speaking to him."

"Then you're friends again?" I asked.

"Like I said . . . I'm speaking to him."

"Do you think the others will tell him about us?" I wondered if they'd mentioned anything to Joe.

"Why should they," Joe said. "It's none of their business."

"They might feel they ought to, out of loyalty. I mean, you're all friends, and live together . . ."

"Give over," said Joe crossly.

"Tell me why nobody says anything to Grant about us. Somebody should, his friends should . . ."

"You're a right one to talk about loyalty!"

I didn't like that, and decided to change the subject. "What else could I do, Joe?"

"What are you on about?"

"Yes, that's what did it." And I nodded my head wisely. "What are you talking about?" Joe was naked except for his briefs. I pointed to them.

"The sight of you naked except for your little yellow scants, Joe, that's what inspired my surrender. I've always had a weakness for yellow knickers."

He saw through my play-acting, and his face reddened.

"Are you going to sit there all night?" he said tightly.

"I suppose not," I said wearily, and started draping my clothes on the back of the little settee. Just as I was getting into bed Joe told me to get him a glass of water.

"Why didn't you ask me before?" I complained. "I've got no clothes on now."

"Neither have I," he said, "go on, get it."

"Get it yourself," I said, and then the whole thing blew up into an argument about Joe's selfishness, and him telling me that I always did what he wanted me to in the end.

"Not any more," I said.

158

"You enjoy being bullied by me, go on, admit it."

"Not since Grant, I don't."

"What do you mean?" he asked.

"Grant does it better than you."

"Then why don't you go back to Grant?"

"I haven't exactly left him."

"But we both know that I can get you back anytime I want to, don't we?" Joe said knowingly.

"Do we?" I asked.

He looked at me, trying to suss out what I really meant. I turned away, and he pulled me round and kissed me savagely. I let him, because I didn't want to talk anymore and it would take his mind off the glass of water. He started to get very rough and threw me onto my back. I hit my head on the wall, but before I could cry out another pain distracted me. He had bitten my nipple so hard I instinctively hit him round the head and tried to pull him off by the hair. He raised himself and slapped me across the face.

"Bastard!" I hissed.

He grinned, pleased with himself. "Get on top of me," he ordered.

I did as I was told. As I did so, he dug his fingers into the skin on my hips and twisted it viciously. It was really hurting, but I kept silent. Then he pulled me off and pushed me down to plate him. While I was doing that he pulled my hair and then grabbed my ears, yanking them up and down painfully, to speed me up. I managed not to cry out, although the pain was making me cry.

When I had recovered I lay down beside him and said calmly, "Enjoy it?"

"I enjoyed it," he said, looking at me to see how I'd taken it.

"Good," I said, and turned over.

I hated him. I was really mad at myself for even starting this thing with him, never mind allowing it to go on. I must have been mad to let him near me again. He was weak, vicious and useless. He was vain and stupid and I hated him. I was glad Grant hadn't found out; I could pull out in time. Grant was worth ten Joes, and I felt the beginning of shame because I had done this to him. But I'd make sure this was the last time, so Grant need never know. If Joe or anyone else told Grant I'd slept with Joe I'd simply deny it. I must have been mad to waste my time with a guy like Joe, it would take me all my time to even speak to him after this. Repeating all of this to myself, I fell asleep.

There seemed to be a lot of banging at Joe's door and I thought I was dreaming. Then I knew I wasn't because the door was open and Grant was standing there. All I could do was stare. "The telly men are here . . ." Grant said and then he saw who I was. After a pause he continued. "Joe, the telly men are here to put your set in . . . you'd better get up."

He went out, closing the door quietly behind him. As Joe fumbled his way out of the bed I lay there dumbstruck. I'd been asking for it; I mean this is what was supposed to happen, but not really, because I had decided I didn't want it to happen and that it was a mistake and . . . But it had happened and now I didn't know what would happen next. I was totally confused, and it was all too much first thing in the morning. I just didn't feel like coping, especially with TV men all over the place. I wanted to get out and see my nice American Gemini again and blow both of them out. It wasn't worth the aggro.

So I hurriedly dressed myself before the telly men appeared. Joe seemed quite happy about the situation, and when I said goodbye, he said he'd ring soon.

"Don't bother," I said, and ran.

CHAPTER TWENTY-FOUR

At work, several black coffees later, I'd calmed down enough to set my mind going again. I decided I would concentrate on Larry while waiting for Grant's reaction – if any. And anyhow, Grant or no Grant, I wanted to see my American Gemini again. He would only be in England about ten days, and if we were going to have a scene I didn't want to waste a minute. I was lucky for once for it all went beautifully.

When I got home from the Kingdom office he phoned. I asked him to come round, and we just picked up the threads of the conversation we'd been having just as if Joe's phone call had never happened. I felt like I was falling in love with him, and I was almost scared to sleep with him in case something went wrong. We talked for a long time, while I played him records of English groups he hadn't heard before. Not that he really listened, he seemed to prefer listening to me. I couldn't believe that there was so much to say to somebody. Occasionally other people in the flat came into my room for things, and, knowing who he was, the normal thing for them to have done was to stay and chat, and ask him things, and generally suss out what a member of an important American group was like. But the vibrations between Larry and I were so charged that they withdrew immediately. It got so late it just had to be time to go to bed. He took my hand and said, "I'm staying, aren't I?" And I said, "Yes, please."

So we got undressed and into bed without any awkwardness and just lay there staring at each other. Then he moved towards me and kissed me and it was so good. It was strange, too, with his long hair flying about above me. It fell into my face as he leant over me, getting into our mouths and eyes. He looked very wild with it loose. We had to pause for a moment while he tied it back, and he told me he wore it loose on stage. It didn't stay tied back for long, but we were so involved with our lovemaking that it didn't matter. It

161

never really stopped, it only subsided, and in between times we talked about our differences.

"I'm kind of scared of the English," he said.

"Why's that?" I asked.

"They're deeper than us, their minds are more together. They are more sure of themselves."

"Well. I'm not all that sure of myself," I said. "I think I'm very much like you."

"Yes, I feel that too."

"I'm rather frightened of America," I said, "though I'd be interested in seeing it."

"Oh, you don't want to do that, it's a terrible place," Larry said. "In fact, I'm ashamed of my country."

"I dug America when I was a kid," I said slowly, remembering all those movies and telly programmes of slick, silver-haired lawyers, and soldiers who looned about on furloughs and then got shot and died in the end. I had envied those beautiful tanned chicks who marched in funny little uniforms and who could toss heavy silver-topped sticks up into the air and catch them with one hand. I tried to explain to Larry how I felt about America now.

"I don't know your country, except that it's big and rich and great. The feelings I had for it when I was a kid have never really left me, and it still intrigues me. But now we hear so much about the bad scenes happening over there that it's frightening. At least it frightens me. Is it really that bad? Have all the good things been swallowed up in the general uptightness? They can't have been, because you're American, and I trust you, and there must be others like you. And all the straight people can't be evil either . . ."

He was silent while he took this in. "You're right," he said. "And of course I love my country, it's just that I don't feel it's mine anymore. It's not just me who feels like that, it's hip people and straight people. It's black people and Jewish people, Wasps and Catholic people. It's parents and kids. It's us and them. It's all of these people and none of them feel like America belongs to them anymore. We've forgotten how to live, you see, and none of us know what to think anymore. It's follow my leader, stamp out individuality. The guts are being torn out of my country, and by the time I'm too old to care anymore, we'll be living in a moral and physical shell. So I grow my hair and play my music. But I don't just play for the bread and power. The really hip audiences in the States dig us, but that's not enough, because that's just trying to convert the converted, and we're not out to convert. We're not on a preaching scene, we're more a mirror which takes in all the hate around us and magnifies it and sends it back even more hateful. People in the sticks don't understand us, so they resent us, and this makes them violent and they try to get their hands on us. We're really only safe playing to groovers or on the television – not that any television company would touch us, they'd lose all their sponsors."

I lay and watched him, he was so serious and intense it knocked me out. After a while I leant towards him and whispered "You're the first American I've slept with."

Larry looked into my face and smiled, and it made my stomach lurch. "You're the first English chick I've met," he said. Then he started to say the kind of things I used to say to people I had fallen for. But I don't say them anymore, because I've learnt to be cool, and careful, and it's often just bed talk anyway. But it was beautiful, nevertheless, to hear him telling me how he's never felt like this before, and I was finally tempted into playing his game when he asked me how *I* felt, because I wasn't sure it was a game for him.

"Well, I'll try and tell you," I said thoughtfully, "I suppose I love you as much as it's possible to love you after only knowing you for two days."

That seemed to please him. "That's a very honest answer," he said. "I like the way you are so honest with yourself. I've noticed it before."

"I'm glad," I said.

"Have you ever been out with someone you can't speak to properly? You know, not being able to communicate with words properly?"

"Yes," I said. "And it's terrible at first. Not being able to say what you want to becomes more and more frustrating, until suddenly it becomes a groove that you can't say what you want to and you just sit there thinking it instead and not getting hung up."

He stared at me without saying anything, and I tried to remember what I'd just said.

"I'm amazed," he said, "I'd never expected a chick to come out with an observation like that."

163

"Really?" I said, surprised, because it had just come straight off the top. I'd never thought about this kind of thing before.

"You know," he said, "that was a beautiful thing you just said."

I seemed to be making a good impression, and it was a nice change to be with someone who appreciated my remarks, instead of treading a verbal minefield like I had to with Grant. Blossoming out, I plunged on.

"It's like we're from different planets and discovering each other," I said.

"Am I that strange to you?" he wanted to know.

"Yes, you are." And he was. Everything about him was different. His sense of humour, his seriousness, his politeness, his intelligence even, were all very different from the English boys I knew he approximated to. As most boys on the scene here had left school very early, they were insecure about the education thing. This was why they tended to be more aggressive and destructive than their American counterparts. Their hunger for the material things they had never had spurred them on and in a sense this is what made their music so much more shatteringly vital, whereas American musicians were generally guys who had dropped out from the good education and the fat family life. Likewise their attitudes, too, were reflected in their music. Larry and I talked about this and from it we discovered all kinds of things we hadn't realised before.

Anyway, as long as I was discovering these differences I was happy, though as the days went past I had moments of feeling sad too, because we were rapidly approaching the time when he'd have to go back. And this made me love him more because he was going away and that would end it, and I got hung up on whether I really loved him or whether I loved him just because he was going away and wouldn't really be around to interfere in my other life. What if he wasn't going away, and Grant demanded me back? In the back of my mind there was this constant feeling for Grant that I couldn't ignore or deny, so how could I say I loved Larry? Perhaps I loved Larry because I knew there wouldn't be time for it to disintegrate or spoil, which it would do in time, seeing it would interfere with work, because work was a bore when you were in love, and love was a drag when you wanted to get on, which I did. But I loved him now, and I needed a bit of love after all the hard-headed scenes I had been going through. I felt I didn't want him to go away, and it made me sad when I heard aeroplanes.

We spent every spare minute we had together, and inevitably I neglected my work. I told myself it didn't matter, because he was going away soon and I didn't want to miss a moment of his company. We were going short of sleep because we had so much to say, and then we'd start making love and before we knew where we were it was morning already. They were going off to Canada the day after they did their Big Tower gig, and on the night they played for us I hardly did any work at all. I made this junior chick take over my desk and kept rushing into the dressing room to sit with Larry. I felt so proud when I watched them play. Larry played the bass, and I liked it best when the musicians took over from the three front men. There was this old poet who leapt about in his underpants waving placards and dancing. It was all very American, as Larry had tried to explain to me, and it just wasn't getting through to an English audience, and I had to admit it wasn't having much effect on me. But when the group played numbers the audience recognised, then they cheered, and all in all it went down really well. Larry looked best on stage, and every time he tossed his hair off his face it gave me a kick to remember it hanging over me in bed. Everyone knew we were having a scene, and kept telling me how lucky I was. But I knew that myself, and I didn't need or want them to tell me. I'd got past caring whether people knew or not which group member I'd pulled. I'd done it and that was enough.

When they finished their last set we rushed home to spend a last few tormented hours together. It all got very desperate, with him promising to come back because he loved me and me pleading with him not to go. He said he didn't want to go, but had to because he couldn't let the group down, and there were all these contracts he had signed, and all the work lined up. When they were back in New York he'd send for me, he promised. So he was coming back, and he was going to send for me at the same time, and I told him I didn't believe him, and it all degenerated into a bitter quarrel which ended in the sulks. Then we fell asleep though we didn't really want to, and didn't hear the alarm clock. Some instinct made me sit bolt upright and when I looked at the clock he had only ten minutes to get to the hotel to meet the others before they split for the airport. He got very irritable because we'd overslept, and this got worse when he couldn't find his elastic band. Then there wasn't time to say any more, so we just kissed.

"I'll write, I promise," he said.

"I'll never forget you," I said, and after watching him walk down the stairs, I ran to the balcony to watch his retreating figure disappear along the road. Gone, I thought, and stamped my foot because it wasn't fair. I knew it would be different when we were oceans apart, and time got to work. And I knew that he knew what I knew, because he was like that. Then I cried. I felt so alone, because we'd been so together, even if it had been for only ten days.

CHAPTER TWENTY-FIVE

I lived and worked like a robot for the next few days, trying to convince myself that it didn't happen. But just when I was beginning to think that I had imagined it, the letter came. Except it was more than a letter, it was an enormous envelope containing lots of little envelopes, five of which had love letters from other chicks to Larry inside them. They were adoring adolescent letters, and the more of them I read the more amazed I became. What was the purpose of sending these things to me? I didn't want to read all this rubbish. What was it supposed to tell me? That Larry was a groovy guy with whom lots of idiot American chicks were infatuated? And that wasn't all, there was worse to come. The rest of the contents were long pretentious poems scrawled in multi-coloured biro, and interspersed with snatches of Dylan songs, which were somehow meant to be apposite to the precious agony of our scene. Here was our whole beautiful thing reduced to this, a superficial capsule of trendy mumbo-jumbo. What could have possessed him to do it? Had he been stoned? It looked suspiciously like a methedrine freak-out. Whatever the reason, it made me very angry, so much so that I threw all the wretched papers at the wall and watched them scatter in all directions. And there was this rambling prose thing about how lately he had been dreaming he was a butterfly, fluttering hither and thither, conscious only of his fancies as a butterfly, searching the eternal search for the flower of life (the word "flower" heavily written in sombre blue biro) and being totally unaware of his human individuality. Then it went on to say that since he had met me, he didn't know whether he was a man dreaming he was a butterfly, or a butterfly dreaming he was a man. Well, his dilemma didn't concern me in the slightest, and the whole thing wouldn't have meant anything to me if I hadn't seen through his butterfly trip. He was mangling an old quotation I knew by a long withered Chinese sage called Chuang Tzu. I had read the book, too. I read all the books,

167

and a lot more which are not even necessary, because that's the way I am, and here he was trying to impress me by mutilating this ancient Chinese's mindstorm without even a hint or mention or tribute. What was the matter with him? Wasn't he able to write in his own words? Couldn't he communicate simply, from the heart, the way we'd done when we had been together, instead of all this garbage of old love letters, Bob Dylan, and over-done obscurities? Had I been mistaken in him? Surely my judgement wasn't that off target? I was disappointed and very annoyed, especially about these love letters. I certainly didn't want them, nor him for that matter, if that was what he was really like. I'll fix that Larry, I vowed, and reached for pen and paper.

I wrote and told him that if he had anything to say to me he was to use his own words. That he should get his quotations right, and here I put in the correct butterfly quotation and the source to show him I really knew. I wrote:

> Once I, Chuang Tzu
> dreamt I was a butterfly
> now I do not know whether
> I am a butterfly dreaming I
> am a man.
> Chuang Tzu (629 A.D.)

The date was sheer guesswork, but he wouldn't know that.

And anyway, I told him, who cared. I told him not to write to me in poems and riddles; it wasn't my scene to sit down and interpret his pretentious ravings. And here were his love letters back, because I didn't want them any more than he presumably did. No wonder I had seemed different to him, I wrote. Compared to these chicks who had written the letters, and from the things they said, and the way they said them, I must have seemed like the one-eyed person in his land of the blind. It seemed I opened your eyes, I concluded, and now you have opened mine, because here you are blind and groping once again, because if you weren't, you wouldn't have sent me those wretched love letters.

I then bundled the whole lot together, single-mindedly charged off to the Post Office and sent it off before my anger subsided and I changed my mind about sending my letter. Let's see what he does with *that,* I thought. Perhaps he would redeem himself with a brilliant reply, but I had my doubts; it seemed letter writing was not his strong point.

I had already started to adjust myself to his absence, telling myself that it had been a ten-day wonder, and now I felt determined to get myself together and catch up on the work I'd let slip. I had to take a couple of days off for the *International* interview, and the chick who asked me the questions took everything I said very seriously, as though it was all weighted with universal significance. But the photographer was great. He was young, blond and turned-on. After the session he took me back to his rich pad and I got stoned with his rich friends. Pretty soon I was back in the old familiar groove again, managing quite well without Larry, and again wondering if I had imagined it all, it had happened so fast. And then I started thinking about Grant.

Then another letter diverted me once again; this was the week for letters all right. This one was from Davey. The Savage were coming back in two days, and would I meet him at the airport. Larry had made me forget Davey's return, and now Davey's return pushed Larry to the back of my mind, and I postponed wondering about Grant.

In two days' time I duly went to the airport for The Savage's arrival, and there was Davey standing in front of me. I'd forgotten how small he was.

"Hello," he said.

"Hello," I replied, and we didn't even kiss.

His voice still had a nasal twang, he didn't seem to have picked up an American accent at all. He was tanned and his fair hair was much longer and curlier, and bleached by the sun. Apart from that he was just the same Davey, and I began to feel exasperated by his coolness. We got into the car that had come to pick up the group, and only exchanged negative small talk in front of the others.

They dropped Davey and me off at my place, and arranged to pick us up later to go to the reception that was being held for them – it was quite an event for The Savage to come back to England as they were pretty well based in America now. Davey looked round my room and said it looked much groovier now, and how was I doing? I gave him a brief summary of my career at The Other Kingdom, and then started asking him questions. He answered them all carefully, and I noticed he was wearing a lot of rings on his fingers. I don't like fancy rings on guys. He told me that although The Savage would still record together, they wouldn't be doing any more live gigs.

"Won't you miss all that?" I asked him.

"Not really," he said, "I've had enough of being snatched and pulled at. The scene in America is more violent than over here, I mean, I never got mobbed here. The chicks over there come up to you after you've played and say "Can I kiss you, sir, could I touch you, sir, would you like to ball me, sir". It's funny the way they call you sir. And the groupies, they're something else."

"Tell me about them," I asked, fascinated.

"Well, it's far more of an occupation with them than it is with the English groupies, they really devote all their time and energy to pulling musicians, especially English ones. They go through incredible hustles to get back-stage or to find out the hotels the group will be staying in, and if they score they sometimes call their friends up to tell them who they've pulled. At first I thought it was rather funny, but now I think it's sick. Though some of them are incredibly beautiful chicks."

Davey had obviously had his share, and I urged him to tell me more about the groupies.

"Have you heard of the Plaster Casters?" he asked me. I hadn't. "Well, there are these two chicks who travel all over the country to take moulds of group members' rigs. A rig is a penis," he explained. "They plate you until you're hard and then thrust it into a container of soft plaster and wait until it sets. It's a bastard getting your hairs unstuck."

I didn't know what to say. I couldn't imagine any chick going through a scene like that. I know I've been through a few impersonal plates myself, but always in private, I'd never be quite as blatant as that or have anyone else around. And what on earth was the attraction of having a plaster cast of some guy's prick? I decided these chicks were pretty perverted, and I told Davey so.

"Yes, I suppose they are in a way," he said vaguely.

I changed the subject by asking him what he was going to do if he wasn't in a group full-time, and he told me he was going to be an actor.

"I've been accepted at an acting school. Of course, I'll have to

170

have voice lessons, but I've always wanted to be a film star. I'm twenty-six now, and I can't be a pop star for ever. I'll still play music – in fact, I'm making a solo record soon – but if I can get into acting, I reckon I've got more of a future."

And I thought, sensible Davey, together Davey, making sure he's not left in the lurch without a career. I agreed, wisely, that he was making a sensible decision, and then we discussed the mind effects acting must have on a person. I noticed how his voice never carried any kind of enthusiasm, it was just a rather thin monotone. I had been aware of this before, but now it was hanging me up a bit. Like the detached way he had told me about the Plaster Casters, he was so cool he hardly existed. He had been involved in a couple of what he called "heavy" scenes, but had cooled them out because they started getting too involved.

"But that always happens to you, doesn't it?" I said, remembering myself. "All the chicks you get involved with end up being desperately in love, and you just don't seem to be able to take it."

He rather gloomily agreed with me. "It's when they start getting very hung up on me that it becomes a drag. It becomes unbalanced, and that's no good."

"But don't you ever fall in love, Davey?" I asked. "It always seems to be them in love with you. I mean, don't you ever flip over some chick?"

"I don't seem to have recently, I must admit," he replied, twiddling his rings. "But don't think I don't know what love is – I do, and it's the most beautiful thing in the world."

This last remark surprised me, and I wondered when Davey had been in love. Thinking back on it I felt sure he hadn't been in love with me, just very involved until it became too involved for his organised mind.

"Yes," I said, thinking of Larry.

Then he brightened up a bit. "How's your love life?" he asked.

I don't like that expression. I gave him a short account and he sighed.

"I knew you'd get onto the group scene sooner or later," he said, matter-of-factly. "And I don't like your hair curly. Why don't you grow it? I was always telling you to grow it."

I didn't reply. I couldn't see that it mattered to him. He was only staying a few weeks anyway, then he was going back to America for

171

another year. They're all over there, I thought. I really must go sometime. Although this rather impersonal homecoming was a bit disappointing, it was also reassuring, for the last thing I wanted to do was to fall in love with Davey again. Though I had known in my heart that this would be very unlikely, because it's never the same the second time round. And I just didn't want another being in love scene, not yet, anyway. I needed a different kind of relationship, not so time-consuming or so involved. More like I had with Grant, and what I should have had with Davey. But as far as Davey was concerned I had changed, and that was weird, because I had been expecting him to change, but he hadn't really, except that I was seeing him in a different way. And I felt very detached.

I was bored at the reception, but Davey seemed to be digging all the big star treatment he'd never had before in England. He told me not to be shy, and I thought he really doesn't think I've changed at all. Six months ago I would have been shy at one of these scenes, but now I was almost bored with the suave guys and dolly chicks, the hustlers and promoters. He thinks I don't know anybody, so I started saying hi to everyone I knew just to show him, and circulated. After a meal we went back home and watched what was left of television. I kept glancing at his face, and had to admit that it was pretty. In that respect things were the same: the more I looked at him the prettier he became, until it amazed me that anyone could have a face like that, and what made it stranger was that the first impression was anything but dynamic, it had something that gradually grew on you until it became unreal because you didn't know how it happened. But none of the vibrations were there, we still hadn't touched and I didn't feel any inclination to. So when we got into bed the only feeling I had was a morbid interest in re-discovering his lovemaking. It was strange undressing and getting into bed like we used to, as though he hadn't been away, and even stranger reaching towards each other in the dark. At first contact I suddenly felt shy, but not for long, because in bed, at least, the old magic was there, holding his frail body once more I could imagine I was in love all over again. He made it so good for me, and I'd forgotten how he gasped and groaned as he came, and it was nice to know how lost he got in the sensation, because it helped me to get lost as well, and until I get lost I can never get there. So I loved him again just for the moment, without any hangups, though by morning I just felt a familiar fondness. It didn't really matter to me whether I saw him again or not. My curiosity had been satisfied and my feelings realised, and everything was cool.

* * *

When I got back that evening I found a note from Davey. Apparently he had come round, and Ted, who had let him in, told him I'd gone to some business party and would probably be back later. So Davey had sat waiting for me until he got bored and left. I was sorry I had hung him up, but that was all. The letter read: "The weak-faced young boy sat huddled in a corner mumbling to himself about self-expression. Suddenly he crossed the room and threw open the window. With one fluid movement he ripped his cock off and hurled it onto the street below, where it burst in a shimmering galactic explosion, drenching the whole of Bayswater in a thick saffron putrescence." Underneath that he'd written "Dear K – sorry I missed ya, praps I'll see yoo again, oo nose. Abbys in you? D. From the poor little lamb who lost his way."

As I said, it was a week for letters.

CHAPTER TWENTY-SIX

I didn't feel mean about Davey. I couldn't change what had happened. He had wanted to take up our scene again in his own particular cool way, and I hadn't been sure. Now I was, and wanted to finish it before it got really started. Davey must have sensed the changes in me, because the next time we met we didn't even talk about it, we just chatted politely to each other about nothing in particular. He rang me before he left for the States again to say goodbye, and we promised to keep in touch, whatever that means.

Then, inevitably, I got back with Grant again. But this time it was obvious that our relationship had shifted into a different phase. I could phone him without being told I was uncool, though I usually waited until he phoned me, which he did regularly. Maybe I had passed some test or other, and he was accepting me as I was; though I was now very different to how I had been when he'd first met me. I reckoned I was pretty cool and didn't get hung up when I didn't see him for days on end because I knew he'd phone when he wanted me. He, of course, hadn't changed at all. He was still aggressive and bossy, but if he had treated me like dirt before, he was treating me like nice dirt now. I felt I was managing to erode his independence thing because I could persuade him to let me do at least some of his washing, if not all of it. And if he didn't try to put me down for merely wanting to do these things for him, he now waited until I had done them and then criticised me for doing them badly, and for not doing anything about minute holes in his socks. He told me I was to find birds for him, birds with big tits, because he liked big tits and mine were too small. I told him I wasn't going to pimp for him, and got very indignant.

"I only want to screw them," he explained. "I don't want to get *involved* or anything like that."

"You never know," I said. "You might meet one like me who digs you and won't leave you alone."

174

"Nobody would be mad enough to do that," he said, very definitely.

"I'm not mad and I like you," I said.

"You *are* mad."

"I'm not!"

"Anyway, you don't like me as much as you say."

"I do," I protested.

"You're always sleeping with other men," he said accusingly. "Not that I care . . . I'm always sleeping with other women."

"Well, if you're sleeping with other women, why do you need me to pull you birds with big tits?"

"Because I can't be bothered to get it together," he said. "I'm only thinking about my mental health. I read that a man of my age needs a lot of sex if he doesn't want to end up disturbed or something."

"Where on earth did you read that?" I asked.

"Never you mind. Just find me lots of birds . . . ones with big tits . . . and we'll get on fine."

"I'll have a look," I said, but I knew I wouldn't. He could find his own birds and as long as I didn't know about them I wouldn't get uptight. But I still didn't like to think of him sleeping around. I was terrified he might find someone he really liked, and get involved. However, he was pretty hard to get involved with, and he claimed he still had hangups about pulling birds, ending up with the ones who wanted *him* rather than the ones he wanted.

"Be careful then," I warned him.

"Why, may I ask?"

"You might catch something. There's a lot of it about, and it's not just posteritis."

"Anything I've had I've caught from you – diseases are your department."

"Well," I said defensively, "I've stopped sleeping with guys now except for you."

I was always telling him that. It sounded nice even if it wasn't true and he didn't believe it. It hadn't been true in the past nor would it be true in the future, because I was about to pull this beautiful boy I'd seen down at the Kingdom. He came every week, and paid at my till. Normally I never look at the customers, just handing them their tickets and change without looking into their faces. But this guy dropped his money all over my till, and as we tried to sort it out I saw his face and got a shock. He looked exactly like Ben from the Satin Odyssey. For a moment my insides lurched and I thought it actually *was* Ben, but when he opened his mouth and spoke I knew instantly it wasn't, for he had this very nasal North London accent. We exchanged a few words and I smiled at him encouragingly as I handed him his ticket.

When the main group started playing, I went to listen. It was The Shadow Cabinet, who have a very heavy sound and this organist I've had my eyes on for some time. They played at the deb dance when I pulled Andy from The Elevation. I looked around for the pretty customer, but couldn't see him anywhere, so settled against a pillar to watch the group. The organist had his back half towards me, and most of that obscured by the speaker columns, so that I could only see the hair hanging over his face, his right hand on the keyboard, and his right velvet leg in a groovy boot working on the pedals. I'd got into the habit of eating a bit of hash fudge when the main work of the evening was over so that I could pass the rest of the time in a slightly stoned state, which made things more interesting. I only took enough to groove to the music, never so much that I couldn't cope with work that came up later. And by The Shadow Cabinet's third number I noted with satisfaction how incredible they sounded, and how completely absorbed in their sound I had become. The rest of the group had their attraction, I suppose, but it was the organist my eyes kept coming back to, and because I dug him, it was like all the sound was coming from him and that he knew what it was doing to me. I couldn't see his face, in fact I couldn't even remember what it looked like except it had attracted me, so I watched his hand instead. And I became very hung up on that hand, watching it playing the notes that were affecting me so much, so much so that I wanted that hand and its owner, and wanted to feel that hand on my body. Then the sound got lost as I went into a fantasy of being confronted by this guy whose face I couldn't see, but whose hand I knew so well, and I knew I'd dig him because I'd dig anybody who could make such groovy music. The fantasy wasn't exactly sexual; it was just an intense awareness generated by the feeling that the god-like figure on the stage was obtainable to me should I have a mind to get it together. I watched his leg for a while and noted his trousers were the same as Jason's. And I watched the long dark hair swinging forward as he leant over to concentrate on particular chords. But his hand was the only available bit of flesh to my sight, the only thing I could identify with, and I ended up just staring at it and listening to it, because the whole sound that was turning me on was coming from it. Wow, I thought, when they finished their set, I want that guy. Not that I was going to do anything about it; I felt very objective about my desire. He'd keep, anyway.

When I turned round I saw my customer walking towards me, and switched my mind to things in hand. I stopped and chatted with him, but he seemed shy and very ill at ease, though obviously pleased to be speaking to me.

"Do you go to The Country Club?" he asked me after a bit.

"Not often."

"Where do you go, then?"

I wasn't sure what he meant. "Where do I go when?"

"Of an evening . . . you know."

"Oh, sometimes I stay in and sometimes I go out," I said unhelpfully. These weren't the kind of conversations that I liked.

"I mean, what clubs do you go to?"

As he persisted I decided to give him a flash answer.

"I go to The Joint to pull group members, to The Speakeasy to eat, and The Revolution to be seen at."

"Don't know those places," he muttered.

"Where do you go?" I asked, fearing the worst.

He brightened up. "Well, on Mondays I go to my mate Pete's. On Tuesdays I stay in and wash my hair. On Wednesdays I block it and go to The White Horse, Thursdays I go to The Marquee, and on Fridays I go to Bluesville 69. Saturdays I come here and trip out, and on Sundays I go up to The Country Club." I presumed blocking it meant getting pilled-up. He grinned and waited for me to compliment him or something.

"And you do this every week?" I was amazed that he should spend most of his time in those sort of places.

"Nearly always . . . I mean, there's not much else to do, is there?"

If he didn't know I wasn't going to tell him.

"Sometimes I stay home and listen to my Dylan records." He paused and fidgeted at my lack of response. "Do you like Dylan?"

"Yes, I like Bob Dylan," I said, and then told him I'd see him later as I had work to do. Also we didn't seem to be getting anywhere

177

very fast. I still wanted to pull him, because he was so physically attractive. But his mind was nowhere, obviously a thickie. It might be nice to change that, I thought. Get inside him and open him up a bit. Kick his mind around and shake it up and see what came out.

Much later, when the rest of my work was finished, I was sitting on the stage talking to Lenny, the DJ, and I saw him wandering about on his own, his shoulders hunched and his hands in his pockets. I waved to him and he came over.

"I forgot to ask your name," I said.

"It's Norman," he replied quickly.

"I'm Katie," I said, "and this is Lenny."

"Yes, I know who you are." He looked at Lenny. "I know who both of you are."

"Hi," said Lenny, putting on his latest West Coast import and freaking out on his headphones.

"Who's on at The Country Club tomorrow, then?" I asked Norman.

"The Daredevil."

"They're not bad," I said. "I might go."

He was now supposed to ask me to go with him.

"I'm going," was all he said.

"Have you got a car?" I asked.

He looked surprised. "Yes, I have."

"What sort?" I hoped he might have a groovy sports car or something.

"A Cortina," he said proudly.

"Oh, that's a drag car," I said, sounding disappointed. He got a bit annoyed.

"Well, it really moves, and it's got lots of room inside."

"What do you want lots of room for?"

"I can give my mates lifts, can't I?"

"Why don't you give me a lift to The Country Club tomorrow night?" I suggested.

He looked a bit puzzled. "Just you?"

"Yes, just me," I said.

"Where do you live?"

"Lancaster Gate," I said.

"Where's that?"

I couldn't believe he didn't know Lancaster Gate. "It's past Marble Arch down the Bayswater Road."

"Oh, I know Marble Arch," he said.

"Where do you live?" I asked.

"Muswell Hill." I was right about him being from North London.

"Well, can you pick me up?" I continued. "I'll get you into The Country Club for nothing. I know the manager."

"Yes, I suppose you do," he said wistfully, "you know a lot of people."

"It's not a big deal to know the manager of The Country Club," I said. "What time will you pick me up?"

In the end I had to tell him the time to come at, and draw him a map of how to get to my pad from Marble Arch.

"Why do you want me to come round so early?" he asked.

"So that we can get stoned first."

A slight shadow of alarm passed over his face. "Oh, I don't smoke pot," he said quickly, "I only block it on pills, or trip out."

"Why don't you smoke pot?" I asked.

"I can't, can I? It makes me sick."

"Well, I've got some tincture; you can try that," I said reassuringly.

He didn't know what tincture was, so I had to explain. I also told him about prescriptions coming to an end because the doctor who handed them out was getting paranoid, and how hash fudge was the new scene.

"Actually, I've taken to eating it in salmon paste sandwiches," I told him, "if you eat hash in one big lot it has a more dramatic effect than by smoking it gradually."

"You seem to know all about it," he said. "I wish I could turn on. All the groovy people seem to."

"Well, don't worry," I said. "We'll fix you up tomorrow."

Then he said he had to go, because his mates were waiting for him. When he'd disappeared, Lenny prodded me. "What was that all about?" he said.

"I'm going to pull him," I told Lenny.

"Is he your scene?" he asked dubiously.

"Everyone is my scene," I said grandly.

"Yes, but pillhead, teethgrinding teenagers from Muswell Hill picking you up in Cortinas . . . surely that's a scene you can do without?"

"He doesn't smoke either," I said, "you forgot that."

"Right," Lenny agreed, "he's not even a smoker – I mean, how will you be able to communicate?" Lenny believes that pot-smoking would resolve the world situation, and claims it is a beneficial herb *not* a drug.

"And his name is Norman," I continued.

"Yes, that's all part of it too."

"And I'm sure he and his mates have punchups with the skinheads in Muswell Hill . . . yes, that's his scene all right, but anybody with a face like that and a skinny body *has* to be my scene, just for a little while."

"Yes, I saw his face," Lenny agreed. "It's incredible."

"Did you see his eyes?" I asked. "Did they remind you of anyone?"

"No," Lenny said.

"His eyes were violet. Nobody I know has eyes like that, not even the guy he reminds me of."

"So what," Lenny said. "I knew an Albino with seven fingers when I was at school."

"Yes, but violet eyes," I said.

CHAPTER TWENTY-SEVEN

When Norman arrived late the following afternoon I was ready with the bottle and spoon. I hoped to get him so stoned that he wouldn't want to go to The Country Club, because I certainly didn't. Norman looked all neat and clean, and his clothes were cheap imitations of the better hip boutiques. He looked very thin today, I noticed, and this thinness was what I liked in men. His eyes were even more startling in normal light, large and violet rimmed with thick dark eyelashes. I couldn't stop staring at them. I tried to get him to take the tincture, but he was very reluctant, insisting that it would make him sick. I got a bit impatient, and swallowed some to show him that it wasn't poison.

"Will it blow my mind?" he asked, defences wavering and wanting the promise of good to come.

"If you take enough it will blow your head right off," I said, and poured him the normal dose, which was a large tablespoonful. He swallowed it, making terrible grimaces and coughing.

"Don't it taste horrible," he said.

"You get used to it, and anyway it's worth it," I said.

We sat around for a bit. He seemed nervous because I was staring at him so much. Finally he couldn't stand it anymore and started glancing behind himself to see what was in the room apart from us.

"Is something wrong?" he asked.

"It's your eyes," I said.

"What's the matter with them?" he asked, in a very paranoid voice.

"Don't you know that you've got incredibly beautiful eyes?" I told him.

Norman gave an embarrassed laugh. "You're having me on."

I looked at him seriously. "You've got the most beautiful eyes I have ever seen."

"What!" he said, and laughed edgily.

"And you've got a beautiful face as well," I continued.

"Don't talk silly," he said.

"No, really," I insisted, enjoying his confusion. "I mean it."

He didn't say anything then for a moment. He started rolling a cigarette, and I thought he might actually be rolling a joint.

"Is that a joint?" I asked.

"Of course it isn't, it's a roll-up."

"Roll-up what?"

"I roll-up straight tobacco . . . you can save a lot of money that way, you know." He lit it and started telling me about the kind of music he liked, and it wasn't very interesting.

"Do you ever listen to soul music when you're stoned?" I asked.

"I don't get stoned, do I?"

"Well, you will in a minute."

"I can't feel anything yet."

"It'll happen soon," I reassured him.

Norman got up and began to fluff his dark hair in the mirror.

"Sorry I didn't have time to freak it out," he said.

I told him I liked it better as it was.

"But it's groovy to have freaked-out hair," he protested. "Look at yours."

"My hair is not freaked-out," I said, annoyed. "These are curls. Great frizzy heads were last year." If he thought my hair was freaked-out now, he should have seen it last year.

"I'm thinking of having it permed so that it's freaked out permanently," he said.

"Don't do that," I said. "I promise you, that's all finished."

He got a bit peeved. "*You* tell me what to do with it then. You know what's in and what isn't."

I went over to him and ran my fingers over his hair experimentally. He shied away a bit. "Let it grow a bit longer and it will be all right."

I sat down again beside him on the bed, so that we were side by side with our backs against the wall. Finding the sides of our arms touching, he moved his discreetly apart.

"Nothing is happening," he said.

"It is, but you don't realise it," I explained.

"Well, I don't feel nothing."

"Well, I'm stoned, so you must be too," I said. I was only very slightly stoned, but I had taken less.

"You know how to get stoned," he said. "I don't. Tripping is the only thing that turns me on."

"What does acid do to you?" I asked.

"Trips are nice. They make me feel all happy."

"Is that all they do?"

Norman looked at me. "What do you mean?"

"Don't you see things, and experience loss of ego?" I thought that would fox him and it did.

"What's loss of ego?"

So I dutifully launched into a long-winded description of a trip I'd taken in the park two summers ago, when I'd felt my soul leave my body and merge with the earth and the sky. I'd been able to feel myself in the grass and flowers, spreading out into everything.

"Oh, I never have trips like that," he said. "I've never had my mind blown."

Christ, I thought, and cannily changed the subject. I wasn't going to be lumbered with having to explain what the psychedelic experience was all about. Let him read Leary. He had the kind of mind that Leary wrote for.

I asked him what his job was, but he wouldn't tell me. He said I'd laugh at him, because I was groovy and had a groovy job, and I would laugh at him if he told me what he did. I said I wouldn't and this went on for a bit.

"All right," he said, "if you must know . . . I'm a postman."

No, I thought, and laughed.

"I said you'd laugh, didn't I?"

"Sorry," I said.

"We can't all have groovy jobs like you."

"There's nothing special about my job," I said.

He was very paranoid because I'd laughed. I decided to calm him down a bit. "Anybody could get a job at the Kingdom."

"I couldn't," he said, "you have to be really *in* to work in a place like that."

"Would you like a job down there?" I asked.

His eyes widened in amazed disbelief. "You mean you could get me a job at the Kingdom?"

"I might," I said, and he laughed delightedly.

"You've blown my mind, you have," he said, and rubbed his hands together gleefully.

I knew I would have no trouble getting him a job but my doubts were mainly concerned with whether I wanted to go to all the bother or not. I wasn't sure yet if he was worth it. Then he said he felt sick and started groaning and saying he felt dizzy. I told him to lie down, he'd soon feel better. He kept apologising about being a drag. And he was a drag, except he was a beautiful drag, and that excused it. He lay face downwards on the bed and I turned the television on. He slept while I watched telly right through to the bitter end, and still showed no signs of reviving. This couldn't go on. Something would have to happen, even if I had to make it happen myself. I shook him and he started up suddenly.

"What's the time?" he asked.

"How do you feel?"

He shook his head. "I wish you hadn't made me take that stuff. I'm sorry I'm such bad company."

"That's all right," I said. "We're too late now for The Country Club."

"Are we?" He looked at his watch. "Yes, you're right, I am sorry. I'd better be going."

I wasn't having any of that. He'd bored me and fallen asleep. He was not going to leave me without making it with me first.

"Don't go," I said. "You can sleep here."

He was embarrassed. "Oh, I can't do that. I wouldn't want you to think I'd come round just for *that.*"

What was the matter with him? Was he a virgin or something?

"Are you a virgin?" I asked.

He got even more embarrassed. "No, of course not. But it's got nothing to do with that. I came round to give you a lift, I mean I didn't come round just to *sleep* with you. I don't want you to think that."

"Don't you want to?" I asked.

"Well you don't sleep with a bird the first time you see her, do you?"

"Why not?"

He got really mixed up. "At least, not with you. It's just that you are so groovy and everything, and I'm not. It's you. You wouldn't want to sleep with *me.*"

"Why don't you find out?"

"I wouldn't even try. I'm sure you'd just laugh in my face if I did.

I've seen the kind of people you go around with at the Kingdom, and I'm not like them. I've seen the way you look at the customers, like they're dirt, and the way you only talk to groups and people who are important."

I tried to prod his imagination along. "Well, why didn't I ask one of my important friends to take me out tonight, then?"

"I don't really know," he said, and I think I believed him.

"I fancied you and I want to sleep with you, it's as simple as that." I don't really enjoy saying things like that, but this seemed to be the only way with this guy.

"I can't think why," he muttered.

"You've got violet eyes for a start," I said.

He started getting uptight, and said I only liked him for his eyes. I said he was wrong, and moved my face up to his face, just to prove it. This was too much for him and he leaned over and started kissing me untidily. Things were looking up when he suddenly checked himself, saying, no, he couldn't, what would I think of him. And then he buttoned all the shirt buttons I'd managed to undo. I was getting impatient, I wanted him, but I wasn't going to spend the whole night persuading him. So I got up and took all my clothes off.

"I'm going to bed," I said. "Are you coming or not?"

He didn't know, so I had to grab him and finally he got worked up enough to agree.

"Don't look," he said, taking off his shirt.

"Why not?"

"I'm too thin."

"Rubbish," I said. "I like thin people."

I lay back watching him through partly closed eyes, and pretending not to. He was very thin, I noticed, and then he was in the bed lying beside me. It was nice to look into his fantastic face, and now he'd stopped speaking it was even better. I ran my hands down his stomach, and he shied away, saying he was ticklish. Without waiting any longer I reached down further and took his erection and squeezed it gently. After a few seconds he took my hand away saying he would come if I did that. So I took his hand and held it against me. Imperceptibly his fingers began to move up and down until he found my clitoris, and in a short time he had me excited.

"Are you ready?" he whispered.

185

Eyes closed, I nodded my head.

His bony hips cut painfully into my thigh tops. He came very quickly with a lot of gasping, and then started kissing me passionately. After lying on top of me for a few minutes, he started again. This time it went on longer, though we didn't change positions or anything. Then we separated our bodies and I moved down and plated him. This made him scream, and must have blown his mind, for he passed out almost immediately after he came. Then when it was all over and I was lying beside him looking into his face perhaps for something that wasn't there, I decided not to sleep with him again. He'd probably be offended, and call me immoral, but that was the way it had to be. He would bore me once I got used to his eyes and his looks. I'd let him down gently though.

Next day I had a few words with Jason and got Norman on the staff as a doorman at the weekends. It wasn't much of a job making sure people didn't get in without paying, but by his standards it was real groovy. At least he told me so when I rang him up to tell him. He admired my little demonstration of power and made a big thing of it. He just didn't know where I was at.

* * *

Theo was going to the States and he rang me up to ask if I would go with him to the airport.

"Does it have to be me? Can't you take one of your hired friends?" I really didn't feel like going. Theo explained that he'd thrown out all his friends except his chauffeur. They had been bugging him, he said.

"It's simply that I'm scared of flying, and I need someone to talk to before I take off."

"What about your chauffeur?" I asked. "You can say what you have to to him, can't you?"

"No I can't," Theo said crossly, "he doesn't listen to me." "Well, it's a bit inconvenient," I said.

"Oh, if you don't want to, that's a different matter. You don't *have to* come round." He sounded very aggrieved.

"Hang on to your mind," I said, "we can't have you going away all hurt . . . when do you want me there?"

"Now," he said, still a little huffy.

So I went round to Theo's. He'd laid out enough clothes to mount a one-man fashion show. I had to take charge of all that, and I made him leave eighty per cent of them behind, and packed the rest for him; he was only going to be away for two weeks. He started hanging me up by making me check and re-check his pill chest, to make sure that the right kind of pills in the right kind of proportion were there, so that every type of future crisis was catered for.

"You see," he explained, "mentally I've got to be very well dug in, so please will you check again?"

I made him take some tranquillisers, although he'd had some already, and once the second lot hit him he was like putty in my hands. Soon we were ready to leave, and we called Robin, whose only concession to his chauffeur status was a peaked cap – the rest of his clothes were scruffy denim – and told him to get the bags into the car. Robin looked very surly today; and without a word, but with a perpetual scowl, he staggered off with the cases.

Theo and I made ourselves comfortable in the back of the Bentley, and with a silent Robin in front, we set off. Sitar music came from the stereo speakers in the back of the car, and I felt slightly foolish as we sailed along. Theo had pulled down the picnic table and was rolling joints.

"Must use up all my hash before I get on that plane," he said. "Mustn't get busted, must we?"

He was rolling a lot of joints, and there was still quite a bit left.

"Why don't you leave it behind?" I suggested.

"What . . .? Leave it for those worms in my place!"

"There's nobody in your pad now, Theodore. You threw them all out. Remember?"

"Yes, but they are still around, don't you see. They're like mice, creeping into my place and nibbling at things. They keep nibbling at my pot when I'm not there to watch them."

"There's only Robin left now," I reminded him again.

Theo started to smoke his joints. "I'm not leaving anything for *him*. He used to pinch my amps when I was on speed."

Theo leant forward and shouted. "And no grooving with your scruffy friends when I'm away, mind . . . you hear me there . . .!"

All I heard was a low-pitched muttering from Robin. I asked Theo what was happening to his script. Last time I'd seen him, he'd been waiting to hear from the studios.

"Have they accepted it?" I asked.

"Well, something better has happened," he explained.

I wondered what this something better could be. Surely the fact that the studios had accepted it was the best thing that could happen to a young writer trying to get his first film scene together.

"Tell me," I said.

"They have turned the rights over to me. I'll be getting it together myself when I come back from the States."

I knew Theo well enough to know what this meant. Projects were never dropped or rejected by him. When the crunch came, they were mentally filed away in his limbo of pending projects. All those agonised weeks on speed, all that mind turmoil, and all that wasted effort. Still, he'd been well paid for it.

"What exactly will you be doing in the States, Theo?" I asked, as he passed me the first joint and lit up another.

"I'm going over there to set up my submarine. I'm going to take my work round all the studios, and see who offers me the best deal. They're bound to want it."

I hoped so. The image of Theo hawking his project round the studios in Hollywood, propped up by his pills, his ego and his unsound reputation, was not a comforting one. Theo had finished the second joint, and there were still three to go. He reached into his pocket and brought out a small bottle of pills I hadn't known about.

"Emergency Mandies," he said, and popped two of them into his mouth. "Flying gives me the horrors, I have to take sleepers to knock me out. These should hit me just before take-off."

I hoped he didn't fall asleep before he got onto the plane.

"Yes, it's sink or swim with this project, Katie," he continued, "I've spent all my bread, and have overdrawn massively to get this submarine scene together . . . yes, sink or swim," he repeated, and after taking a couple of drags on his third joint fell back into a kind of coma.

When we got to the airport Robin and I hoisted Theo out of the car and directed him into the departure lounge. I kept talking to him to keep him awake while Robin disappeared into the loo, to have a fix, I suspected. Theo had managed to order himself a double brandy, and he sat there clutching it in his hands, while his head fell this way and that. I hoped people wouldn't think he was drunk, and asked him how he felt. He was in a drugged funk about his imminent departure. I told him it was time to leave, and he suddenly leapt out of his chair and vaulted over the low coffee table. He stood stupidly in the middle of the lounge wondering what had happened while the other people stared at him in amazement. The brandy had shot into the air when he'd leapt up, and now he looked at the empty glass in surprise.

"What's this?" he said, and returning to his chair he told me to get him another. Fortunately his flight was being announced and there wasn't time. Before he could drift off again, I got him to his feet and looked around for Robin. The big suitcase had already gone through customs, so I picked up his briefcase and steered him to the departure gate.

"Bye bye Katie," he said, totally bemused, and I watched him weave his erratic path off.

I found Robin sitting at the wheel of the Bentley, and after complaining about his unhelpfulness, we drove back home in silence. I finished off the other two joints while I was at it. I didn't see why Robin should have them. When he dropped me off, I told him I'd be coming round from time to time to check up on things for Theo. He gave me several shifty looks and said he knew what he had to do. I told him I would make sure, although I would do nothing of the kind. I had no intention of wasting my time watching the goings-on at Theo's during his absence. I just said it to make Robin uptight, because I didn't like him.

CHAPTER TWENTY-EIGHT

There are some things which are a capital offence in my books, and calling round without phoning first is one of them. So when Norman started to do this, action had to be taken – and quickly. I decided to disappear for a week, as this would cool him out without me actually having to *tell* him. That sort of thing is so embarrassing. I phoned Grant to see if I could stay with him for a while. It didn't matter if he said no, because I had other friends I could stay with, but I wanted to see what Grant said first. I'd never asked him to do anything for me – it was always the other way around. And I wanted to stay with Grant, to see what he was like *all* the time, and to have a small sample of what living with him would be like. I felt sure that our scene had moved off the battlefield and into the peace talks, so to speak, and there was much more tolerance between us now we understood each other's terms. When I rang him I found him surprisingly co-operative.

"I suppose so," he said, "how long for?"

"I'm not trying to move in," I quickly explained. "It's just for a few days . . . there's someone I'm trying to avoid."

He came back like a shot. "I've told you about those people, haven't I?" he shouted triumphantly. "You will get involved, won't you? I knew you'd come running for help sooner or later."

"Well, if it hangs you up, don't bother," I said. I mean, I wasn't going to let him think I *depended* on him.

"No, no, it's all right," he said grandly. "You won't be a nuisance, I'll see to that . . . besides, I won't be there tonight."

"Where will you be then?" I demanded.

"I'll be sleeping at the office tonight. Roland Johns is ringing from the States at some time. It's about the group's trip to America."

What? Relation going to America?

"I didn't know the group was going to the States," I said.

190

"Of course you didn't. Nobody knows," Grant said, "it's very hush hush."

"Will you be going with them?"

"Mind your own business. I'll speak about it when I'm good and ready."

"OK," I said, "and thanks for letting me stay."

"Don't mention it," he said airily.

So, I thought, Relation are going to America. Don't think about it, you mightn't like what comes into your head, and you'll get hung up, like you always do when people you dig go away. So I put it out of my mind, though it made me feel rather grim. Certainly not in a mood to handle Norman with the lightness I'd hoped for. Just as I was getting some things together for my departure, one of Norman's friends rang up.

"Is Norm there?" asked this awful voice.

"No," I said, and put the phone down. What a name. Norm! And then there was a knock at the door and Norm himself was there, committing another capital offence.

"Oh, hello," I said, in a bored voice. "I'm afraid I'm just going out."

"Shall I wait?" he asked, after a pause.

"No," I said. "I won't be back tonight or tomorrow or for the rest of the week."

He gave me a doleful look which made me feel impatient.

"You don't love me, do you?" he said, not looking at me.

"You shouldn't ask things like that," I said.

There was a tense pause as he watched me putting things into a carrier bag.

"I knew you were just using me, I said so," he burst out.

That wasn't strictly correct, but I couldn't see the point in arguing.

"Yes," I said, trying to remember what I needed to take.

"You're not groovy at all, you're just *wicked*."

I looked at him, into his incredible eyes that didn't matter any more.

"Am I?" I asked, not feeling wicked at all. "If I'm wicked, then there's no need to like me. In fact, better to leave me alone all together."

"You think you know it all," he flashed defiantly. "You think you know where everything's at . . . well, you don't, see because I've sussed you out. You impress people with the way you look and the way you talk, but you're nothing, because inside there's nothing, and you have nothing to give anybody."

I'm sure he's wrong, I thought, as I threw a few more unnecessary things into my bag.

"Sometimes there's nothing and sometimes there's everything," I said. "It depends who I'm giving it to."

He gave me a bitter look.

"I thought you were going to give something to me, but I suppose I'm not good enough. I loved you and you conned me."

"You'll learn," I said, putting on my coat. "It's good for you."

"Will you see me again?" he asked suddenly.

"No," I said. "And you'd better go now, because I have to lock the door."

"Didn't you like me at all?" he persisted.

I looked at him and considered for a moment.

"Well, you have incredible eyes," I said, and that got rid of him.

"My eyes have nothing to do with it," he shouted, and dashed out of the room and down the stairs. I waited until I was sure he had gone and then split. I didn't feel good at all.

* * *

Bill let me in when I got there and said Grant had told them I was coming. Everyone except Grant and Joe was watching the new telly in Joe's room. Joe came in much later and told us all he'd been having dinner in this millionaire chick's pad in Belgravia. He started going on about how groovy the pads in Belgravia were and how this chick wanted him to move in with her. During this, all the others somehow left and I found myself alone with Joe. To try and change the subject I asked him what this American trip was all about, but I didn't get much out of him. He said yeah, it was almost certain that they'd go to America, but a lot depended on the call Grant was expecting. In America they were bound to make it in a big way, and I thought, yes, they were good and any good group going to America usually made it there. And, of course, once they'd made it there, they would make it here too in a big way, so he really had something to be cocky about. He told me when he came back he'd get himself a really big pad in Belgravia, with fitted carpets, soft lights and expensive furniture. It would be somewhere he could bring his new groovy friends back to without being ashamed. Not like this house, he explained, where he had to share with all the others and put up with their habits. Sure, this place was all right, for *now*, but when he came back things would be different. He'd have beds that came out of walls, perspex baths, and goldfish in the toilet tanks.

"Places like that cost money," I said.

"Yes, I know," he said. "That's why I'm wondering if I shouldn't move in with this chick in Belgravia – until we go away, that is. She'll pay for everything and I can just lie around in luxury. The only hangup is she'll expect me to sleep with her all the time, and that's a bit too involved for me."

Same old Joe, I thought.

"It sounds great," I said, bored by Joe's ambitions. Everyone wants to live in expensive pads, but they don't talk about it until they are ready to put their money where their mouths are. I intended to live in a groovy flat as well and share it with groovy people, and in time I reckoned I would be able to get it together. I had enough money to move into a sort of interim pad, better than my Bayswater scene, and this I intended to do very shortly. I rather fancied a Chelsea address.

"If I made it in the States and came back and got a big pad together, would you like to move in with me?" Joe asked suddenly.

"Why should I do that?" I asked.

"Well, we get on together, and you wouldn't hang me up by being possessive, and you could look after me . . . and, of course, you're a groove in bed."

The perfect scene, I thought. Groupie glory. Living with the best in the best possible way. The idea definitely appealed to me, but Joe didn't.

"We'll see when you're rich and famous," I said.

Joe looked surprised. "What does that mean?"

"It means that I can't really see us living together."

"Why not? Don't you dig me?"

"Not any more."

"But you dig what I am," he said confidently. "And you'd do so even more if I was very big."

"No, that doesn't really matter any more. Besides, there's always somebody bigger," I added.

"Well, I think you'll be missing out," he said, a bit put out.

"I'll take my chances," I said.

Joe thought for a minute, then gave me a puzzled look.

"Don't I turn you on at all?" he asked.

"I've told you, not any more."

We sat in silence for a moment.

"What are you doing here, anyway?" he asked me finally.

"I'm staying in Grant's room for a few days."

"Is he here?" Joe asked.

"No, he's at the office waiting for the call that'll make you rich and famous."

"Oh yeah, I forgot," he said absentmindedly. "Why are you staying in Grant's room for a few days?"

"Because I don't want to stay in my flat at the moment."

Joe grinned. "Having problems with some geezer?"

"Nothing much."

"Still having it off with Grant?" Joe gave me a nasty leer.

"You won't go down too well in Belgravia, Joe, if you use expressions like that."

"What do you see in him?" Joe asked, ignoring my remark.

"In Grant?"

"Yes. I've heard the way he speaks to you and I don't know how you stand it."

I smiled tolerantly at him. "You know I like to be bullied, Joe, you were always telling me that. Besides, he does it so *well.*"

"Does he talk like that to you *all* the time?"

"Not really. He's changing a bit now."

"In what way?" asked Joe, looking eagerly at me.

"Well. we've reached the point where we don't have to play so many games now. He's managed to get me to behave in certain ways which keep him happy. He thinks he understands me and I think I understand him . . . but really neither of us knows very much about each other; just enough to keep us interested."

Joe looked very intrigued. "Does he play games?"

"Oh yes, very clever ones."

"Does he say nice things to you . . . you know, does he tell you he loves you and that?"

"What?" I laughed at Joe thinking of Grant as weak and imploring

194

when he was alone with me. "Grant say he loves me? You must be joking!"

"But doesn't he ever say things to you when you're in bed?"

"Well, we talk. But he never speaks when we're making it, if that's what you mean. In fact, he's the most silent love-maker I've ever met."

Joe's eyes lit up. "What's he like, then?"

"He's good."

"Is he really?"

"Yes, he's very good."

"Better than me?"

"Yes," I said. "You could learn a lot from Grant."

Joe looked a bit resentful. "In what way?"

"Well, he's got more imagination, for a start." I was enjoying this, and it was so easy, because it was the truth. "And he's got it all worked out."

"Got all what worked out?"

"His positions and things. And he's energetic and gentle at the same time, and it always seems to happen just right. It's like he's really thinking about it all to make it good for you and yet he's digging it as well. He's not like some of the stoned zombies you find who don't really seem to care what happens in bed as long as it's something. That's important, you know, Joe. You once told me that it didn't matter whether a chick did or didn't anymore, it was the way she did it that counted, that's what you said. Well, the same applies for guys. It's not enough for them to do it, they've got to know *how* to do it too, if the whole operation is going to make any sense."

"Are you speaking about me?" Joe looked very uptight.

"In a sense," I said.

"Well, I'm very straightforward in bed," he said defensively.

"You're just lazy," I told him.

"Well, what are these positions and things you're telling me that Grant is so good at?" he demanded.

"Do you *really* want to know?"

"Sure I do."

"Well, we start off like this," and I lay down on Joe's bed to demonstrate a position. "And after a while we move to this," and I threw both of my legs in the air. "Then at some stage I lie on my tummy," and I moved accordingly. "And we often do it sitting up," I sat on the bed with my legs at angles. "Then he sometimes plates me for a bit, or I plate him." I lay back on the bed. "But we usually finish up like this," I moved into a sideways position, "Or this," and I arched my back, "though I often plate him last as well."

Joe had been watching me in amazement. "Oh, I could never get all that together. I couldn't be bothered."

"Like I said, you're lazy."

He gave me an anxious look. "Do you think I should vary things a bit?"

"Yes," I said, "and you need a bigger bed too."

"We managed in it."

"Just about."

Joe thought for a moment, and then leant towards me with a confident look on his face. "Listen," he said, "you know what it's all about, so why don't *you* show me all of Grant's tricks." He took hold of my hand. "I never knew all *this* was going on in Grant's room."

I took my hand away. "That's not my scene, Joe. You had your chance once, but now it's too late."

"But I've been missing out," he said.

"Buy a copy of the *Kama Sutra* or something," I said.

"Oh, come on," Joe pleaded, "I won't tell Grant, promise I won't."

"He's already found out once, and you did that deliberately. You wanted to stir it up between us." I had been stirring it up too, but he wasn't to know that.

"That was different."

"You're right, this time it doesn't happen."

"But I thought you were my friend?" Joe looked genuinely hurt.

"I am," I said, though I didn't see where friendship came into it.

"Look, Katie, I like you, really I do. I feel I can talk frankly about things like sex without getting too hung up . . . so why don't you show me what you and Grant get up to? I mean, he's not even here."

"I've shown you, haven't I? There's no need for you to get worked up about it because of me. Find a chick and work it all out on her. Have a go at that rich chick in Belgravia you were talking about."

I got up and went to the door. Joe was looking at me as if he couldn't believe I was serious.

"Where are you going?"

"To bed."

"But Grant's not here," he said, all confused. "I mean, he won't be back tonight, and you don't want to sleep alone, do you?"

"Yes, I do," I said. "Goodnight."

And I left him to his imagination.

CHAPTER TWENTY-NINE

I got back to the house before Grant the next evening and didn't know whether to expect him or not. I sat in his room reading, and then, suddenly, there he was, exploding into the room, throwing his attaché case on the mattress and squirting air-freshener all over the place.

"Hello," I said.

"Hmmm," he replied, and sat down and started doing his football pools. Then he brought out a copy of *Tit Bits* and ogled at the pictures of semi-naked girls.

"That's a good one," he said from time to time, flicking over the pages. Then he turned to me. "Got any food?"

"Some," I said.

"Right, I'll have a sausage sarnie and a yogurt."

I knew his diet pretty well by now, so I'd got myself prepared and was able to produce what he'd asked for.

"That's better," he said when he'd finished. "You can take a gold star for that."

"Oh, *thank* you, Grant," I said.

"Don't patronise me, now."

"No, Grant," I said meekly. He looked at me sharply. "Did you sleep here last night?"

"Yes, you said I could, didn't you?"

"I know what I said ... thought you might have slept with Joe, that's all."

"Well, I didn't." This was the first time he'd mentioned me sleeping with Joe. "You might have come back."

"I told you, I had to wait for a call from America. So there was nothing stopping you."

"Except for the fact that I don't want to sleep with him anymore," I said. "And while we're on the subject of Joe, I didn't *want* you to find out the other time, you know."

198

"Don't give me that," he said. "You've got a very devious mind, and I can see straight through you."

"Then you'll know it's you I really care for," I said facetiously. "Besides, you're always telling me you don't mind what I do or who I sleep with, and anyhow, I always come back to you, don't I?"

"Oh yes, I know you'll always come back to me," Grant said confidently. "But sleeping with Joe that time, that was pushing it a bit, you must admit."

"I don't see why, if you care as little as you claim to."

"It annoyed me that he managed to pull you again, because it made him more big-headed and difficult to deal with. It's him that's trying to prove something, not me."

"I'm sorry," I said. "I really didn't think it mattered."

"It doesn't," he said. "Just don't do it again."

"No, all right." I waited a moment. He seemed to be talking to me in a straight way for once, I thought jump in while he's in the mood. "Tell me, Grant, if you really don't care, why do you go on seeing me?"

"Well," he considered, "you boost my ego by being so persistent. If you hadn't been so persistent I'd have blown you out long ago. And it's a convenient relationship because you keep me amused, do as I say, and don't hang me up. Those are about the only compliments you'll get out me, my girl, so don't ask any more question."

I didn't need to. It was a bit of a drag that I'd had to sleep with Joe to find out my position, but it had made Grant react, and I still had him, so I reckoned everything was cool. I told Grant about my conversation with Joe last night, and he laughed, hugging his sides with delight when he heard that I'd told Joe that he, Grant, was better in bed than Joe.

"What did he say then?" asked Grant.

"He wanted me to demonstrate how you made love," I said.

"And did you?"

"Well, I leapt about in a few different positions on his bed, saying we did this and that, but he wanted me to try them with him. He said he wanted to learn your technique."

"No one could learn my technique. Every girl that sleeps with me wants to marry me, and that includes you."

"Does it?" I asked. I hadn't really thought about it.

"You know it does. You'd marry me like a shot if I asked you to, only I'm not going to."

The thought of Grant asking me to marry him was very strange, and I couldn't really imagine it at all.

"Anyway, what happened?" he asked.

"I told him I didn't want to, and came and slept up here."

"Oh good," he said, losing interest.

"Joe says he wants to live in a luxury pad in Belgravia," I told Grant.

"Yes, that would be good for his ego. Did you know Wyatt is moving out?"

"Where's he going?" I asked.

"Somewhere over in North London. I'll tell you something, I'm not going to live here much longer. I want to get away from this lot, it's a hangup having to live *and* work with people at the same time. Besides, I need a bigger room to impress the birds."

"I'm going to move soon as well," I said.

"Well, get it together then," he said swiftly. "Find a good flat and I'll share it with you. Separate rooms, mind, none of this living together."

"That's cool," I said, and it was, because living with one guy must be very restricting if it's on a marriage basis. Much as I dug Grant, I had never been faithful, and didn't think I ever would be, even though I liked him best. But I would like to share a flat and be near him, and this arrangement sounded ideal.

"Right," he said, "that's settled. And I tell you what, it might be better to wait until we get back from America, so if you like you can have Wyatt's room until then. And bring your television." Grant's old television had broken down some time ago, and been thrown out of the window.

"OK," I said. The idea of moving in with Relation certainly appealed to me. They would be nice guys to live with, and when people asked me where I lived, which they always seem to, it would be great to be able to say "I live with a group, Relation".

Then Grant started telling me about a big row they'd all had, and how a lot of things had been sorted out.

"They got uptight because I was telling them what to do. They thought I was becoming power mad and they ganged up on me. You see, I get paid out of their bread and they resent it when I try to get them together. This is really Roland Johns' scene. He should be doing this, but it was left to me. As a group they are something else, but off-stage they're pretty untogether, and they need someone like me to get them to the top. If I didn't believe they could make it, I wouldn't waste my time with them. As it is, I'm going to do everything I can to see that they get there. Anyway, we've sorted it out; I'm not paid by them anymore. I'm Roland Johns' assistant now. I have more authority and that'll be a help . . . so just watch how I move those guys from here on in."

Grant sounded very impressive. His eyes shone and his whole presence registered iron determination.

"Are you going to the States with them?"

"Probably . . . but I'm not sure yet."

Although I didn't want Grant to go away, I did feel it would be good for him to go to America. He would learn a lot and make important contacts, and he had the kind of energy and attitude Americans respected. And the group would certainly need someone like him to look after things for them; you just don't send a group into that particular jungle without protection. So it seemed certain to me that he would be going, and I knew that this was something I would have to sort out for myself in my own way. And anyway, I was used to people going away. America seemed to be my biggest rival.

I moved into the house a week later, and it was as if I had always lived there. A pattern seemed to establish itself almost immediately. I hardly bothered to go on gigs with them; it didn't seem necessary or even very desirable unless it was something very special. When they weren't away on gigs Grant would come into my room and watch telly and get me to cook for him. None of the others seemed to have any steady chicks around – even Bill and Wendy's scene had disintegrated – and they would crowd round the things I was cooking for Grant in the small kitchen. If they weren't hungrily criticising my efforts, they were pinching and nibbling at it when I wasn't looking. I didn't really mind, because I liked them all, but I wasn't going to offer to cook for them. Grant would shout at them if he caught them at it, and he also kept them out of my room, though when he wasn't around they'd knock at my door and ask me things, or invite me to come and smoke with them, and it was easy to fit into the life there. I got used to taking messages from the different chicks who kept phoning up, and I could tell from their reactions which chick would be phoned back and which one wouldn't. And when chicks came round I enjoyed sussing them out, and trying to guess which one would last and which one would be dropped. Grant was either rude to these chicks or ignored them completely, and although he kept going on about wanting a bird with big boobs and suspender belts – his latest thing – he never seemed to bother to do anything about it. I slept with him when he told me to, and this was a good arrangement, because we often went to bed at different times anyway. He'd either march out of my room saying, "see you" or he'd stop and consider by the door and say "you may join me in half an hour" and then disappear, without bothering to wait for a reply. I didn't have any more incidents with Joe, who had got himself involved with a friend's wife and was causing a lot of aggro in that direction.

When Grant went to bed early I often looned down to The Joint with the others. We'd sit at a table specially reserved for us, and all these different people and faces would come over and say hello and talk. I got to know a lot of people that I'd really only had contact with over the phone before, and working for the Kingdom gave me quite a lot to say about things. I soon felt very much at ease and was part of these happenings around me. I could go over to faces at other tables and sit down and talk to them like it was the most natural thing in the world, and when the group was away some of these faces would ring me and take me down to The Joint for a meal. This was usually cool. it was like we had an understanding or something because they didn't try to pull me right away, rather things were left hanging in an open-ended sort of way which either of us could tie up together should we have a mind to. I mean, they would have pulled me if I had indicated that I wanted to be pulled, but they knew who I was, and that I had some scene going with Relation, so I never accepted any invitations back to pads, because once you do that you are virtually saying yes, I'll sleep with you. And now I don't sleep with people just to sleep with them because it just doesn't seem to work out for me, and anyway, it's better to have scenes with people who really turn you on. This meant that from now on I would be doing the choosing, and, while they had to be faces, it didn't matter whether they were lesser or greater faces provided I dug them and their music or the scene they had going.

So, quietly behind all the talk and hustling conversations, I filed away all the likely future prospects in the back of my mind. Top of my list was that organist from The Shadow Cabinet who really did things to my mind every time I watched him play.

But I had my scene with Grant and that was enough right now. We were getting on quite well, though I sometimes got a bit uptight with his lack of affection outside bed hours. I accused him of not caring at all, and he said he did care, but not too much about physical things. His scene with me gave him more than that, he said. He'd been through the whole thing of telling a chick he loved her, holding hands and kissing, because that's what chicks wanted, and it kept the whole thing running smoothly. But it had been a nuisance to him, he'd never been in love, and didn't think he ever would be, because he didn't believe in that kind of love. It was a mind trap people lumbered themselves into, with no happy ever afters, and full of obligations and hangups which stopped a person doing their thing. There was no need to be like that with me, he said, and it was nice to be able to be himself as he really was. Anyway, I liked him like that, so why should he bother with all the crap?

I presumed that he was indirectly telling me about the chick who had written all those uncool letters. I hadn't seen any more arrive since I'd been living there, nor had I seen any in his room, so I supposed he'd blown her out because he hadn't been able to cope with it all. And now he'd told me all this, I knew I could never expect to hear nice things from him. He'd only be saying them to keep me happy, and we'd both know it. However, I thought, maybe it's better to know somebody digs you without their having to tell you in words.

I used to brood about this when I was alone and taking stock. Half the time I was pleased to be having this sort of uncommitted relationship with Grant which gave me the necessary amount of freedom not to feel tied down, and the rest of the time I really wanted to feel more secure about him, and believe that he really cared. So I was satisfied and dissatisfied at the same time. Also I wasn't absolutely sure if he was going to the States with the group, and this made me feel precarious as well. I only found out for certain the night before they were due to leave. There had been hustles over passports and visas and smallpox injections, and everyone was over-excited. Grant marched into my room and I asked him what was happening.

"I'm going with them," he said. "I didn't see any point in telling you before."

A familiar panicky feeling welled up inside me, but I quickly put it down. "Oh, that's good," I said.

"I knew you'd only brood if I'd told you before."

"Won't I brood now?"

"No," Grant said, "you won't have time. You'll be too busy enjoying yourself while I'm away. And don't think *I'm* not going to pull anything I can get my hands on," he added.

"I'll miss you," I said.

"No you won't," he said firmly. "We'll only be gone two months, and by the time I come back I'll expect you to have a flat together for me to move into."

That cheered me up a bit, and we started discussing where the flat would be, and how much we should pay for it. After that was all sorted out he began to give me instructions about looking after the house, and how I wasn't to let anybody stay here and not to hold wild parties. Then I helped him pack, and he kept running around the house telling people things and reminding them of all the useless and important things they mustn't forget. When we were finally alone in his room I asked him if I was sleeping with him tonight, although I'd slept with him last night and was quite prepared for a refusal.

He looked at me first without speaking. "If you come to bed immediately," he said abruptly. "I've got to have a good night's sleep."

So I got into his bed and we went through another last time. Only it wasn't as bad as with Davey or Larry because Grant *really* was coming back soon, and we would be living together then. And even if he went away again, he'd come back, because if he came back once he'd come back twice. And he'd come back to me because he didn't get involved with chicks, he only slept with them, and I was the only one he could have a scene with. That's what I told myself as I told him I loved him. He laughed, and told me not to get sentimental over him, as he'd probably come back with a dose.

Next morning he was leaping about, and soon the whole house was up, and I lay there listening to them all getting ready. It sounded much like when they set off for any gig, except more so, and then they all came in and said goodbye to me, and I said goodbye and have a nice time and those sort of things. Finally Grant re-appeared all dressed up in his velvet suit and shades and picked up his attaché case.

"Got to impress the Yanks," he said, and there was a pause. "Now don't forget what I told you."

"I won't," I said. "Are you going now?"

"Yes. I might write, but I can't promise. Be good."

And he was gone, and then they were all gone, and the front door went bang.

CHAPTER THIRTY

Yes, it's sometimes funny sitting in alone, with the house empty, and knowing that they aren't just away on a local gig, wondering where they are now, and how they're going down in America. It's not that I'm brought down or sitting waiting for letters from Grant, it's just a strange feeling that suddenly occurs from time to time. I manage to follow their tracks from the American rock papers, and I'm not surprised to read glowing reports about their appearances, because I felt it was inevitable that people would like them. And an incidental piece of information I pick up while reading one of the papers is that Larry, my American Gemini, has been admitted into Bellevue Hospital, claiming he's Bob Dylan. He never did reply to my letter, and it's not surprising, as it seems he has freaked right out now, and I wonder if I ever knew him at all. Besides that I'm kept busy at the Kingdom, and new things are coming my way as well. I have been approached by a French promoter to help set up a Pop Festival in France, similar to the one in Rome, except smaller and better organised. There is enough front money to do everything properly this time, so I can put my experience to good use. Occasionally I go to view prospective flats, but there is no sweat in this because I have plenty of time and I want to choose wisely, and anyway groups always stay in America longer than they plan, especially if they are going down well. Wendy comes to see me quite a bit and we get smashed and analyse things. She hasn't made The Joint scene yet, and I keep promising to take her. I'm still going down there to eat, sticking around until the group has played and then just grooving around from table to table, talking and listening, but not committing myself in any way, even though everyone knows Relation are in the States and guys know I could be available.

David, the photographer who took my picture for International magazine, dropped round with some copies for me, and told me he was doing some pictures of Liza Bellamy and two of the Jacklin

H. Event in a couple of days' time. Jacklin H. Event are the biggest group around still playing live gigs, and have just come back from the States, where they spend most of their time. There are three of them, they're thin, wild and freaky and have a reputation for scoring thousands of chicks. I said I know Liza well, and could I come along? He didn't see why not, and arranged to pick me up from the Kingdom offices on his way to the studio. When we arrived, Liza was there, in a low-cut semi-transparent lace dress that reached her ankles. She didn't look too pleased to see me, although she gushed hellos in all directions. The two guys from the Event were an hour late, and Liza was getting a bit uptight. When they finally appeared they both looked very stoned, and gave incoherent answers to the interviewer. Then David started hustling them into the main studio, where there was a large bed with a Casa Pupo cover on it under the spotlights.

"Right," said David, "I want you to all start getting it together on there," and he indicated the bed. Liza gave a delighted laugh, and looked at the two Event. They mumbled something to each other, and didn't move.

"Come on, don't be shy," David encouraged.

"Well, *I'm* not shy," said Liza, and lay down invitingly.

The blond guy from the Event, Keith, who sings and plays the bass, carefully took off his patchwork boots and joined her, and then the other guy did as well, only he kept on his boots and his long black velvet coat. With his pink sunglasses, he looked rather incongruous lying there so fully dressed. Liza turned to him and ran her hand down his leg. He didn't move, he just kept staring at the ceiling.

"Come on, get it together," called David, fiddling with his equipment.

Liza turned to Keith and kissed him on the neck. He stared at her tits, which were almost falling out of her dress, and then wriggled towards her. She entwined her legs with his, and they started kissing in a self-conscious way. The other guy just lay there with his arms crossed, making no effort to join in.

"What about you, Sam?" asked David, "are you just going to lie there? OK, that's cool, it looks quite freaky like that," and he fitted his face to the camera.

"That's great, that's great," he shouted, "a bit more, a bit more, don't mind us, let yourselves go."

Liza was virtually on top of Keith, who was much smaller than her, and we could hardly see him.

"Give him a chance, darling," called David, "he's supposed to be in the picture as well, you know." Still clinging together, they rolled towards Sam, who was still lying motionless.

"That's it, I'm going to start now, just keep going like that."

But before David could take one shot, Sam suddenly got up off the bed and walked towards where I was sitting on the sofa. Everything stopped, and Liza and Keith separated.

"What's the matter?" asked David.

"I need a drink," said Sam. "A vodka will do."

"OK, OK, get him a vodka," David told his assistant. Keith had also got up off the bed, leaving a slightly ruffled Liza spread out on her own. Sam was shaking his head and telling David he didn't want to go on with it, and Keith was agreeing with him. Liza joined them, and they all stood muttering together. I couldn't catch what they were saying, but Sam seemed adamant in his decision. After drinking his vodka he said he had to be going, and Keith put his boots back on and followed him out of the door.

"Well," said Liza, in an astonished voice, "how do you like that? I'd never have expected *them* to be so coy. I expect he got uptight because I was giving Keith all the attention. Or maybe it was because you were here," and she looked at me.

"I don't see why that should have put them off," I protested.

"You'd be surprised," said Liza, draping her fur coat over her shoulders.

I had to admit I had been surprised as well. I'd have thought they'd have both leapt on her, being the type of guys that one assumes have no inhibitions at all. I left the studio wondering why Sam had been so unco-operative and what he was *really* like.

It wasn't long before I saw him again. They arrived down at The Joint the next night, and you *knew* when the Event arrived. A kind of reverent hush settled over the place when they entered, and everybody was looking at them without appearing to. Jacklin was with this chick he's had for some time now, but Sam and Keith were alone. There were a couple of other guys with them, and they all looked pretty smashed as they weaved their way to a table that was instantly available to them. I was sitting at a nearby table with this friendly booker I know, and watched them all knocking back a lot of hard booze. The manager of The Joint came over and sat with them for a bit, and gradually other people came over and said hello, and shook hands, but nobody else sat down. When the group that had been playing duly finished their set, there was the usual discreet stampede by other musicians to get to the stage, so that they could be first in line for the jam sessions which invariably take place. After about twenty minutes of jamming, Jacklin himself got up and walked over to the stage. The guys up there immediately stopped, and the guitarist offered his place to Jacklin. Then the other two staggered over, and there they all were, tuning and conferring, while everyone in The Joint applauded and gathered round. They started up, and went into this long instrumental thing, with emphasis on Jacklin's incredible guitar sound, which lasted for three quarters of an hour. It was a single melody line that they developed and improvised on, with a lot of tempo changes, and I stood watching their intent sweating faces as their full, emotion-laden sound swelled around me.

They finished abruptly, and went to the bar. After them, nobody dared follow onto the stand, and the DJ started up the records. I waited for a moment, and then followed them out. I saw them all standing together, and went straight up to Sam.

"Hello," I said. "I met you at the studio yesterday."

He swayed slowly on his thin legs, and peered at me through the pink glasses. He took my hand and leant towards me.

"Who are you?" he said, and I noticed how quiet his voice was.

"I'm Katie," I said, and found myself talking into a great frizz of dark hair, because he'd come too far forward. He moved back a little still holding my hand, and regarded me.

"You're nice," he said, and moved his head towards me again. I thought he wanted to say something else, so I leant towards him, and found myself being kissed, very softly, on the mouth.

"You're *very* nice," he said, and kissed me again. He was pulling me, and I was flattered because this one had an especially bad reputation for chicks, which made him even more attractive. I mean, he could walk up to any chick, take her hand and say "you're nice", and he'd have scored.

"You're nice too," I said, and wondered if he was. The others had all spread out a bit, Jacklin had gone into the restaurant with his chick, and Keith and Danny, the roadie, were talking in a little group of people. Sam stepped back a little, still keeping hold of my hand, and bowed over and kissed it several times, like an old-fashioned courtier. Then he kissed me on the cheek, and ran his hand down my waist and hips. It was all rather overwhelming, and there were a lot of people watching.

"We're going in a moment . . . are you coming?"

"All right," I said.

"We're just waiting for Keith and Danny to score some chicks. They shouldn't be long."

You're right they shouldn't, I thought, and this brought me down to earth a little. While guys like this were over in England, not doing too much work, they spent most of their time getting smashed and scoring chicks. They scored so many chicks and got so smashed that one chick was pretty much the same as another. I was just another pull as far as this guy was concerned, and an easy one at that. But it worked the other way as well, if I turned the whole situation round. I had gone up to him, because of who he was and the group he played in, so that he could score me should he want to. And it was a groove that he did, and was making it so obvious in front of everybody at The Joint.

We were ready to go, and swept out of The Joint like a royal party or something. I was with Sam, and Danny had a chick he'd just scored plus her friend who was obviously meant for Keith. Danny's chick wasn't very pleased with the arrangement because, as they were getting their coats, I heard her say in an uptight voice, "How is it you always score the singer and I always end up with the roadie?" Then they went into a groupie thing about whose turn it was to pull the group member, and who should chat up the roadie, so that once he had himself a chick, the friend could tag along until she could move in on the group proper. These chicks seemed to have a system that worked, but it wasn't my scene at all. They weren't very special to look at, in fact if they hadn't been wearing groovy clothes they would have been rather plain and uninspiring. As it was, with their see-through bits of silk, eccentric eye make-up and long wigs, they didn't look too bad.

In the taxi Sam sat beside me, and apart from telling me that he was smashed out of his mind, he didn't advertise his presence. I watched the other two chicks going through kissing and fondling scenes with Keith and Danny. I wondered whether I was like them, I mean, we were all groupies together, me in my different way, and they in theirs. Did they care that it was only for tonight, with a vague future maybe, because they would probably be replaced in twenty-four hours, if not sooner. It wouldn't matter that much, because for these chicks, once was a kind of forever. I watched their intent faces and their uninhibited movements, and I thought, this is where they're at, these chicks have no hangups about what they're doing, *they* know what they are here for, even if I am not sure.

I couldn't honestly convince myself that I wanted a scene with this guy Sam. He was so smashed that he wouldn't remember me by tomorrow, either. I knew I could steel my mind to accept that, and be just as dedicated as these other two chicks, but did I have to? Why should I let him use my body tonight, and forget my face by tomorrow? I'd been seen leaving with him; so as far as pulling him was concerned, that was already an established fact. I examined him doubtfully from the corner of my eye. His features were basically unattractive, and he looked very wasted. His eyes couldn't seem to open properly, though with his thinness, his clothes, and especially his long curly hair, the effect was rather dramatic, and of course, he was one of the Event. His mind had probably registered that he'd scored a pretty chick for tonight, and now that was settled, he could drift off into his stoned reverie until he arrived, and then go through all the necessary changes until it was time for me to be a warm accommodating presence beside him in bed.

I still hadn't made up my mind as to whether I wanted to sleep with him or not when we got to their flat. It was a beautifully furnished place, with a lot of antiques, and an expensive sound system. We went into a large sitting room where a plump, fortyish guy, wearing glasses, lay dozing. He woke up as we entered, and nodded, though nobody introduced him. He got up and went to a corner and sat down in an armchair. Before going back into his doze again he took a great swallow from an half-empty bottle of whisky he had taken with him. Sam seemed to have revived a bit. As soon as we were inside he started fussing round the room, straightening rugs and emptying ashtrays. He made Keith's chick stand up while he re-arranged the cushions of the sofa they were

211

sitting on, and when I stubbed out my cigarette he emptied the ashtray into the fireplace.

"What's the matter with you?" I asked.

"He's an old woman," Keith shouted, and stretched out with his head on the chick's lap. The chick framed his face with her hands and he had her undivided attention.

"Roll a joint, you," Keith told her, and called to the plump guy in the corner to give her the gear. The guy came over without a word, and passed the chick a plastic bag with skins and hash inside. Then he went back to his corner, and I wondered who he was.

"I can't stand mess," Sam said, and tried to straighten some books on the shelf and fell over.

"But it's terribly tidy in here," I said.

Sam picked himself up and crawled over beside me. "It's a doss house, I can't stand this filth any longer." There's something wrong with him, I thought.

Danny's chick had hardly sat down before she was whisked off to a bedroom. Sam took hold of my hand, and started kissing me rather lazily, and then, as if remembering something, he broke off, and put some tapes on. He got very confused with the reels, and spent a long time fiddling with the knobs, complaining that the balance was wrong.

"It's all right," Keith said, and passed me the joint he'd ended up rolling himself, because the chick didn't know how. I took a couple of drags and passed it to Sam. He frowned at me severely.

"That's not the way we do it here," he told me, and took a couple of very deep pulls. "Watch." After blowing the smoke out, he placed the joint on a gold ashtray and passed it on to Keith's chick. "That's the way to pass joints . . . no mess, you see."

I nodded. I noticed the guy in the corner seemed to have a persistent cough, and every time he coughed he took a slug out of the whisky bottle. Apart from the cough and the occasional gurgle of the bottle, it was as if he, or we, were not there.

Then Keith and Sam went into a long technical discussion about a group they had discovered and were recording. It was somehow reassuring to hear them talk like that, and good to know that they were involved in music as much as I'd assumed. Keith started singing to one of the tapes to demonstrate the way he thought the harmony should go, and Sam asked me if the track we were listening to would make a good single. I said it would if the backing were a bit more organised, and then it became a three-way conversation. Keith's chick sat there looking bored. She didn't want Keith to be distracted from the scene she'd come for. She began rubbing her hand up and down his thigh and after a while she connected, and he turned back to her.

"I'm going to bed now. Coming?" Keith said to her, and in a moment they had split to the bedroom.

Sam was stroking my back as he listened to his tapes. He seemed quite happy to lie there without going through any pre-bed fondling, and I didn't encourage him because by now I had decided not to sleep with him. It was going to be interesting to see what kind of hustle I'd have to go through to get out of this. The whole set-up here was too premeditated for me, and I wanted to give him a jolt by leaving him chickless tonight. He'd probably dismiss me as a waste of time if he ever managed to remember both me and the incident. On the other hand, I was tempted to have him, if only to see how he worked out in bed, and he was a drummer, and I'd never had a drummer before. Maybe if he worked at making me stay, I'd stay, I told myself. But he'd really have to let me know he wanted me, and put some effort into it. I'd got involved in a sort of moral issue with myself because the assumptions under which some of these guys operated for once got on my wick, and I had decided to make an issue of it with this particular one. Besides, people who knew I'd pulled him would make remarks, and I'd tell them I'd turned him down, that I hadn't wanted to sleep with him, and see how they liked that. Everybody has their protest bit, and this was my protest, my way of hinting that people should qualify in some way if they wanted to have scenes with me.

I nudged Sam. "Who's he?" I asked, indicating the plump guy in the corner.

"He's Dennis He's our bodyguard."

"Do you need one?"

Sam shook his head seriously. "You wouldn't believe what would happen if we didn't have Dennis to look after us. That guy gets paid a lot of bread just to keep us in one piece."

"He's not very busy, is he?" I teased.

"It's not always so quiet here," Sam said ominously.

"Would he protect you from me if I grabbed you?"

Sam grinned and put his arm around me. "He'd tear you limb from limb." I could see his eyes hotting up as he stared at me, and I reckoned it was time to go. I got up and said so. Dennis turned to look at me, and Sam stumbled onto his feet and followed me out into the hall looking very surprised.

"Why are you going?" he asked.

"It's late."

He tried to take my coat away from me. "You don't need that. Stay for a while."

"I can't," I said, and firmly pulled my coat away from him. He took hold of me and kissed me on the mouth very hard. I almost changed my mind because I liked it and he seemed to be actually trying. But I pushed him away.

"I'm not going to sleep with you," I said.

He laughed. "Why not?"

"Because I'm not an easy pull."

Sam frowned. "Then why did you come back with me?"

"Well, you are one of the Event," I said, matter-of-factly.

Sam didn't like this at all, and his lips tightened. "Is that the only reason?"

"I think so," I said.

He thought about this for a moment. "Well, can't you stay anyway?" he said, and he moved in and kissed me again, but I stopped him before he could get into it. He could persuade me if he tried talking to me, because I'm a sucker for words and would probably have believed all his lies. But getting at me physically wasn't going to do the trick.

"Why are you being so uncool about it?" he asked.

"I'm not uncool. I'm just going home."

Sam couldn't sort it out at all. He shook his head as if trying to clear it. "But when you came back with me . . ."

"Yes, I know what you thought. But why should I sleep with you?"

"I don't know," he said, "I just thought you would, that's all."

"Who am I?" I suddenly asked.

"What do you mean?"

"I mean, what's my name."

"What's your *name*. . .?" he laughed, and I could almost hear the clicking as his mind tried to fit the face to the name.

"I know," he said at last, "your name is Katie."

"You're wrong," I lied, "you don't even know who I am."

His face kind of drained a bit. He was so sure he'd guessed correctly. "I don't know . . . I really thought it was Katie."

He may have guessed, but he wasn't sure. I wasn't standing for any of this anonymous fucking business. I put my coat on and we stood looking at each other. I wanted him to say something that would make him seem a bit more real, but he didn't know what was happening except that I was being unco-operative and he wasn't used to that.

"Well," he said, "all right then."

I knew he wasn't going to bother any further. A freaky little scene that had unsettled him for a night, that's all it was. Or was it? I walked to the door and he followed me.

"Goodbye," I said, stepping outside.

"Goodbye," he called. "Have a nice time." And he closed the door very quietly behind him. Well, I told myself, as I walked down the hall, I wouldn't have got very much out of him, except maybe the clap. And I can't be doing with the clap when there's that organist from The Shadow Cabinet to be pulled. Yes.